"I wanted you to remember me on your own. If you didn't, I wasn't sure you'd ever believe me."

"Why the hell wouldn't I?" Josh asked.

"Because what we did…" Paige hesitated, unsure how to explain her own fears. "I know we probably weren't the first operatives to…have sex on a mission. I'd be a fool to believe that, considering the stresses. But you were always so damned hard-line about personal involvement."

"Until that night," he concluded for her. "Why would I have changed my mind?"

She had wondered that a thousand times. Once for every day he'd been missing. Because she had always remembered what had been in his eyes when he laid his gun on the ground and looked up at her. She had always known there was some connection between that look and his subsequent disappearance. And the most obvious was that he had known he would never see her again.

Dear Harlequin Intrigue Reader,

The days are getting cooler, but the romantic suspense is always hot at Harlequin Intrigue! Check out this month's selections.

TEXAS CONFIDENTIAL continues with *The Specialist* (#589) by Dani Sinclair. Rafe Alvarez was the resident playboy agent, until he met his match in Kendra Kincaide. He transformed his new partner into a femme fatale for the sake of a mission, and instantly lost his bachelor's heart for the sake of love....

THE SUTTON BABIES have grown in number by two in *Little Boys Blue* (#590) by Susan Kearney. A custody battle over cowboy M.D. Cameron Sutton's baby boys was brewing. When East Coast socialite Alexa Whitfield agreed to a marriage of convenience, Cam thought his future was settled. Until he fell for his temporary wife—the same wife someone was determined to kill!

Hailed by *Romantic Times Magazine* as an author who writes a "tantalizing read," Gayle Wilson returns with *Midnight Remembered* (#591), which marks the conclusion of her MORE MEN OF MYSTERY series. When ex-CIA agent Joshua Stone couldn't remember his true identity, he became an easy target. But his ex-partner Paige Daniels knew all his secrets, including what was in his heart....

Reeve Snyder had rescued Polly Black from death and delivered her baby girl one fateful night. Polly's vulnerable beauty touched him deep inside, but who was she? And what was she running from? And next time, would Reeve be able to save her and her daughter when danger came calling? Find out in *Alias Mommy* (#592) by Linda O. Johnston.

Don't miss a single exciting moment!

Sincerely,

Denise O'Sullivan
Associate Senior Editor
Harlequin Intrigue

MIDNIGHT REMEMBERED

GAYLE WILSON

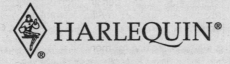

HARLEQUIN®

TORONTO • NEW YORK • LONDON
AMSTERDAM • PARIS • SYDNEY • HAMBURG
STOCKHOLM • ATHENS • TOKYO • MILAN • MADRID
PRAGUE • WARSAW • BUDAPEST • AUCKLAND

ISBN 0-373-22591-1

MIDNIGHT REMEMBERED

Visit us at www.eHarlequin.com

Printed in U.S.A.

ABOUT THE AUTHOR

Gayle Wilson is the award-winning author of fifteen novels for Harlequin. She has lived in Alabama all her life except for the years she followed her army aviator husband—whom she met on a blind date—to a variety of military posts.

Before beginning her writing career, she taught English and world history to gifted high school students in a number of schools around the Birmingham area. Gayle and her husband have one son, who is also a teacher of gifted students. They are blessed with warm and loving Southern families and an ever-growing menagerie of cats and dogs.

You can write to Gayle at P.O. Box 3277, Hueytown, Alabama 35023.

Books by Gayle Wilson

HARLEQUIN INTRIGUE
344—ECHOES IN THE DARK
376—ONLY A WHISPER
414—THE REDEMPTION OF DEKE SUMMERS
442—HEART OF THE NIGHT
461—RANSOM MY HEART*
466—WHISPER MY LOVE*
469—REMEMBER MY TOUCH*
490—NEVER LET HER GO
509—THE BRIDE'S PROTECTOR†
513—THE STRANGER SHE KNEW†
517—HER BABY, HIS SECRET†
541—EACH PRECIOUS HOUR
561—HER PRIVATE BODYGUARD††
578—RENEGADE HEART††
591—MIDNIGHT REMEMBERED††

* Home to Texas series
† Men of Mystery series
†† More Men of Mystery series

FOR YOUR EYES ONLY
CIA
AGENT PROFILE

NAME: Joshua Stone
DATE OF BIRTH: December 28, 1960
ASSIGNED TEAM: External Security

SPECIAL SKILLS: Skilled in a variety of the martial arts and hand-to-hand combat, counterterrorism training, light and heavy weapons expert, mountain warfare expert.

AGENT EVALUATION: Highly valued and experienced antiterrorist operative whose disappearance during a covert operation forced the reassignment of his female partner.

CURRENT ADDRESS: Unknown
STATUS: Missing in action…

FOR YOUR EYES ONLY

CAST OF CHARACTERS

Paige Daniels—She had survived her first and only mission for the External Security Team, but she had returned from it without her lover and partner. Just when Paige thought she had finally put that nightmare behind her, she discovered that some memories—and some men—are far more difficult to forget than others.

Joshua Stone—The most legendary operative of Griff Cabot's elite team, Joshua Stone disappeared with a biological toxin worth millions on the black market. Had he turned traitor? Or had something so terrible happened to him that dark midnight that even Stone, with all his skills, couldn't escape?

Jack Thompson—Why was his name on a folder in the top-secret files at the CIA? And why couldn't he remember anything about the life he had led before he'd awakened from a coma in an Atlanta hospital?

Carl Steiner—He wanted the nerve agent in CIA hands, and he was willing to use anything or anybody to achieve that.

Andy Rombart—There is nothing more dangerous to a secret than a good cop with a couple of troublesome murders on his hands. And Andy Rombart was a very good cop.

Dr. Helen Culbertson—Could she reach the secrets locked in Jack Thompson's mind? More important, would she survive the attempt?

To Phoebe Robinson—
for her unceasing support, her kindness and generosity
of spirit, and most of all for her friendship.

Prologue

"What's the first thing you're going to do when we get out?"

Paige Daniels turned her head and found Joshua Stone's gaze on her face rather than on what was going on in the village square. And despite the seriousness of what was happening out there, his eyes seemed full of amusement.

"I haven't allowed myself to believe that we're going to get out of here," she admitted. "Not yet, anyway."

"You have to have faith, Daniels," Josh chided, the creases at the corners of his eyes deepening as he grinned at her.

She turned her head, looking again at the men who were searching for them. They were moving systematically from building to building through the bombed-out rubble.

Armed primarily with out-of-date Soviet-made weapons, these rebels were as ill-equipped as were most of the Vladistan forces. Of course, there was nothing that said an old bullet couldn't kill you as dead as a modern one.

"Okay…" she whispered, still watching the manhunt, "then first I'm going to take a hot bath."

She heard a breath of sound beside her and recognized it as laughter. Her lips tilted in response, but this time she resisted the impulse to turn and look at him. Looking at

Joshua Stone had proven too disruptive of her peace of mind during the weeks they'd spent together.

After all, he was her partner. A professional relationship. And so far it had been highly professional.

Despite her initial doubts that anyone could live up to the high regard in which Stone was held at the CIA, she had discovered that his reputation for ingenious planning and meticulous execution was well-deserved.

Partner. And nothing else, she reminded herself.

Even if there *had* been anything between them, now was not the time to allow herself to become distracted by it. Actually, she was determined that no one would ever know exactly how big a distraction Joshua Stone had been. Especially not Joshua Stone.

"Can't say you don't *need* a bath," he said. "There is a certain primitive charm, however, in listening to your nightly efforts at hygiene. A real exercise in creativity."

"Mine in making them or yours in listening?" she retorted.

Without warning, he moved closer. His concentration on the scene outside had intensified, in spite of the absurdity of the conversation they were having. And she had known all along that he had begun it to keep her mind off what was going on. Paige pressed back against the wall, allowing him greater access to the crack through which they had been keeping an eye on the search.

"All mine," he said, his gaze still directed outside. Then he added, "And believe me, Daniels, I'm *very* creative."

He was so near that she could feel his breath against her cheek. They had existed in this same kind of intimacy for weeks, compelled into physical proximity by the demands of the mission and by their living conditions. Despite that enforced closeness, things had never gotten anywhere near any other kind of intimacy.

At the beginning, if Josh Stone had attempted to initiate

some sort of physical relationship, it would have made her uneasy. And she would have resisted. By now she was curious, to put it mildly, why things had never progressed beyond the easy camaraderie they shared. Stone's notorious self-control? Or the fact that he didn't find her desirable? She had to admit his lack of interest had piqued hers, despite her determination not to succumb to his reputed charms.

They had talked about everything under the sun in the long, cold evenings they had spent together. And she had been fascinated by the breadth of his knowledge on subjects ranging from rock and roll to Eastern mysticism. Not once, however, had the talk turned personal. Not until now.

She turned toward him again, at least as much as the close confines of their positions allowed. Josh was still focused on the soldiers outside, and the slant of late afternoon light coming in through the crack illuminated his face.

His skin had been darkened by the never-ceasing wind of this rugged, mountainous country. He hadn't had a haircut in the four months they had been here. His hair's natural curl was obvious as it had never been when he was able to keep it close-cropped, which was the way he preferred to wear it. And it was almost as dark as the hole they were cowering in, as black as the thick lashes that the shadowed those pale blue eyes.

His features, taken individually, weren't extraordinary. Actually, they were harsh. Hard-bitten. His face was dominated by its bone structure: a Roman beak of a nose, high cheekbones, and a determined jaw. Tonight the shadow of several days' growth of whiskers gave it a truly cutthroat aspect.

Joshua Stone was certainly capable of cutting a throat or two if he felt doing that would be in the best interests of his country. Perfectly capable, she thought, her eyes still examining that unusual combination of features.

They were not a satisfactory explanation of why this man

had proven so compelling to her. Maybe it was the contradictions that fascinated her. His almost forbidding looks hid a reckless, devil-may-care personality. And those austere features included a mobile mouth that tilted into a smile at the slightest provocation. During the four brutal months they had spent in this devastated country, Josh had never lost his sense of humor or his patience. And she had sorely tried both.

He turned his head, meeting her eyes. "What *is* that you do every night?"

Think about you. "Sponge bath," she said aloud.

"That's my girl," he said, turning back to the view through the crack. She watched the visible corner of his lips lift. "Sponge bath, huh?"

"I prefer not to become one of the great unwashed."

"Implying I have?"

"Well…" she said, drawing the word out.

Suddenly his body, which was pressed against hers, tensed. Paige's gaze flew back to the slit in the wall. One of the soldiers was coming toward them, his eyes sweeping the area in front of him, rifle held at the ready. She didn't need the warning glance Josh shot her before he turned back to the crack.

Unconsciously, Paige held her breath as the soldier approached. Like most of his comrades, his boots were old and broken, his uniform a collection of mismatched garments, which had probably been purchased from Soviet military surplus long before the rebellion had broken out. None of which meant he wouldn't know how to use the weapon he carried. Or wouldn't be as willing to kill for his country as Joshua Stone would be.

As she would be? Paige wondered. She had gotten brave enough one night to confess to Josh that she'd have a real problem killing any of these people if they were forced to fight their way out of this beleaguered republic. After all, she had said, these aren't the bad guys.

And she had not forgotten his answer: *"Good guys or bad, if they shoot you, Daniels, you'll be dead. Believe me, whatever you may feel about them, they won't hesitate to kill you."*

She blocked the ongoing mental debate about what she would do in that worst-case scenario. It wouldn't happen, she told herself, just as she had since they had begun this. She wouldn't be faced with that decision. Not now. For all intents and purposes they were through, their mission complete. All they had to do was get to the border, which was less than five miles away, and wait for their contact to pick them up.

All they had to do. Those had been Josh's words. And he didn't seem to feel that the fact that those five miles were crawling with rebel forces searching for what they were trying to smuggle out of the country would make any difference.

The soldier shouted something over his shoulder. Despite her familiarity with the languages in the region and the crash course the CIA had given them in this specific one just before they'd left, she couldn't understand the idiomatic dialect he was using. However, the sweeping gesture that urged the others to join him was universal.

She glanced at Josh again. Without looking her way, he held his semiautomatic up in one hand and pointed to it with the other. Only then did she realize she didn't have her weapon out.

Pushing against Josh to let him know he had to give her some room, she unbuttoned the middle buttons of her parka and reached inside, her palm closing around the metallic weight of her own pistol. She held it for a second or two, and then she made herself pull it out. By that time there were two other soldiers converging toward their hiding place.

The building she and Josh had taken shelter in had once been some kind of government office. The top stories had been destroyed in one of the Russian air strikes, as had most of the rest of the village, with the exception of an old stone church, which was fairly intact. That had been the first place Josh had considered, but he had rejected it in favor of this one.

This particular building had collapsed inward, spilling structural debris from the top floors into the basement. The subfloor of the bottom story had been left partially intact, however, and it was under that part, sheltered against one of the outside walls, that they were hiding. The foundation had cracked as the building came crashing down, and they were looking out through a narrow separation that had opened up between the subfloor and the stones of the cellar.

They had had to crawl through a maze of fallen beams, broken boards and plaster to get into this corner. At the time, she had been relieved because it had seemed incredibly safe. Directly over their heads, the subfloor sloped toward the center of the basement, leaving just enough room for her to stand upright and be able to look out. Josh, who was taller by a good five or six inches, had to stoop to see out of the crack.

Two other soldiers had now joined the one outside. There could be no doubt that their attention was on this structure. One of them walked forward, stepping up onto the boards directly above her and Josh. Paige ducked her head, closing her eyes as a rain of dirt and broken mortar showered down on them.

The soldier's boots echoed across the wooden floor above. He was making his way slowly because of the treacherous angle at which the boards inclined and the danger that the damaged floor might collapse under his weight. Which wouldn't be a good thing for him or for them, Paige thought.

If he did make it across, on the far side of the cellar, clearly visible, was the set of steps they had climbed down this afternoon. The top ones had been exposed by the shattered floor joists, and from there the path she and Josh had taken across the debris-strewn basement wouldn't be hard to follow. Their footprints would be obvious in the dust that had filtered down after the building's collapse.

She felt Josh shift so that he was facing the opposite direction, looking behind them now. His movements had been painstakingly careful and almost noiseless, so as not to draw the attention of the soldiers outside. He was trying to get into a defensive position if the one who was in the building found them.

If that happened, Josh would be counting on her to take out the others before they could come inside. And then he would expect her to prevent the soldiers on the other side of the square from joining in the fray. Moving as quietly as Josh had, she raised her weapon, training the muzzle on the two men waiting outside.

Above their heads, the footsteps stopped. Paige didn't know if that was because the soldier had found the broken beams too dangerous to cross or because he had spotted the cellar steps.

She heard him call out something to the others. One of the words had been stairs, she knew, but she didn't get much of the rest. Under the assault of adrenaline, her mind seemed numb, focused only on the two men outside, who were her responsibility.

She put her left hand around the stock of the pistol, steeling herself to pull the trigger. That's all she had to do. *Point and squeeze. Don't think. Just point it and keep squeezing until it's over.*

As the two began to move forward, she could hear the

other soldier behind her now, much closer than he had been before. He must be at least part of the way down the steps, and unconsciously, she tightened her grip on the gun.

And then, suddenly, the two outside began looking over their shoulders. Shifting her gaze to that direction, she watched a military transport pull into the village square. The sound of its engine finally reached her ears, a few seconds after the men outside had become aware of it.

The truck seemed as dated as the rebels' weapons, but given its olive drab color, there was no doubt what it was. Or, after a moment, why it was here. There were distant shouts, and the troops who had been searching the rubble began to trot toward the truck and clamber up onto the open bed. One of the soldiers standing outside the building where she and Josh were hiding turned back and called to their companion.

There was an exchange of shouts. Holding her breath again, Paige listened as the searcher's footsteps began to retrace his route over the broken boards above their heads. The dust dislodged by his passage this time was less than before.

Then the soldier jumped off the subfloor right in front of the crack. Paige flinched involuntarily with the thud his combat boots made when they hit the ground.

As the three began to walk toward the truck, one of the others threw an affectionate arm around the shoulders of the man who had been in the process of descending into the basement. Consoling him? And then, laughing at something he said in response, the three began to jog toward the truck.

Neither she nor Josh said anything until the rebel forces were all aboard. As soon as they were, the transport began to move, lumbering out onto the main street with a belch of smoke from the exhaust and an ominous grinding of gears. As the sound of its laboring engine faded into the twilight, silence descended over the remains of what had once been a thriving community.

"Close call," she said. Her heart was beginning to slow, beating in her chest rather than crowding her throat.

"The very best kind," Josh said softly, his eyes still scanning the deserted village.

Looking for what? she wondered. Someone left behind to secure this place? To see if anything suspicious popped up after the rest of the unit departed?

The two of them wouldn't show themselves, of course. Not until he was sure there was no one there. The Joshua Stone she had come to know in these four months took nothing for granted.

"What does that mean?" she asked, willing her voice to steadiness. "The 'best' kind. As far as I'm concerned there isn't a 'good' close call."

He turned, his eyes examining her features, which she imagined showed the strain of the last few minutes. "A *good* close call is one you survive, Daniels. A little danger gets the juices flowing. Keeps you young," he said.

Paige felt as if she had aged ten years while she'd been waiting for the soldier to discover them. "You, maybe," she said. "I don't think danger has that same effect on me."

"So what effect does it have on you?"

She hesitated a moment, and then she said truthfully, "It makes me glad to be alive."

"And makes you appreciate life in a way you don't think about too often," he suggested.

He was right, of course. She was very glad to be alive. She wasn't sure, however, if that equated to *feeling* more alive. Or to feeling younger. As for those flowing juices, there didn't seem to be enough moisture in her body to work up a good spit. Her mouth was dry, hands trembling. Only with that observation did she realize that she was still holding her weapon.

"Think it's safe to put this away?" she asked, lifting the pistol as she glanced up to find Josh's eyes were on her face. They were again illuminated by the light which filtered in through the crack. For the first time since she'd known him, their blue seemed dark. Mysterious and unfathomable.

And his face was set, harder than she had ever seen it before, a tic visible in the tightness of his jaw. As she watched, his lips flattened. Then he turned his head, looking out through the narrow opening once more. She felt the breath he took, deep and uneven.

"Is something wrong?" she asked.

He turned to face her, his eyes assessing. Then he stepped back, bending and laying his weapon on the concrete floor. He shrugged out of the camouflage backpack he was wearing, propping it carefully against the wall. Her eyes followed those movements. When Josh straightened, she expected some kind of explanation. Instead he simply looked at her again.

Unspoken permission to put her own gun away, as she had asked? If so, she wasn't averse. Especially since she understood that would mean Josh felt they were no longer at risk.

They would probably wait out the night here. It was as good a place as any, especially since the village had already been searched. In the morning, according to plan, they would head for the border, deliver what they had been sent here to retrieve, and then get the hell out of Dodge. And despite Josh's teasing, that hot bath was going to feel very good.

She lowered her pistol, unwrapping the nearly bloodless fingers of her left hand from around those of the right. She usually kept the weapon in the side pocket of the fatigue-type pants she wore, and she wanted it back there, out of the way. She doubted Josh would approve. The location was not particularly handy, not if she needed the gun in a hurry.

Given her ambiguous feelings about engaging in any kind

of shoot-out with the rebel forces, however, that was okay by her. She'd leave the quick-draw responses to people like Joshua Stone.

She looked down to guide the insertion of the barrel back through the opening of her parka. Josh's hands were suddenly there, preventing her. Surprised, she looked up, expecting to find that she had somehow misinterpreted what she had thought was permission to put her weapon away.

As she hesitated, trying to understand, his left hand took the pistol and shoved it into the pocket of his own jacket. And then his right hand slipped into the opened placket of her coat.

Holding her eyes, he began to unbutton her shirt, fingers moving quickly over the task, as if this were something he had done a thousand times. He probably had. But not with her.

As soon as he had undone two or three of the buttons, his hand flattened and pushed inside the opening he'd created. And his palm encountered not bare skin, of course, but her long johns. She could tell by the sudden widening of those blue eyes that he hadn't expected the thermal underwear, despite the climate.

"Think you could possibly have on any more clothes, Daniels?" he asked, the teasing note back in his voice.

She was almost too shocked by what had happened to formulate an answer. And more shocked when his palm moved upward to cup the softness of her breast. As it did, his eyes dilated slightly, the pupils expanding outward into that rim of sapphire.

She wasn't wearing a bra. She wasn't all that well-endowed to begin with. Besides, Josh was right. She had on so many layers of clothing as protection against the cold that she had known no one would ever be able to tell. Now, of course...

Josh's thumb and forefinger found her nipple, pebbled

with cold and the aftereffects of fear. It seemed to have hardened even more now with anticipation. Watching her face, he rolled it between his fingers, the pressure almost enough to be pain. And almost ecstasy. As the sweet, hot heat began to roil through her lower body, she closed her eyes, exhaling through her mouth the breath she hadn't realized she was holding.

"You like that?" he asked softly, increasing the pressure.

She nodded wordlessly. The juices he'd talked about flooded her body in a molten stream of sensation as he touched her.

"Then tell me," he demanded. "Tell me you like it, Daniels. I need to hear you say it."

"I like it," she whispered, knowing only now that this was what she had been waiting for for four months. Right or wrong. Smart or very stupid, she had been waiting for Joshua Stone to touch her. Waiting for him to claim her body. To possess it.

She wanted him to do those things. Most of all, she wanted him. Wanted him with a need so sharp it, too, verged on pain.

"I've been wanting to do this for a long time," he whispered, seeming to echo her silent confession. "A very long time. Every night I'd listen to the rustle of your clothes, and I'd imagine I was undressing you. And then I'd hear that cloth moving over your skin, and I'd imagine my mouth there instead. My tongue touching all the places you were bathing. But *I'd* be bathing them. Caressing them. Caressing you."

He had put his cheek against her forehead, and his mouth was moving beside her temple, his whiskers abrasive. His breath was warm and moist as it stirred over the fragile skin, which had already dampened with a fine dew of perspiration just at the thought of what he was saying. Another sensation to add to the dominance of his fingers, which had never ceased their movement over and around her nipple.

"All those cold nights, I'd lie in that bed thinking about how warm I'd be if you were under me, your skin sliding, wet and slick, against mine."

The last was so soft the words were little more than breath. Less sound than the suggestion of it. And the images they produced were as seductive as the husky timbre of his voice. His mouth on her skin, warm lips gliding over her cold, shivering body. His tongue touching all the intimate places that no man had ever touched in that way before. No one before Josh Stone.

Compared to him, she had known she was inexperienced. Maybe that had been one of the things she had found so exciting. She had known that if he ever made love to her, it would happen in exactly this way. He wouldn't ask permission. Or give her warning. He would simply take her. Dominating. Controlling.

And even if she had no idea what she wanted, he would know how to please her. She had understood from the beginning that he would be this kind of lover. She had wanted him to be.

He lowered his head, putting his lips against her neck. His tongue followed the blood as it pulsed through the artery there. Then it traced to her ear, dipping inside, and slowly trailed downward again, until his mouth encountered the top of her shirt.

Think you could possibly have on any more clothes, Daniels? he had asked. But what she had put on, she could take off.

She wanted his lips and his tongue on her body. Moving over the hollow of her collarbone and across the small, highly sensitized swell of her breast. Circling her nipple, just as his fingers had caressed it, their movements sure and unhurried. So sure. So knowing. As his mouth would be.

She turned her head, bending her knees a little so she could put her lips under his. His head tilted to accommodate the kiss, his mouth fastening hungrily over hers. There was nothing tentative about the movement, but he didn't push his tongue inside as she expected. His lips played with hers, making contact and then breaking it, only to touch her mouth again at a slightly different angle. A series of small weightless kisses, which gradually gave way to something else.

His mouth opened, his lips moist and warm, trailing languidly over hers. Breaking off and then coming back to hers again. And again. And yet again.

Only after what seemed an eternity did his mouth fully open and his tongue contact hers. Her lips had already parted, ready for the invasion that was not an invasion, but the long-awaited answer to an unspoken invitation.

His head turned slightly, the alignment again perfect. He eased her against the wall at her back, one arm around her waist. His fingers deserted her breast and worked at the buttons of her clothing, a barrier between them that neither wanted there.

He never released her mouth, however, plundering it even as he unfastened and pushed aside layers of fabric. He eased her parka over her shoulders, guiding it down her arms, and she let it fall to the floor.

She should have felt the cold, but she didn't. She was aware of nothing but the movement of his mouth and his hands. After he had tugged her shirt out of her pants and unfastened the last of its buttons, it followed the jacket to the floor. Only when he pulled the top of her thermal underwear over her head did he break the contact of the kiss, just long enough to accomplish that task.

"Your turn," he said, his mouth again over hers, so that the words were muffled by her lips, almost lost against them. Her mind seemed drugged by his kisses, so that she didn't respond for a moment. And he didn't wait.

He unzipped his parka, shrugging out of it and dropping it onto the floor beside hers. And then he took her hands and put them against the buttons of his shirt. Finally, she seemed to comprehend what he wanted her to do.

Her fingers trembled over the simple task, and after a moment his hands lifted, brushing hers aside as he pulled the shirt out of his pants and then apart, those two actions almost simultaneous. And as soon as he had, he leaned against her.

His bare chest pressed against her breasts, flattening them, and her breath released in a low moan. She was conscious on some level of the cold, damp stones behind her, but she was far more conscious of the warmth of the solid wall of his chest, hair-roughened, moving enticingly against the front of her body. Against the hardened peaks of her breasts.

Her arms went around him, spread hands caressing. Following the corded muscle of his shoulders and the long, elegantly sculpted back and narrow waist. Trailing up the smoothly ringed column of his spine.

They were completely naked above the waist, and oblivious to the cold. Their bodies were pressed tightly together. Hands exploring. And it wasn't enough. Not nearly enough. Not for either of them.

His palms cupped under her hips, lifting her into his erection. She gasped again as she felt the undeniable proof that he was as aroused by what they were doing as she was. *A little danger gets the juices flowing.*

Was that what this was all about? A reaction to what had just occurred? To the close call they'd had? *And if it were?* she asked herself, the intellectual question almost unimportant as her palms moved over the warm, smooth skin of his back. Did she really care about his motives? Were hers any purer?

This was about two people coming together after a long and tantalizing physical awareness. Maybe that's all it was for him, despite what else it was for her. And if, as his reputation indicated, this was all Joshua Stone was ever willing to give, she would take it. Her decision. And her choice.

She arched her back, changing resolution into action. His hands were still cupped under her hips, and as she moved, he pulled her closer, groaning as their bodies came together, as close as they could get physically, given the situation.

And then he released her, dropping her back to the ground so quickly she staggered. His hands, working at the fastening of her pants, steadied her by the simple expedient of grabbing a handful of their fabric.

Then, he was unbuttoning and unzipping with a frenzied urgency. Her hands found the waistband of his trousers, working as hurriedly, as desperately.

Given that frenzy, she expected him to take her standing up, pressed against the wall behind her. Instead, he bent, putting one knee on the floor, and pulled the two down-filled parkas together to form a makeshift pallet at her feet.

When he looked up, the slant of fading light from the crack over his head fell on his eyes, highlighting them. Their pupils were wildly dilated now, either from the darkness in the cellar or because of what was happening between them.

She could barely see the rest of his features, but his mouth was set again, almost stern, unsmiling. And for some reason a jolt of anxiety moved through her stomach. That was not the way a man about to make love should look.

When he held up his hand, inviting her to join him on top of the two parkas, she never thought about refusing. She put her still-trembling fingers into his strong, dark ones, letting him pull her down to the spread coats. As his body lowered over hers, moving as if he had all the time in the world, the last thing she saw before the subtle remains of daylight faded away into night were Joshua Stone's eyes looking down into hers.

And no matter how many times she recreated that scene during the next three years, she found she could never quite be sure what had been in them.

Chapter One

"Special Ops is asking for you."

Paige glanced up from the magnifier through which she was studying the latest satellite images of a site along the Russia-Afghanistan border. Her boss hadn't stopped at her desk. He had simply tossed the paper that held the message he had delivered down on it and then disappeared into his own office.

Special Ops, she thought, wondering how long it had been since she had heard those words. *Not nearly long enough.*

She wished she could treat the summons as casually as Pete Logan had. Instead, the phrase created an unwanted frisson of anxiety. Almost in self-defense, she looked down through the magnifying glass again, ignoring the paper Logan had dropped on her desk and trying to bring her concentration back to the photographs that had come in only an hour ago.

She had been totally absorbed in them before the interruption. After all, this was her job. Being at the beck and call of Special Operations was not, she thought fiercely, feeling her anger build, despite her attempt to focus on the satellite images. The days she had spent with the spooks were over and done. Long gone. Long forgotten.

Which was why, of course, her ability to concentrate was

all of a sudden shot to hell, she thought in disgust. She pushed the magnifier away, the motion almost violent.

Special Ops. What the hell could Special Ops want with her? She glanced at the paper lying on the outer edge of her desk, as reluctant to pick it up as if it were something vile.

The print was facing the other direction, and she couldn't quite manage to decipher the upsidedown signature of whoever had issued the request. After a fruitless few seconds of trying, she reached out and turned the paper around, her eyes automatically scanning the one-line message before they fell to the name at the bottom. It was one she recognized.

Her gaze lifted to the door of Logan's office, but she resisted the impulse to go in and ask if he knew any details. Even if he did, it wouldn't change anything. She knew that. She would have to answer this summons, no matter how unpleasant reentering that world, if only for a little while, might be.

Too many memories, she thought. Too many ghosts. And she wasn't looking forward to resurrecting a single one of them.

"Why now?" Paige asked. "I told you people everything I knew when it happened."

"*You* people?" Carl Steiner repeated pointedly, his tented fingers resting under his chin. His dark eyes were amused.

She understood why he had questioned her wording. She had once been one of the people assigned to the CIA's Special Operations Branch, which Steiner was now head of.

"I told Griff," she said. "It's in the incident report."

"Tell *me*," Steiner said. He hadn't raised his voice, but that was obviously an order. As an assistant deputy director, he was entitled to give them.

Paige didn't know why she would hesitate to tell him. Other than the fact that she couldn't see any point in bringing something to life that had been stone-cold dead, maybe even back when she had reported on it to Griff Cabot. Nearly three years ago, she realized with a sense of disbelief.

It didn't seem possible it had been that long since she had sat in this room pouring out that painful story to someone she considered a friend. Her eyes rose to study the face of the man who now sat behind Cabot's desk. A man who *wasn't* her friend and never had been.

She didn't have any reason to dislike Carl Steiner. Not any concrete one, anyway. When the External Security Team had been disbanded, however, there had been a lot of rumors that this man had had a major role in that decision.

They had all known, intellectually at least, from the moment of Cabot's death that the demise of his team would follow. But when the order had come down, none of them had been prepared. The team and their relationships to one another had been too important. Too much a part of who each of them had been then.

"I want you to tell me about Joshua Stone," Steiner said, his eyes on her face.

Paige had no idea what it might reveal, but that same sensation she had felt when she had heard her boss say Special Ops lurched through her stomach again. Just at the sound of the name. *His* name.

"He disappeared," she said. And then nothing else.

She didn't know what Steiner wanted from her. Or why they were bringing this up after all this time. Joshua Stone was almost certainly dead and buried in some frozen wasteland thousands of miles from here. There was no reason not to let him stay buried, she thought, resenting Steiner's stirring of the ashes of her life. Particularly these.

"Circumstances?" Steiner prodded, glancing down at a folder in front of him.

Paige's eyes followed his, wondering if he were looking at Griff's report. And wondering if Cabot had written down everything she had told him. Even those parts she had clearly intended to be for his ears only.

Maybe there ought to be an official designation within government communications for the kind of conversation they had shared that day. She had never told anyone else the truth about what had happened in Vladistan. No one but Griff. And no matter what Steiner said, she knew she never would.

"We had completed our mission," she said. As soon she uttered the word "mission," her mind had gone back, reliving those long-ago events, in spite of the fact that she had sworn never to revisit these memories.

Steiner hadn't given her much choice, however, and she supposed it would be better just to get this over. Tell him only as much as she wanted to and no more. And trust that Griff hadn't betrayed her confidence about the rest.

"We were supposed to meet our contact the next day," she continued, forcing the words through her throat, which seemed constricted. "There was more rebel activity along the border than we had expected. We had to hide a few times from patrols, the last time just a few miles from the border. We knew we were cutting it close, but…it hadn't been an easy assignment."

Her voice faded, thinking how true that was. The area had been unstable when they had been sent in, and in the months they had spent there, everything had fallen apart. Including their in-country support. At the last, it had been just her and Josh.

"Go on," Steiner prompted.

"And then…Stone disappeared," Paige said, her voice softer than she had intended. More emotional? People like Steiner didn't like emotion, not of any kind. That's why they were here. Why they were the ones in charge.

"You woke up the morning before you were to cross the border and found that Stone was missing."

She nodded, determined not to remember the events of the night before that discovery. She had done that too many times. Especially during that first year.

A long time ago. Just saying those words in her head was a form of comfort, putting distance between her life now and what had happened then. *Do it,* she told herself. *Tell him the rest and be done with it. Put it behind you again.*

"Russian tanks rolled in less than four hours later, and Griff, through our contact, ordered me out. I wasn't given any choice about whether I wanted to leave or not."

"And exactly what did you do in those four hours?"

There seemed to be accusation in the tone of the question, and Paige's eyes narrowed against it. "I tried to find Josh. We had to get out before the Russians came, so I tried to find him."

"And the nerve agent?"

That's why they had been sent into Vladistan. To find and bring out a deadly neurological toxin, a new class of nerve agent for which there were no antidotes. It had been developed in one of the old Soviet weapons complexes, located in the region. When the rebellion started, the fear in the West was that the rebels might use the agent against the invading Russian troops, provoking a nuclear retaliation.

And then suddenly, feeling stupid that she hadn't figured it out before, Paige realized this was what Steiner's summons was all about. There was again unrest within Vladistan. Some people were already predicting another rebellion. Had that nerve agent now shown up in the wrong hands?

It could, of course. It could have at anytime during the last three years, she supposed, because when Joshua Stone had disappeared, that lethal toxin had disappeared with him.

"Josh was carrying it in his backpack," she said. "I never saw it again." *Or him.*

She had told Griff the truth about what had happened between them. A truth that might even be included in the folder Steiner had in front of him, but she didn't intend to mention her personal involvement with Joshua Stone unless Steiner brought it up. The uneasy silence built until he broke it.

"When you woke up," Steiner said, his voice flat, no longer questioning, "Stone was gone."

Paige nodded.

"And you never saw him again?"

Something about the question bothered her. Not the words themselves, which were only the truth, but the nuance of tone in which he had asked. Was that skepticism she heard?

"Griff believed Josh must have been killed shortly after he left the building where we had taken shelter. The whole area was in chaos. Full of rebel patrols."

"Yet Stone, an experienced operative, left the safety of your hiding place. And he left it alone, leaving you asleep."

"Maybe he heard something and went out to investigate."

She had tried for three years to come up with a viable explanation for Josh's actions. That was the only one that made any kind of sense to her. She could tell by Steiner's eyes that it made none to him.

"Or maybe he had an appointment," Steiner said. "A highly lucrative one."

At the time of his disappearance there had been elements within the agency who suggested Joshua Stone had seen an opportunity to make a fortune and had taken it. A new and very lethal nerve agent would bring millions on the terrorist black market. Stone had both the skills to get it out of the country, and, with his External Security Team experience, the contacts that would be necessary to sell it.

Griff Cabot had never credited that explanation for Josh's disappearance. Cabot had always had complete confidence in the integrity of his team. Stone, however, wouldn't have been the first CIA operative to have gone rogue, Paige admitted. And there had been something about his eyes that last night...

"If you're suggesting that Joshua Stone turned traitor, then you need to review his record," she said aloud, blocking that niggling, disloyal image. "Griff Cabot, who knew Stone better than anyone else, dismissed that possibility out of hand."

"Griff would never admit that one of his operatives had gone bad. I'm afraid I'm not quite that...trusting."

"If you seriously believe Joshua Stone sold that nerve agent to the highest bidder, then how do you explain why it's never been used?" A shot in the dark, Paige acknowledged, but she had heard nothing in the last three years to suggest it had.

"Maybe whoever bought it is biding their time, waiting for the right opportunity."

"Or maybe whoever killed Stone never found the toxin," Paige said. "Maybe they never realized what he was carrying."

"I confess I prefer your scenario to mine," Steiner said. "I suppose only time will tell which of us is right."

"It seems to me that three years is time enough to tell. Joshua Stone wasn't a traitor."

"And I sincerely hope you're right about that, too," Steiner said, closing the folder and getting to his feet. "If we need any further information, we'll be in touch."

His face was unreadable, but it was clear from his words that he considered the interview to be at an end. Paige knew she should be relieved, both that it was over and that his questions had been no more probing. For some reason, however, there was a letdown after the abruptness with which this questioning had ended. The whole thing seemed anticlimactic, especially in the face of the frightening suggestions he had made.

Paige stood, pushing the heavy leather chair back from

the edge of the desk. She wondered if she should offer him her hand and decided, illogically, that she didn't want to shake hands with Carl Steiner. She didn't want anymore contact with him than was necessary. She reached the door to his office and then, very definitely against her better judgment, she turned back.

Steiner was still standing behind his desk. He was looking down at the file he had just closed, the tips of the fingers of his right hand resting on top of it, as if it might spring open if he didn't hold it shut.

"Why now?" she asked again.

His dark eyes lifted, questioning.

"Why bring me in to talk about this now?" she asked.

There was the smallest of pauses, not even enough to call suspicious, unless you were already suspicious. "The region is becoming unstable again. This is a loose end that was never satisfactorily resolved. The agency doesn't like those. Since you were the last person to see Stone alive..."

A loose end? Somehow Paige didn't think he meant the disappearance of Joshua Stone. Steiner's concern was almost certainly for that incredibly dangerous chemical weapon, which had gone missing in a region noted for being a powder keg.

As she watched, the thin lips of the head of Special Ops moved into what was supposed to be a smile. It seemed cold, lacking in feeling. Maybe someone like Steiner didn't really feel. Maybe that's what made him good at this. And maybe that's what had made her such a failure.

"Good luck," she said, barely avoiding sarcasm.

She put her hand on the knob and opened the door, stepping out into the deserted hallway, and then closing it carefully behind her, deliberately not letting it make any noise.

She hadn't believed him, she realized. Intuition, maybe, but she thought Carl Steiner was lying about wanting to tie up loose ends. Something had happened, something besides the ongoing instability of that area. Something that had re-vived the mystery of Joshua Stone's disappearance.

However, whatever was happening in Special Operations these days, she told herself determinedly, was no longer of any concern to her. And thank God, it was also no longer her responsibility.

JACK THOMPSON hunched his shoulders, holding the evening paper he'd just bought over his head as he made a run for the cab that had finally pulled up to the curb in front of his office building. He hated rain. Especially cold rain. It made all the bones that had been broken ache with a renewed vengeance.

He jerked open the cab door, slid in across the cold vinyl of the back seat, and then slammed it shut against the down-pour. After he gave the driver his address, he settled grate-fully into the taxi's stale warmth.

He'd take a couple of extra-strength aspirin when he got home, he decided, and turn up the thermostat. He had some stronger stuff, but he saved that for the headaches. He hadn't had one of those in almost three weeks, he realized, and he hoped to God he never had another.

He gazed out the window as they began to move, watch-ing the twilight-darkened streets rush by through the screen of raindrops on the glass. A car had pulled out from a park-ing place on the opposite side of the street at the same time the cab had, and its headlights briefly haloed the droplets with rims of gold.

"Rain's a bitch," the driver said, "but I hear this stuff'll turn to snow tonight. I ain't looking forward to that either."

Jack pulled his eyes from the wet gleam of the sidewalks, which were reflecting the lights from the stores behind them, and glanced at the back of the driver's head.

"I hadn't heard about the snow," he said.

"Not from around here, are you?" the driver asked, meeting his eyes in the mirror. "Originally, I mean."

"No," Jack said. His accent was different enough that it sometimes evoked comment, although Atlanta was pretty cosmopolitan these days. He wasn't from the South, however, and anyone who was spotted that immediately.

"Where you from?"

He knew the driver was only making conversation, maybe to relieve boredom, maybe in hopes of a larger tip. And Jack could have supplied the facts easily enough. Trying to feel some connection with them, he had gone over the information the cops had provided a million times.

He knew everything on those sheets by heart. And none of it felt real. Or meant anything to him. That would pass, the doctors had assured him. That feeling of disassociation with who he was. Simply the lingering result of the head injury. And, they had said, he was lucky its effects hadn't been more severe.

"Don't push it," the psychiatrist he had seen at the last hospital had warned. That had been just before Jack had been released from the rehab center, his physical injuries healed, even if his memory hadn't yet returned. *"If it comes, it comes. If you try to get it all back, if you push too hard, then...who knows what may happen?"* the doctor had said, shrugging.

Jack could remember wondering exactly what he meant by that. He had made it sound as if Jack's brain would implode or something if he tried to force the return of those memories.

Still, he knew they were there, lying just below the surface of his mind. Sometimes, especially in dreams, they were so close he could almost touch them. It was like looking down into a dark pond and seeing things beneath the surface, murky and unclear, but definitely there. Just a little too far down to reach.

"Hey, buddy," the cabbie said.

Jack's eyes came back up, meeting the questioning ones in the rearview mirror. The cabbie was looking at him as if he thought Jack was some kind of nutcase. People did that sometimes. They seemed to pick up on the fact that there was something wrong. That something about him didn't fit anymore. Jack never was quite sure how they knew, but their eyes always looked at him just like this guy's were now.

"Des Moines," he said.

"Yeah?" the driver said, his voice relieved. "Could'a fooled me. That don't sound like the Midwest."

Jack smiled, and then he deliberately turned his head, looking out the window again as the rain-glazed streets swept by. He had heard that comment a couple of times before, and it had bothered him enough that he had even checked it out. Not so much because of the accent, but because of the way he felt.

So he had paid one of those people-find agencies on the Web to do a search for a Jack Thompson from Des Moines. It had all been there. Exactly like the cops had told him.

Then why the hell can't I remember any of it? Why the hell doesn't any of it feel as if it has a damn thing to do with me?

There was no answer from the gathering darkness to either of those questions. Just as there hadn't been for the past three months. And he was beginning to be forced to think about the possibility that there never would be.

PAIGE KNEW as soon as she opened the door to her apartment that someone had been there. A hint of something alien lingered in the familiar air. It took her a second or two to identify the smell as cigarette smoke.

Maybe not the smoke itself, she acknowledged, taking a deep breath, but the whiff of it that clings to a chronic smoker's clothes and hair. She stood before the door she had closed behind her, wondering if there was someone else in her apartment. A burglar? Or another, more dangerous kind of intruder?

It felt empty, however. She knew intuitively that whoever had been here was now gone. If she had come home half an hour later, the heating system and the filters would probably have taken care of the faint odor, and she would never have known.

The first thing she did was to take the semiautomatic out of the bedside drawer where she kept it. Although she was grateful to have it in her hand, it felt almost as alien as the ghostly scent she was chasing. Then, despite her sense that there was no one here, she checked out all four rooms, opening closets, looking under the bed and behind the shower curtain.

Nothing seemed to have been taken or disturbed. Despite that, she couldn't help but feel as if she had been invaded. Violated, somehow. This was her home, and someone had come into it without her permission.

It wasn't until her hand was on the phone to report the break-in, that she remembered the call to maintenance she'd made. More than three weeks ago, she realized. It had been her first request for repairs since she had moved in. Was it possible, she wondered, that the maintenance staff had let themselves in without notifying her they were coming?

Which should be easy enough to check out. She walked over to the light switch by the door that led from the living room into the kitchen. It controlled the overhead fixture in the kitchen and had started malfunctioning a few weeks ago.

Of course, she could walk across the kitchen and turn on the overhead light by using the switch beside the sink, but since these were newly constructed apartments, something going wrong so quickly had seemed strange. She had been afraid it might mean faulty wiring, which had made her nervous enough to call.

She pushed the switch up now, and the fixture in the middle of the kitchen ceiling didn't respond. Which didn't necessarily mean maintenance hadn't been here, she acknowledged. Just that they hadn't fixed whatever was wrong.

Paige walked back to the phone, shrugging out of her coat and throwing it over the back of the couch as she did. She took the resident manager's card out of the drawer of the end table where the phone was sitting, and laying the pistol down, she punched in his number. She'd feel better knowing that he had sent someone up here today, she thought, as she listened to the distant ring. A hell of a lot better.

When he said hello, she got right to the point. "This is Paige Daniels in 1228. I was just wondering if you sent somebody up here to look at my kitchen light switch?"

"Hold on a minute," the manager said. In the background she could hear the sound of papers rattling and finally he came back on the line. "It's gonna be a while on that, Miss Daniels. The crews are taking care of emergency situations first—heating and plumbing problems. You did say the other switch still works?"

One part of her mind was assimilating his denial and his questions. The other part was trying to figure who had been here if not maintenance. "It works," she agreed. The hand that wasn't holding the phone closed over the pistol again. "Look, are you absolutely sure no one's been up here today?"

"The switch start working again? Sometimes wiring does that. Probably just a short. If I were you, I'd just keep it off until we can get somebody up there to take a look at it.

"Would it be better to throw the breaker?" she asked, realizing only now that it was possible what she had smelled hadn't been tobacco smoke. Maybe it had been hot wiring.

"I don't see why you'd need to do that. Besides, that breaker probably controls some other stuff, too."

"I'm a little nervous because I smelled smoke when I

came in from work,'' she said, readily discarding her original theory.

''Just now?''

''About five minutes ago.''

''You still smell it?''

She took a breath, drawing air in through her nose. She had been inside long enough now that she couldn't smell anything. Coming in from the fresh air outside had made the scent of smoke obvious. Now however...

''I'm not sure. Look, could you just come up here and check out that switch? Maybe something's hot under the plate.''

There was a moment's hesitation. She couldn't blame him. It was Friday night, already late because she had stopped for dinner on the way home. And maintenance wasn't his job. Of course, keeping the complex from burning down probably was, at least as far as his employers would be concerned.

''I'll be right there,'' he said, apparently reaching that conclusion at the same time. ''You understand I can't fix the switch, but I *can* make sure nothing's smoldering under it.''

''Thanks,'' Paige said. ''I really appreciate this.''

She put the phone down and walked back over to the wall plate. It looked innocent enough. No telltale threads of smoke escaping from behind the ubiquitous plastic rectangle. She was probably being ridiculous.

She took a quick look around the apartment. There were a few dishes in the sink and her coat was out. She walked across to the couch and picked it up. She opened the drawer of the phone table and slipped the pistol inside before she carried her coat over to the hall closet and hung it up.

After she had shoved the dirty plate and cup from breakfast into the dishwasher, she headed back to take another look at the switch plate. She put her nose close to it, inhaling deeply, trying to find any trace of what she had smelled before. It seemed to have vanished, however, and she straightened, blowing the air she had just inhaled out in a small sigh of frustration.

She was headed back to the bedroom to look into her closet again when the doorbell rang. Maybe maintenance was slow, but the resident manager seemed to be on the ball.

Paige hurried to the door and looked out through the peephole. It was the same guy who had showed her the apartment six months ago. She turned the latch and the knob at the same time, a two-handed operation, and threw open the door.

"Hi," he said. The shoulders of his jacket were dark from the rain. He was carrying a small screw driver, and he had a pager on his belt, revealed by the open windbreaker.

Just as she had earlier, he stopped on the threshold and, lifting his nose, scented the air like a hunting dog. "Don't smell a thing," he said, smiling.

"Maybe it's a false alarm, but I definitely smelled something when I came in."

She didn't mention that her first impression had been cigarette smoke and that she had thought someone had been in here. Right now all she wanted was for him to make sure that during the night her apartment wasn't going to go up in flames with her inside it. Little enough to ask, she told herself.

He walked over to the switch and made the same sniff test she had made. She expected another comment about not smelling anything, but he didn't make it. Instead, he walked into the kitchen, and she heard him open the circuit box. There were clicking noises, and the light in the kitchen went off.

When he came back, he said, "Let's take a look."

He placed the tip of the screwdriver into one of the tiny Phillips head screws and began to unthread it. When he had finished with the first screw, he took the other one out, slipping the plastic plate off the wall. There was no whiff of smoke from the rough cut opening behind it. There was only a tangle of wires, none of them smoldering.

The manager put the screwdriver and the cover plate on the floor, carefully laying the screws on top of it. He bent so that he was on eye level with the hole in the wall. Then he reached into it with one finger, pushing around amid the wires.

"Nothing hot. No smoke. I think that it probably—" His voice stopped, as his finger probed deeper into the hole. "What in the world?" he said, the words almost under his breath.

Hearing them, Paige edged closer, anticipating a glimpse of a frayed or burnt wire. She couldn't see anything, however, and other than bending down and putting her head next to his as he poked around in there, she wasn't likely to.

Almost as soon as she thought that, he inserted his thumb as well as his index finger into the hole, fumbling among the wires. And when he straightened, he brought something small and dark out of the opening. He laid it on the palm of his other hand.

"Never seen anything like *this* before," he said. "Not in a wall switch. Maybe they were going to put in a dimmer and then changed their minds. Cost overruns, maybe. They must have decided to go with a less expensive option."

He held the object he'd retrieved from the faulty switch out for Paige's inspection. She didn't need a closer look. She had recognized it immediately. What the resident manager had just taken out of the wall of her apartment was the latest version of a very sensitive listening device. At some time during the six months she had lived here, someone had bugged her apartment.

SHE SPENT most of the night tossing and turning, everything that had happened running endlessly through her head. She

replayed Steiner's words, examining each of them, even trying to remember the expression on his face when he'd said
them. And every time she did, she came back to the same
comment. Something that hadn't reverberated as strongly
then as it should have.

Of course, at the time she hadn't known that the agency
was bugging her apartment. She still didn't *know* that, she
admitted, trying to be reasonable. What she did know was
that there had been a very sophisticated listening device
planted in her wall, exactly like the state-of-the-art ones the
CIA used.

She couldn't know how long the bug had been in place,
but the light switch had started acting up after she'd moved
in. Maybe a couple of months ago. Maybe a little less.

And another thing she knew was that someone had been
inside her apartment today. To put the device in her wall?
Or to check on it because it had stopped working?

Or had they been there for some reason totally unrelated
to the bug. To search the apartment? To read her computer
files? She hadn't found any evidence of either of those
things, but she knew that whoever the agency sent would be
good at what they did.

And "good at what they did" brought her back to the
other significant thing that had happened today: Steiner's
summons and the comments he had made as she had been
about to go out his door. *This was a loose end that was
never satisfactorily resolved. Since you were the last person
to see him alive…*

She thought all the pertinent questions about that mission
been asked back then. And as far as she knew, they had
been answered to the agency's satisfaction. Or at least to the
satisfaction of anyone who had known Joshua Stone.

Had a trusted operative disappeared in order to sell that
nerve agent on the black market, as Steiner implied? There
was no denying such a sale would have been a huge temp-

tation for some people. *Not* for Joshua Stone. She would never believe that.

Griff Cabot had believed that Stone had been captured by one of the opposing sides in the rebellion. If the Russians had taken him prisoner, they might have tried to arrange a trade, exchanging Josh for one of their own compromised agents. Washington usually agreed to such deals to get their people home, and Cabot would have done his best to influence them to make that decision. As far as Paige knew, no such offer had ever been made.

The strongest likelihood, given the time frame, was that Josh had heard someone outside the cellar that night. He had gone to investigate and been captured by the rebel forces.

Maybe they had taken him with them as they retreated from the Russian advance, intending to interrogate him later. Or maybe whoever had captured Josh hadn't known about the theft of the toxin. Maybe they had simply killed him, leaving his body and the backpack he'd carried in the snow, never knowing what a valuable prize they'd lost.

Whatever happened, Joshua Stone, the most experienced member of the External Security Team, had disappeared forever on that mission. And Paige Daniels, the novice, had escaped from Vladistan as Russian tanks rolled across its border. She had escaped, and Josh had not. Maybe, as she had always believed in her heart, because he had gone out into that dangerous darkness to protect her from whatever he had heard.

Lying in her bed, eyes open and staring, the haunting images of that night played again through her consciousness. The same night he had made love to her for hours, until she had finally drifted into a deep and exhausted sleep.

She hadn't allowed herself to indulge in this particular exercise in futility in a very long time, but she didn't deny those memories tonight. And they steeled her determination to prove Carl Steiner was wrong. She was as convinced today as she had been then that Joshua Stone hadn't been a traitor.

By bugging her apartment the agency seemed to be trying to implicate her in whatever they imagined Josh had done three years ago. And she knew she hadn't done anything wrong on that mission. Nothing except sleep while someone took her partner. Nothing except survive when he hadn't.

Now someone in his own agency was trying to blacken Joshua Stone's name. And there was no one from the External Security Team left to defend his reputation. No one but her.

She had failed him once before. No one had ever seemed to blame her, but she had always blamed herself. And after three long years, she had discovered that the ghost of Joshua Stone was one she needed very badly to put to rest.

Chapter Two

Reactivated.

Paige stared at the screen, trying to make sense of what she was seeing. As she tried to think what else that word could possibly mean, she fought a surge of emotion she didn't want to feel, not after all this time.

She had started her search as soon as she'd gotten into the office this morning, trying to discover what had set Steiner off. Something must have come to light fairly recently that had made him question Stone's disappearance. Something that had made him call her in. Something that had made them plant a listening device in her apartment. *Something.*

She had spent most of the day scanning page after page of the tedious situation reports that had come in about Vladistan during the last four months. Because of her work in Sector Analysis, she was already familiar with most of this material. And on closer examination she had found nothing that might be construed as having anything to do with Josh or with the nerve agent he had been carrying when he'd disappeared. The computers had been next, and she had cross-referenced everything she could think of that might apply to the region, to the rebellion, or to that particular mission. And again, she had come up empty.

It was only then, an exercise in nostalgia perhaps or

maybe because she had run out of ideas, that she had tried to access the old External Security Team files. Unbelievably, she had found that the access codes had never been changed. The files themselves were intact, even though the team hadn't even been in existence for more than two and a half years.

The bureaucratic mind works in mysterious ways, Paige had thought, as she typed in Joshua Stone's name. When the file came up, she had discovered the reactivated notation. And the date it had been made was less than four months ago. She scrolled through the whole thing, trying to find more recent additions or changes, but there were none.

Which made no sense, she thought in frustration. Why activate a dead file and then do nothing with it? Or was the reactivation simply a clerical error? Did somebody key in the wrong access number? Things like that happened, even at the CIA.

And she might have been willing to believe they had in this case, if it hadn't been for Steiner's questions yesterday. If you put these two things together, they had to mean something. Something obviously connected to Joshua Stone's disappearance.

Reactivated. There was nothing else there. Nothing after that one entry, which had brought a dead file back to life and out of limbo where it should have remained. Why would someone reactivate a file and then not put anything in it? That made no sense. Unless...

When the explanation hit her, producing a rush of adrenaline so strong her hands began to shake, it *all* made sense. Because it fit the pattern. *And* the bureaucratic mind-set. Joshua Stone had been a member of External Security, and she knew what had happened to the other operatives on that team.

As far as she could tell, she was the only one who was still working for the agency. After the fiasco in Vladistan,

she had requested a move back into Sector Analysis. Griff
had tried to talk her out of leaving, but the transfer had gone
through.

Then Cabot had been killed, and the elite antiterrorist
team he'd assembled stood down. Since she hadn't been a
member long enough to have participated in any of the black
ops missions the EST was famous for, Paige couldn't represent any threat to security, and she had been allowed to
stay in the CIA.

The other agents, however, had been destroyed—at least
on paper. And then they had been carefully resurrected. Recreated as totally different people, their original identities
erased. Their agency records had been purged, so that no
one could ever trace those men, or what they had done, back
to the agency.

In most cases, their names had been changed and they
had been relocated. At least a couple of them, like Jordan
Cross, had had their physical appearance altered as well.

Now she was looking at the agency's file on Joshua Stone,
a man who had been presumed dead *before* the team was
disbanded. It had been reactivated, brought back to life less
than four months ago. Then nothing had been added to the
folder, so maybe...

Paige closed the file and backtracked. There was no "list
all" feature on these kinds of secure files, so when she
reached the main directory, she typed in the date when the
designation on Stone's file had been changed. Then her
hands hovered over the keyboard as she stared at those numbers, almost afraid of what she might find. Finally, holding
her breath, she hit Search.

And was bitterly disappointed when there were no results,
other than in the folder she had just closed. There was no
other file with a matching date in this entire section of the
records. There shouldn't be *any* recent dates, of course, since

the team was no longer in existence, but that didn't explain why someone had changed the designation of Josh's folder.

She couldn't be wrong about this. It fit. It made sense. Maybe she was just rushing the bureaucracy, giving them more credit for efficiency than they deserved. After all, it might have taken them a while to decide what to do.

She typed in the following day's date. And when there were no results for that one either, she typed the next date in the blank. Then the next, working methodically now.

And finally, ten days after somebody had brought Joshua Stone's file back to life, there it was. A matching date. In the middle of all the inactive folders of a now-defunct, highly secretive special operations team was a brand new file. A new name. *But not a new man,* Paige knew with absolute certainty.

"Joshua Stone," she said softly. "Fancy meeting you here."

NOT MUCH DOUBT, Paige thought, her eyes focused on the man seated across the crowded restaurant. Not much doubt left at all, despite the obvious physical changes.

This was the closest she had come to him. Close enough to study his features. However, even at a distance, his mannerisms had seemed heart-stoppingly familiar. The set of his head. The understated, almost elegant power of his body. Something about the way he used his hands. Even their shape.

She knew in her heart that this was Joshua Stone. The blue-black hair was threaded with gray, and then there were the scars, slightly reddened as if they were still fairly new. One crossed his right brow, causing a break in its thick black line. The other ran from the corner of his lips, slanting downward across his chin to disappear under his jaw.

Even the structure of the bones seemed slightly altered, as if they had been broken and then put back together, the fit not quite as perfect as it had once been. His nose had definitely been reshaped, molded into something less arrogant. The result was no less compelling or attractive, but it *was* different.

She had been trailing the man who called himself Jack Thompson for almost two days, but she hadn't approached him. She had told herself that she wanted to be sure she wasn't mistaken. That this wasn't some kind of bizarre coincidence. That's what she had told herself, although she had known the truth about who he was, almost from the moment she had seen him again.

Now there were no more excuses. The only thing left in doubt was what she wanted to do about what she'd discovered. Because she knew that no matter what Griff Cabot had believed three years ago, Joshua Stone wasn't dead.

She didn't know where he had been during those years, but there was no mystery about where he'd been the last couple of months. He had been living in Atlanta, working for one of the international brokerage firms headquartered here. Paige had wondered if the company was a front for the CIA or if it was simply a legitimate business that had some reason to cooperate with the agency by placing one of its ex-agents—an operative the CIA wanted to hide—on its payroll.

She didn't suppose that really mattered. It was just something to think about instead of all the other things she'd been trying not to think about since she'd discovered Joshua Stone wasn't dead.

She looked down at the unappetizing salad in front of her, wondering why she had ordered it. *Because other than eating, there isn't any excuse for being here.*

Josh had eaten in this small neighborhood café both of the nights she'd been trailing him. He had stopped in on his way home from work. Having tried it now herself, she couldn't say much for his choice.

She poked at a piece of lettuce with her fork, finally spearing it, along with a piece of ham and a small slice of cheese, on the tines. She dipped the combination into the watery looking salad dressing, and then raised the fork to take a bite. She looked up as she did, directly into Joshua Stone's eyes.

She wondered if he felt anything remotely resembling the jolt that had given her, even from across the room. She looked down quickly, but she was forced to admit that this must have been what she was hoping for when she had come in here tonight. Hoping he would notice her. Hoping he would make contact, despite whatever rules the CIA had set up for his relocation.

She supposed that what the agency did with members of the EST worked like Witness Security. Contact with anyone from their former life would be forbidden. Even with a former partner.

She realized that she was still holding the forkful of food halfway to her mouth. Pretty telling, she supposed, but after all, Josh should understand. It wasn't often one was confronted with a ghost.

She wondered what he was thinking. That this was an accident? A fluke? Or that the agency, maybe even Steiner himself, had sent her?

She put the fork down on her plate, unable to make herself take that bite. And then slowly she raised her eyes again, prepared now to make contact with his.

Josh was eating, his concentration seemingly on the newspaper that was folded to fit beside his plate. Just as if he hadn't seen her.

But he had. There was no doubt in her mind about that. Which must mean that he didn't want to acknowledge her. Not in so public a place. And he was probably right about that.

She knew where he lived. She could approach him at his

apartment building. Or maybe on his way home, which was even safer, because it would give him the opportunity to decide where they should talk.

As she was thinking all that, the question she had been trying to deal with was still stirring in the back of her mind. For the past three years, she had tried *not* to think about Josh Stone because she had believed he was dead. Had he ever, during all that time, thought about her? After all, he had always known where to find her. Which must mean...

She turned her head, looking out at the street through the rain-streaked plate glass window beside her. Which must mean, she continued doggedly, no matter how painful she found the conclusion, that Josh had consciously made the decision not to try to see her again.

That decision would have nothing to do with whatever rules the CIA had set up for his disappearance. Joshua Stone didn't play by the rules. Few of Griff's agents ever had. That characteristic was almost a requirement for the EST. If Josh had *wanted* to contact her, he would have. And since he hadn't, she would have to assume he hadn't wanted to.

She could deal with that. She could deal with almost anything, she decided, feeling anger build again, as long as whatever was going on with Joshua Stone and the CIA didn't get her called into Steiner's office for the third degree. Or didn't make the agency bug her apartment.

She wanted an explanation for those two things. A truthful explanation, which she would never get from Steiner. Eventually, she damn well would get it from Josh Stone. After all, she thought with a trace of bitterness, he at least owed her that.

While Josh finished his dinner, and he didn't hurry over the meal, Paige drank the rest of her coffee, savoring both its warmth and the subtle stimulation of the caffeine. She couldn't keep her gaze from touching on him occasionally, and after a while she stopped trying.

His eyes were still locked on the newspaper he had brought in with him, acting as if he were completely unaware that Paige was sitting across the room. Of course, Josh was better at this game than she was. He always had been.

As soon as she saw the waiter bring his bill, she signaled for hers. She handed her server a ten, without taking the check he presented and waving away his attempt to make change. She slipped into her coat and headed straight toward the door, making no effort either to avoid or to pass near Josh's table.

He had made it clear by meeting her eyes that he was aware of her. And he had made it equally clear, by ignoring her, that he didn't want them to be seen together.

When she stepped through the door, she realized the rain that had plagued the Georgia city for most of the past two days had finally stopped. However, it must have dropped ten degrees while they'd been eating. She turned up the collar of her coat, holding it around her throat with one gloved hand.

She began to walk the three blocks to Josh's apartment, her eyes searching every foot of that distance for somewhere she could wait for him. It would need to be out of public view and yet within hailing distance of the sidewalk where he would pass. An alley or a recessed doorway. Actually, anything hidden or relatively sheltered from the eyes of passersby would do.

She could always wait beside the steps that led up to the front entrance of his apartment building. That was almost as public as the restaurant, however, and she suspected Josh wouldn't be any more eager to be seen with her there.

Finally, having found nothing better, she went down the short flight of stairs that led to the basement entrance of his building. She leaned against the damp concrete block wall, not fighting the memories the feel of it evoked, and looked up at the steps he would have to climb to reach the front door.

She wasn't sure he would notice her standing down here. And she still wasn't sure she would speak to him if he didn't. Actually, she admitted, she wasn't sure about much of anything.

Except that Joshua Stone wasn't dead. And that he had never sought her out during the three years that had passed since she had last seen him that night in Vladistan.

WHEN PAIGE finally heard footsteps, unconsciously she pressed more closely against the wall, her body hidden in the shadows as she listened. The footsteps passed by the front entrance and then by those that led down to the alcove under the stairs where she was hiding. She looked up in time to watch the man whose steps she'd been listening to walk by. It wasn't Josh, and she took a breath in relief.

Maybe he had stopped off somewhere on the way home to do some shopping or an errand. Or maybe he wasn't coming home because he suspected she would be waiting for him. And *maybe* a whole hell of a lot of other things, none of which she would have answers to unless Josh gave them to her. He obviously didn't plan to do that unless she approached him and asked for them.

What was wrong with her? she wondered suddenly. What was she doing here, waiting for a man who had made it clear he didn't want to see her? For some reason, she closed her eyes, fighting the sudden sting of tears. And she couldn't understand why she had this ridiculous urge to cry.

After all, the reason she was here wasn't personal. Their former relationship had impinged on her professional life. She was convinced that someone had bugged her apartment because of her association with Josh Stone, and she wanted to know why. She wanted answers that made sense. Answers from him.

The footsteps that approached this time didn't move past the entrance. She opened her eyes, ears straining to follow them. When they started up the front stairs, her heart jolted again, as strongly as when Josh had met her eyes across the restaurant.

And those reactions, after three long, silent years, made her furious. Not at him, but at herself. Using that anger, Paige stepped out of the shadows, looking up at the man climbing the stairs. At the man she had known as Joshua Stone.

Perhaps he noticed the movement. Or maybe the intensity of her stare made some kind of psychic impact. Whatever drew his attention, Josh looked down, again right into her eyes. Despite the distance between them, she could see his widen. Then they narrowed slightly, just as they used to when he was trying to figure something out. *And this one shouldn't be too hard.*

She didn't say anything, and neither did he. Their gazes held for maybe twenty seconds, and then he came quickly down the stairs he had just climbed. He glanced over to where she was standing a couple of times as he made the descent. To keep an eye on her? Afraid *she'd* disappear? she wondered, not even bothering this time to deny the corrosive bitterness she had fought during the last two days.

But disappearing wasn't her act. That's what he did. What he *had* done, she amended. He had just…disappeared.

Josh walked over to the top of the flight of steps leading down to the covered basement entrance where she was standing. He stood a long moment, unmoving, still looking at her.

"You were in the restaurant," he said finally.

She nodded, not trusting her voice to sound anywhere near normal. And, damn it, she wanted it to. She wanted it to sound calm and rational and unemotional.

"Were you waiting for me?" he asked.

How about for three years. Which wasn't completely fair, she admitted. Most of that time she had believed Josh must be dead. So that didn't constitute waiting, exactly. Besides, they had made no commitments. Not even...

"Is something wrong?" he asked. "Are you in trouble?"

"Steiner's asking questions about you," Paige said.

Despite her fear that her voice might betray her reaction to seeing him again, to being this close to him, the statement had sounded perfectly natural. Cryptic, perhaps, but at least she didn't think her tone gave away her inner turmoil.

"Steiner?" he repeated, as if puzzled by the reference.

"He took over when..." Paige stopped, suddenly unsure, maybe because of that seemingly genuine puzzlement, exactly what Josh had been told.

"You know about Griff," she said, not phrasing it as a question. If this was an agency hide, and everything she had found in the computers indicated it must be, then of course, Josh would know about Cabot's death.

They became aware at the same moment that someone was walking toward them. A man and a woman were approaching, moving toward him. Josh turned his head, openly watching them, which surprised her.

The couple walked passed the entrance, deeply engrossed in their conversation. Josh waited until their voices could no longer be heard before he looked down at Paige again. Even in the dimness, his eyes were as blue as she remembered them.

"Look, I don't know what you're talking about," he said. "Those names don't ring any bells. Maybe you've got me mixed up with somebody else."

She supposed she should have been expecting that denial, but she hadn't been. Maybe he was part of some witness security deal, with the formal constraints that imposed, but he was also her partner. Her lover. Or he once had been.

And he owed her more than this. They all did. From Steiner on down.

She had been lied to throughout this entire deal, and it infuriated her. She'd spent so many damn hours during those three years regretting the things she had done. Regretting even more the ones she hadn't done. Too many hours lost out of her life to be fobbed off with this crap.

"I don't think so," she said almost mockingly. "I don't think I've got you mixed up with anyone else."

He took a breath, his lips pursed slightly. She tried not to remember what they felt like moving over her skin in the darkness. Tried and failed, and for some reason that made her even more furious.

"Look—" he began again, his voice still reasonable, not reacting to the obvious anger in hers.

"Your name is Joshua Stone," she said, interrupting whatever lie he intended to offer. "You were a member of Griff Cabot's External Security Team. You and I were on a mission in Vladistan when you disappeared. That was three years ago. And then, less than four months ago, they put you back into the computers as Jack Thompson. I've seen the file, so 'You've got me mixed up with someone else' won't work, Josh. Not with me."

"Vladistan?" he repeated, and she wondered why he had picked that out of all the rest. "In...Russia?" he questioned.

"A republic of the former Soviet Union." Paige corrected. She sounded like some geography professor.

"Who is 'they'?" he said, ignoring the lesson. "Who put me back into the computer?"

He had asked those questions in exactly the right tone. As if he really *didn't* have a clue what she was talking about. Of course, Josh had always been good. So damn good at everything.

"The company," she said. That was the nickname for the CIA that almost everyone who worked for the agency used.

"Debolt?"

Which was the name of the firm he was working for here in Atlanta. Again the tone of his question held exactly the right note of confusion. She laughed, mocking his skill. The sound of her laughter almost prevented her from hearing his next question.

"After the accident?" he asked. "Is that what you mean?"

"What accident?"

The word had shocked her for some reason, jerking her out of her very satisfying anger. But the concern in her repetition was the wrong response, and she regretted it as soon as she had given it voice. She had wanted to convey her absolute certainty that she knew who he was and knew that he was lying to her. And then she had bit on that ploy like an amateur.

"The wreck," he said. "Is that what this is about? Insurance or something? If so, maybe you've got the right guy but the wrong name."

There was enough information there, and the tone reasoned enough, that she had to stop and think about what he had said. Accident. Wreck. Insurance. Wrong guy. Except, of course...

"Not Debolt," she said again, rejecting the scenario he had just dangled in front of her. "The CIA. And you *know* what I'm talking about, Josh, so let's stop playing games. Maybe you're only doing what they told you to do, but don't expect me to buy it. Maybe I didn't spend as many years in special ops as you did, but I spent long enough to know how to do a computer search. Joshua Stone dies, and Jack Thompson is born. It's all there. Right in the External Security files for anyone who wants to look for it. And I think that means you've got a problem."

He said nothing for a long time, his eyes still considering her face. Trying to read it, maybe? She didn't care if he was.

She was telling the truth. A truth he needed to hear. If she could find him, then a lot of other people could as well.

"I think you'd better come in," he said. "We need to talk."

The strongest emotion she felt when she heard that invitation was satisfaction. She had forced him to listen to her and to stop making those ridiculous denials. She started up the basement steps, expecting him to lead the way over to the street-level set of stairs and up to the building's front entrance.

Instead, he stayed where he was, watching her face until she reached the top. When he still didn't move, she stopped beside him, looking into his eyes. She didn't know what she had expected to find in them. Embarrassment that he'd tried to put her off like that? Admiration that she hadn't bought that cock-and-bull? Maybe even some memories.

They held none of those things. They were interested. Reflecting the same deep intelligence she remembered so vividly, but nothing else. Not even, it seemed, an admission that they had once been more to one another than professional associates.

"I take it I'm supposed to know you," he said.

Just when I was about to give you some credit, Paige thought. Her mouth tightened in frustration. She broke contact with his eyes, looking past him, focusing on the row of cars parked across the street. An exercise in gathering control, like counting to ten. And then it became something else.

"They're taping us," she said, her eyes coming back to Josh's. "Someone in a car across the street is filming us."

"Filming?" he repeated, turning around and staring at the car that was parked along the opposite curb, its motor running.

What Joshua Stone had just done was against everything Paige had been taught when she'd been brought over to Special Ops. Griff's people were carefully trained. They had to be because the things they were called on to do were not only dangerous, but potentially embarrassing for their government as well.

And one of the cardinal sins was to have your picture taken. To have your face caught on camera. That was especially true while you were on a mission, but the rule applied at any time. Any place. And Joshua Stone, the best agent she had ever known, had just blatantly violated it.

As shocked as she had been by his turning toward the man who was video recording their meeting, she was even more surprised when he began walking toward the car. The camera was still pointed toward them, still filming. Josh stopped at the near curb and looked both ways before he stepped out into the street, not even seeming to hurry.

Was he going to ask them to stop shooting? Or was he going to try to get the tape? Which called into question, she supposed, just who Josh thought the two men in that car might be.

Paige's guess was that they were from the agency. Either they had followed her here, which probably wouldn't have been too difficult, despite the routine precautions she had taken, or they had already been running surveillance on Josh.

She couldn't quite figure out why they would be doing that. Why would the CIA be keeping tabs on one of their own? Especially on someone who was no longer working for them? That almost made it seem... Almost made it seem...

Her mind was racing again. And even as it did, Josh reached the car. He opened the door and said something to the man with the camera. Paige was too far away to hear the words, but the man lowered the recorder and looked up at Josh, answering him.

She was already fumbling to open her purse where her weapon was, her hand moving almost without her volition. She had started toward the street when Josh reached out to take hold of the camera, as if he intended to wrest it from the man who was apparently reluctant to give it up. Paige began to run, closing the distance between her and her former partner.

Her gun was in her hand, but she prayed she wouldn't have to use it. If the men in that car were fellow agents...

And then the guy with the camera came up out of the front seat, still holding onto it with one hand. With the other, he was reaching into his pocket.

Paige's heart rate accelerated, knowing she was going to have to make a decision about whether to shoot within the next ten seconds or so. It was a decision she didn't want to have anything to do with. One she didn't have enough information to make. And one that would inevitably be influenced by what had once happened, a long time ago, between her and Josh Stone.

She stopped, gripping the semiautomatic with both hands, willing them not to shake. She drew a bead on the chest of the man who was struggling with Josh over the camera.

Her concentration, however, was on his other hand. And then, moving almost in slow motion, that hand began to come out of his pocket, bringing something with it.

Chapter Three

This isn't supposed to be happening, Jack Thompson thought.

He couldn't even begin to explain why he had come over to confront the two men. When he had seen that camera, for some reason he had been overcome by an overpowering wave of anger.

The doctors had warned him. They had said that a tendency to impulsive and risky behavior was a fairly common result of head trauma. He hadn't paid much attention, because up until now he hadn't sensed any lack of restraint within himself.

Up until now, he thought grimly, aware that the guy he was struggling with for control of the camera was reaching into his pocket with his other hand. And he knew with cold certainty, a feeling which tightened all the muscles of his stomach, that the cameraman was going for a gun.

Something Jack wished he had. He could almost feel the solid, reassuring weight of a weapon in his hand. Except he didn't have a gun, and he couldn't remember ever having touched one. Couldn't *consciously* remember, he amended, because somehow he knew that he had. And he wanted to again. Right about now would be a real good time.

The fumbling hand finally emerged from the side pocket of the guy's coat. And he hadn't been wrong, Jack thought, seeing what it held. He wished to hell he had been. He also wished that he hadn't started this. What could it possibly matter that someone was videotaping him while he was talking to a woman? A stranger. It sure wasn't worth getting killed over.

He willed his fingers to release their grip on the camera they were struggling over. The unexpected loss of opposition unbalanced the cameraman. He staggered backward, crashing into the open door of the car. Both hands rose automatically, almost shoulder high, as he tried to regain his balance.

For a split second, Jack realized, the hand with the gun would be out of firing position. With that recognition some primitive part of his brain took control. His right leg kicked up, the toe of his shoe connecting with the cameraman's arm, exactly at the point on his elbow where the nerves were joined.

The guy's hand opened involuntarily, and the gun flew up and back. Jack was no longer watching it. Without seeming to plan the move, he dove forward instead, his head spearing the man's midsection, right over his diaphragm. The blow drove the cameraman backward, slamming him again into the door.

The air came out of the guy's lungs in a satisfying whoosh, and then he seemed to collapse, hanging over Jack's back like a limp balloon. Jack crawled out from under him, dumping him off to the side. Before he let the man fall, however, he ripped the video recorder out of his unresisting fingers.

He looked around for the gun, but he couldn't see it. And as long as nobody else could either, that was okay. He turned back to the car to take care of the driver.

Despite the dome light, which had come on as soon as he'd jerked open the door, the interior of the car was fairly dark. In the dimness Jack's eyes searched for the guy's hands, expecting to find one of them filled with a weapon.

If the man was carrying a gun, he apparently hadn't had time to get it out. Or maybe he hadn't wanted to. Because both hands were raised in the traditional gesture of surrender. The driver's eyes were widened, focused on something behind Jack.

He turned and found the woman who had followed him from the restaurant standing almost in the middle of the street. Her feet were slightly apart, and she was holding a semiautomatic pistol out in front of her. Both hands were wrapped around the butt, the left supporting the right, to keep it steady. Classic shooter's stance, Jack noted approvingly.

She wasn't aware of that approval, however, because her eyes weren't on him. They were moving back and forth from the driver to the man he'd just downed, who was still writhing on the ground, trying to suck air into his empty lungs.

Before he had turned, Jack had been thinking about tossing the woman the video recorder to hold while he took care of the driver. Looking at her now, he decided he preferred to have her behind him with that gun. She looked like she knew how to use it. The guy in the car seemed to believe that, too.

"What the hell were you doing?" Jack asked him.

The driver shook his head, his eyes still locked on the woman with the pistol.

"Okay, easier question. Who are you?"

The driver's lips whitened as he pressed them together, and he shook his head again.

"Fine by me, buddy," Jack said. "You can explain it to the cops. You got a phone?" he asked, turning his head just enough to make it obvious he was talking to the woman behind him.

"Yes," she said.

"Dial 9-1-1. Tell them to get somebody out here to pick these clowns up. They can explain to the cops why they were filming us. *And* why they pulled a gun when I objected.''

There was no response. Jack waited, listening for sounds that would indicate she was doing what he'd asked. Finally, realizing she wasn't, he turned to look at her again.

She hadn't moved. Her face was set, her eyes and the gun still on the driver. Jack realized the guy on the ground had stopped making that unpleasant wheezing noise.

A belated realization, because as soon as that thought formed, the man made his move. He leaped up from the pavement and shoved Jack away with his left hand. His concentration on the woman, Jack hadn't been prepared for the blow. With its impact, he staggered a step or two to the side, just enough to allow the man to get by him and to jump back into the car.

The driver stomped on the gas, sending the sedan, tires squealing, fishtailing out of the parallel parking space, the passenger-side door still open. They were halfway down the block before the cameraman managed to get it closed.

The smell of burnt rubber lingered in the air, and there were a couple of marks on the pavement. They had left the gun, lying somewhere in the shadows. And the camera, which Jack was still holding, almost absently, in his left hand.

There had been no shots as they made their getaway. He turned again, a complete about-face this time. Although she still had both hands around it, the woman had lowered the gun until it was out of firing position, her eyes following the car that was now careening around the corner.

''Why didn't you call the cops?'' he asked.

''What if they were on our side?''

''*Our* side?''

''I think they were from the agency,'' she said.

In the commotion he had almost forgotten the story she'd tried to tell him. That easy distractibility was another product of his injury. One that would eventually pass, they had promised. Until it did, he would just have to learn to cope with that occasional inability to stay focused. Considering that someone had just pulled a gun on him, he supposed this time he had an excuse for his wandering attention.

"CIA? Why would you think that? You just said *you* worked for them."

"They bugged my apartment. I think they may have been following me."

"And filming you?" he asked, holding up the camera.

"Filming one of us," she corrected.

"You know why someone would want to do that?"

She turned her head, looking toward the direction in which the car had disappeared. Even the smell it had left behind had begun to dissipate. She straightened, removing her left hand from the weapon. Then, her eyes coming back to his face, she put the pistol back into her purse.

"Maybe," she said.

"Then *maybe* you should tell me what it is."

"ARE YOU TRYING to tell me you really don't remember me?" the woman asked.

"Not even vaguely," Jack said, his voice almost mocking, pretending an amusement he didn't feel. "I don't even remember *me,* which is a lot more disconcerting."

She shook her head, her eyes on his, obviously attempting to read them. "What does that mean? That you don't remember you?"

"Amnesia," he explained.

"Amnesia," she echoed, her voice full of disbelief.

He should be used to that by now, but he wasn't. Not entirely. "The rarest kind," he said. "The one-in-a-million kind that wipes out any recollection of who you are."

There was a small silence. Apparently, she was finding it

difficult to assimilate the information. "Any recollection? Are you saying you don't remember *anything?*"

"I'm saying I don't remember who I am or anything about my past. I remember how to do things. And all the factual information someone would normally accumulate throughout a lifetime seems to be intact, but any sense of self is missing. I can remember the capital of North Dakota, but not my own name."

"You must have remembered enough that—"

At that break, he looked up from the drinks he was pouring. There was a small crease between her brows, and her brown eyes were still incredulous. It was a look he had seen often enough in the last few months not to be mistaken about it.

"Then how do you know who you are?" she finished. "How did you know you're Jack Thompson?"

He was aware that wasn't the question she had begun, but at least it was one he could answer. "When I came out of the coma, they were calling me Mr. Thompson. It didn't ring any bells, but neither did anything else. I couldn't remember my address. Where I went to school. My family. Not even whether I had any."

"Do you?"

"My parents were killed twelve years ago. They died together in a plane crash. My dad was ex-military, a guy with lots of missions in Nam, who had never stopped flying. When he could finally afford it, he bought his own single engine. It killed him and my mother with him."

"You remember that?"

He supposed the recitation must have sounded as if he did. "I remember being *told* about it. Sometimes I've even thought I had some...independent memory of it. But I was never sure how much of that was the result of trying so hard to remember it. The result, maybe, of trying to make it feel real."

"No wife?" she asked. "No children?"

As she voiced the questions, her eyes surveyed the apartment, at least what was visible of it from the living room where they were standing. He allowed his to follow, touching on the pristine neatness of the kitchen. The lack of clutter. The total lack of anything personal in either of the two rooms, not even photographs. There was nothing here that indicated family. Nothing that said this was a home.

It was more like a stage setting. He had always felt that. And had felt the inherent emptiness of the life of the man they told him he was. He had thought that was another product of the amnesia. That terrible sense of incompleteness.

"No," he said. "No wife. No children."

Her eyes had returned to his face, and she spent a few seconds studying it before she asked, "What caused the coma?"

"Car wreck. I was driving too fast. Drinking too much."

He thought he had managed to say it without revealing any emotion. He picked up the scotch he had poured for her and carried it across to where she was standing. When they had first come in, he hadn't invited her to sit down. He didn't now. As far as he was concerned, this wasn't a social visit.

"I slammed head-on into a bridge abutment," he said.

Her eyes flinched from the brutality of the words, and that surprised him. He lifted the glass, offering it to her with a gesture that was almost a salute. As she took it from his hand, he noticed that her fingers were trembling. Aftereffect of the adrenaline rush they would both have felt earlier? Or whatever emotion had made her eyes react as they just had?

He was glad she hadn't offered the meaningless sympathy most people did when he was forced to reveal what had happened to him. Actually, she hadn't said anything at all. She had watched his eyes, not seeming to judge, and so he finished it.

"They put me back together, well enough that everything

functions pretty much like it used to. I set off metal detectors at airports, but the moving parts all work. The only permanent damage was to my brain. Apparently the area that controls memory got…short-circuited or something.''

''Maybe there are things you don't want to remember.''

He laughed, the sound soft but derisive, and then he turned and walked back to the table where he had left his own scotch.

''Selective memory loss?'' he questioned. ''Believe me, if that were the case—''

''I didn't mean that,'' she interrupted. ''I meant trauma. Something that your subconscious wants to block. Something that's too painful to remember.''

''Like hitting a concrete wall at a hundred miles an hour.''

There was another small silence.

''Or something else,'' she suggested, her eyes on his face.

''Except that's *not* the kind of amnesia this is.''

''How do you know?''

''Believe me, I know. This is something I've researched. And because it's so rare, I've even *been* researched.''

In the beginning he had read everything he could get his hands on. All the clinical descriptions. None of them had told him much, except how unusual this was. What they couldn't tell him was how to get his memory back. Or how to get his life back.

''You said that before,'' she said. ''The rarest kind. What exactly does that mean?''

''With most brain injuries, people don't remember the events that happen immediately before the trauma. Those memories never come back. Or if they do, they're…faulty. Distorted. That's the most common kind of amnesia. Pretty standard with any concussion.''

''And the other kind?''

She had seemed to be listening to every word, her concentration on what he was saying complete. The ability to do that was almost as rare as his condition. And then he wondered how he knew that. It was the kind of thing that had been frustratingly unanswerable throughout this entire ordeal. Her question, however...

"Another variety, the kind *you're* talking about," he said, "involves memories that people block because they don't want to remember them. Can't bear to remember. A trigger might be sexual abuse in childhood or seeing something so horrible, like a particularly brutal murder, that the brain can't deal with it. The remembrance may lie buried for years, even forever. Or something may happen one day that brings it all back."

"Suppressed memories. I understood those are suspect."

"Most of the criminal cases where those kinds of memories have surfaced have hinged on the question of whether there actually was a memory of an event or whether someone implanted in the person's mind the idea that there was. A therapist can create memories, even unintentionally, where there aren't any. There have been well-documented abuse cases where that's happened. To the person remembering those events, however, they seem as real as if they *had* actually happened."

That was a phenomenon that he understood a lot better now. As he had tried to remember things he'd been told were a part of his history, they had begun to embed themselves in his mind. Like the images he had formed of his mother and father from the pictures he'd been given. The crash site. His reaction to it. Sometimes it seemed as if he *did* remember all of that.

"And then there's the truly bizarre kind," he said, putting that question aside to complete the explanation he'd begun. "The one-in-a-million kind. Complete amnesia. The knowledge from a lifetime of experiences may still be there, but there's no memory of how it was acquired. I have certain skills, like using a computer or driving a car or knowing a foreign language, and yet I have no idea how I learned them. No memory of learning them."

Just like knowing what to do about the gun the cameraman had drawn. And reacting automatically to the violation of the camera itself. Mindless rage from a damaged brain? Or a reasoned response based on a background he knew nothing about? Or, if what this woman had suggested earlier was true, based on a training he couldn't remember.

"I guess that makes some kind of sense," she said.

"What makes sense?" he asked, puzzled by her response.

"That they would create this alternate identity for you. That's what they did for everyone else, but..." She shook her head, still watching him. "I don't know how they managed the amnesia."

"*Managed* the amnesia?" he repeated, suddenly feeling his anger build, again flaring out of proportion to the cause.

He walked over and took the fingers of the hand that was not holding her glass. She didn't resist, not even when he placed them against the small depression in his skull, just behind his temple. Her eyes reacted, however, recoiling almost exactly as they had to his description of the accident.

"Are you suggesting someone deliberately bashed in my head in *hopes* it would result in amnesia?" he said. "If so, apparently they weren't satisfied with that. They broke a few other bones. Just for good measure, I guess. I have plenty of pins and screws in various places. If you need more proof, I'll be glad to show you those. Or at least I would if we knew one another a little more intimately."

The last had been pure sarcasm, but her eyes reacted to those words, too. He wasn't sure what the reaction was this time, but there had definitely been one. And then, as suddenly as it had appeared, it was gone. Controlled.

"My name is Jack Thompson. And I had an automobile accident." The words were soft, but he said each one so that it was distinct, his emphasis very sure. "It was my fault.

And I've verified my identity in every way I can think of. Fingerprint matches from the military. Computer searches. Distinguishing marks. They all fit a man named Jack Thompson.''

"They can do that," she said earnestly. "They can do all of that. They can do anything."

He took a deep breath and then blew it out in frustration. "They? The CIA, I suppose. Then I guess my question is why would *they* go to the trouble?"

"To hide you," she said.

"To hide me," he repeated, sarcasm deliberately back in his tone. "To hide me from who?"

There was another silence, this one lasting several long heartbeats. "From someone who thinks you could take them to the location of something that's extremely valuable."

He held her eyes, seeing nothing but sincerity in them. She believed what she had just said. Which meant either she was a nut—and the fact that she had been following him around with a gun in her purse didn't make a convincing argument she wasn't. Or it meant he should at least listen to what she had to say. After all, she had listened to him. And God knows, his amnesia wasn't half as interesting as what she was spouting.

Although he was having a hard time reconciling Jack Thompson with some guy who was supposed to be a CIA spook, he didn't have any other plans for the evening. The apartment was starting to warm up and the scotch was doing its part to mellow him out after the incident in the street.

If this woman thought she could explain why those two clowns had been filming them, then he was more than willing to listen. More than willing, he thought, looking down into her face. Because there was something about her eyes...

And then the feeling was gone. An elusive wisp of memory, perhaps, which had suddenly snapped like a thread that has been stretched too tightly. And it had left nothing behind.

Those kinds of images drifted through his brain periodically, teasing it. And then they drifted out again, usually before he had gotten a good look at them. It was frustrating as hell, and it made his head hurt. The psychiatrist's warning echoed, unwanted.

"I need a couple of aspirin," he said.

She looked disconcerted. Maybe his comment had been a non sequitur. When one of those flashes of recollection occurred, he had found that he seemed to lose track of what was going on around him. Maybe he had this time.

"After I take them," he offered, "we can talk."

"Do you think you might have more than a couple?" she asked, her lips almost smiling. More relaxed, anyway.

"Enough that we can both indulge? I think I can manage that. I'll be right back. Why don't you have a seat."

He motioned toward the couch, and she nodded. Her eyes were brown, surrounded by a sweep of long black lashes, which were darker than her shoulder length hair. Her skin was a smooth ivory, very light for a brunette, her features delicate and finely made. Attractive, he acknowledged. Damned attractive.

Aspirin. He had been going for aspirin. He pulled his eyes away, realizing that the silence had stretched uncomfortably as he had studied her. "Be right back," he said again.

NOTHING HAD CHANGED about the face reflected in the bathroom mirror. It was the same one that had stared back at him this morning before he had left for work. Same face. Same scars, he thought, putting the tips of his fingers on the one that slanted across his chin. Same man.

Except something *had* changed. He couldn't quite figure out what, and he knew it would drive him crazy until he did, but something was different. And after months of trying to fit into this skin, that was pretty damned frustrating.

Some adolescent James Bond daydream? Was that what had appealed to him about the story she had told? Or was it that if he bought into this CIA conspiracy scenario, he didn't have to acknowledge in how many ways he had screwed up his life.

He hadn't been driving drunk. It had been the government who had bashed in his head because they were trying to give him amnesia so he wouldn't remember he was a spy.

Despite the growing headache, the lips in the mirror, surrounded by a slight five o'clock shadow, lifted in derision. Nice, he thought. Too bad he couldn't quite buy into it.

Whatever the woman who had followed him was after, however, she was good. He would give her that.

He opened the medicine cabinet and took out the bottle of aspirin. After struggling a few seconds to line up the arrows on the child-proof cap, he succeeded in opening it. He poured two of the oblong tablets into his palm.

He stared at them a minute, still thinking about what had happened in the street, and then he put them in his mouth. He set the bottle down on the sink and cupped his hands, filling them with water from the faucet. Before he could lift them, the tablets had begun to dissolve, leaving a bitter taste on his tongue even after he'd washed them down.

He closed the cabinet door, and the man in the mirror stared back at him once more. *Jack Thompson, he repeated mentally. My name is Jack Thompson.* It didn't mean a thing. The name created no intellectual or emotional response. It never had.

Joshua Stone. There was no more resonance from that than there had been from the other. His eyes again traced over the face reflected there. Following the line of each scar. Examining the shape of his nose and chin. They had already done a lot of reconstructive plastic surgery. And he was scheduled for more. If he wanted it.

He wasn't sure he did. What did it matter if they returned

his face to the way it had been before, since he couldn't remember what it had looked like then? And if there was no one else who remembered it either?

Except, if the woman in his living room was telling the truth, she remembered it. And she remembered him. Which would mean she was someone he should remember.

And he didn't. Nothing other than that fleeting sensation that had something to do with her eyes. Memory? Or admiration? Or nothing more than relief that with her here, this would be one night he wouldn't have to look in the mirror and wonder who the hell the man staring back at him really was.

Chapter Four

"My name is Paige Daniels, by the way. I was your partner on that mission to Vladistan."

She had been sitting on the overstuffed sofa when he came back from the bathroom. She had taken off her shoes, probably because they were damp from the rain. Her feet were up on the couch, legs curled to her side.

He hadn't answered her comment until she had swallowed the aspirin he'd brought her. It was a good thing he had stopped in the kitchen for a glass of water to wash them down with, since she didn't seem to be making much headway with her drink.

"A mission for the CIA?" Jack said, taking the water from her hand and setting it down on the coffee table. He hadn't really meant for the question to come across mockingly, but he could tell from her face it had.

"What you did out in the street just now," she said. "Do you think you learned that being a broker?"

He had no idea where those skills had come from. They had simply been there, ready to be used when he'd needed them. That, combined with the now-familiar feeling that he didn't fit into his own skin and the fact that he was being followed by men wielding a video camera, probably meant he should at least listen to what Paige Daniels had to say, even if it seemed far-fetched.

Damned far-fetched. He picked up his own drink and, looking down into the scotch, he swirled the glass so that the liquid touched the rim on one side and then on the other.

"You used to do that all the time," she said.

His eyes came up, and he found she had been watching him. Then her gaze fell to his glass, following the slow swirl of scotch as he tilted it back and forth.

"I always thought that one day you'd miss." Her tone was colored by amusement, maybe even a hint of nostalgia. "And it would finally spill over the side. I waited for that to happen, but it never did."

"Sorry," he said.

He stopped the unthinking movement, deliberately ignoring the trip down memory lane. Was she trying to convince him that she really did know him? The observation could just as easily have been spur-of-the-moment. If so, he admitted, it was inspired, because this really was something he did all the time.

He lifted the glass and tossed back what was in it. He wasn't sure straight scotch was conducive to clear thinking; however, he could still feel the dregs of the adrenaline that had flooded his system during the scuffle out in the street.

And the feeling hadn't been unpleasant. Perhaps more importantly, it hadn't been unfamiliar. He hadn't realized that until after the incident was over, and he wasn't sure what it meant. If there was anything he had learned in the last three months, however, it was that his feelings were about as reliable as anything else his brain dredged up to throw at him.

After all, he had felt all along that something was wrong about what the cops had told him. Something hadn't *felt* right about being Jack Thompson. The persona they had supplied hadn't fit, and somewhere inside, he had known that from the beginning.

He hadn't known why. Or what to do about it. And he

wasn't sure that what this woman was telling him would provide an answer to either of those questions. Still...

"So what was this mission about?" he asked.

"We had been sent to retrieve something. Something the government was afraid would fall into the wrong hands if the revolution succeeded."

"Did we?" He had noticed the omission, but he supposed that until he decided to buy the story she was selling, details like that didn't matter too much.

"We..." She paused and took a breath before she continued. "We retrieved it, but Russian troops overran the border sooner than we had expected. And...you disappeared."

"Disappeared?" he repeated. The note of skepticism back, no matter how much he tried to control it. "In the middle of a Russian invasion?"

"The night before. No one ever knew what had happened to you. At least, that's what they told me."

"I disappeared in the middle of a revolution, and the CIA told you they couldn't find me."

"*I* couldn't find you. I was the only one in country. Until I was ordered out."

"You got out, but I didn't."

She nodded, lips tightening. She looked down at the drink she was holding, as if she had forgotten about it. Maybe she had, because it appeared untouched. As he watched, she took a tentative sip. It was no more than that. She held the scotch in her mouth a few minutes, not savoring the dark, smoky taste, but enduring it. And when she swallowed, it was with a grimace.

Not a scotch drinker. He would bet she was not much of a drinker at all. And he wondered why she hadn't turned down his offer. Maybe, like him, she had been in need of something steadying after that encounter with the two men and the camera.

"Okay, just to make sure I understand this, I disappear.

You can't find me. The CIA says they can't find me. And now you *have* found me after..." He raised his brows, questioning.

"Three years."

"And you found me because they put a new name on my file?"

"Not a new name. A new file," she said. "It's what they did for the others. I figured they might have done it for you, too. And when I looked, they had."

"The others?"

"The External Security Team."

"And we were both members of that...team?"

She had said all this while they were outside, standing by the front steps. Now, as he clarified it, he watched her expression, trying to assess how much of what she was telling him was the truth and how much was pure garbage. Even if he eventually decided it *was* garbage, he supposed he needed to know why someone would want to spin this fairy tale.

"You had been a member a lot longer than I was," she said. "That was my first mission in the field. And it wasn't really black ops."

He thought he understood the term, but he would have liked to hear her interpretation of it. He would have liked to hear a lot of things, but she was only going to give him whatever information she'd been instructed to reveal. *Instructed by whom?* he wondered, unsure where that cautionary thought had come from.

"That's what this team did?" he asked. "Black ops?"

She nodded. "Mostly anti-terrorism. Some commando-type operations against out-of-control dictatorships."

"Assassinations?"

Despite the cold sibilance of the word itself, he was surprised to discover he didn't find the idea offensive. In his opinion, there were too many madmen in the world and not nearly enough people with the balls to go after them.

"Sometimes," she admitted. "If the situation was dangerous enough to warrant it. That *wasn't* what our mission was about."

"We were just retrieving something," he said, repeating the information she had given earlier.

She nodded again.

"Which was?" Maybe it was time to get to that bottom line she'd been deliberately avoiding.

"A new nerve agent."

"As in…chemical warfare."

She nodded once more, holding his eyes.

He knew, and didn't know how he knew it, that Vladistan was a region with a long history of unrest under communist rule and a much longer history of democracy before the Soviets had come to dominate the area. He could imagine that the State Department had been frantic at the thought of the rebels there using chemical weapons against the Russians, who had repeatedly threatened nuclear retaliation against any such attack.

"We retrieve the nerve agent," he said, "but in the shuffle, I disappear. And then somehow, three years later, you think the CIA has given me amnesia so they can hide me?"

She didn't say anything for a few seconds, and when she finally answered, he was surprised by the admission.

"That doesn't make any sense."

He laughed. "It didn't to me, but I figured you had this all mapped out before you showed up."

"I didn't know you had amnesia *before* I showed up," she said, a hint of sharpness in the reply. "It confused me."

"It hasn't been a particularly enjoyable experience for me either."

She smiled, hiding the upward tilt of her lips behind the glass as she took another sip of scotch. And made another face.

"I have bourbon, if you prefer," he offered.

"This is fine. Actually, I'm not much of a drinker."

He didn't respond to a confirmation of what he had already surmised. "Okay, so now you *don't* think the CIA cracked my skull in an attempt to induce amnesia."

"Moral considerations probably wouldn't stop them, if they thought they had anything to gain. But...the possibility of inducing amnesia that way seems like a long shot, even for them."

"So why are they tailing me? Or tailing you? *If* that's who those two guys were."

"The agency has been bugging my apartment. And Steiner called me in, after a three-year silence, to ask about that mission. I just put all that together."

"How did you know they had your apartment bugged?"

"I found the bug. It was the kind the agency uses. Voice activated. The latest model."

"Not exclusive to them, surely."

"Maybe not," she admitted. "Maybe I put two and two together and got five."

"How'd you find it?"

"When I came home from work one day last week, I thought someone had been in my apartment. I called to see if it was maintenance. To make a long story short, when we checked out a faulty light switch I'd complained about, we found the bug."

"We?"

"The manager and I. He didn't even know what it was."

"And you think they planted it that day?"

"I'd had trouble with the switch, going back a couple of months. So it may have been there a while."

"Then...why did someone come to your apartment?"

"I don't know. Maybe it had stopped working. Or maybe they just thought it had," she said, meeting his eyes. Hers seemed amused. A little embarrassed, perhaps. "There wasn't much going on in there for them to listen to."

"I guess the same thing could be said—"

For here. That's what he had been about to say. There wasn't much conversation at his place either. Except tonight there had been. And suddenly, he found himself wondering if someone could be listening to what they were saying right now.

She was still looking up at him. His expression must have revealed something of what he was thinking because her eyes widened. He shook his head, putting his finger over his lips.

"—about most people who live alone," he said, finishing the sentence he had left dangling.

Her eyes scanned the apartment, but he knew there wasn't much point in that. He would have to make some sort of search later on....

Only with that thought did he realize how deeply he had already bought into this. Believing they might have been on a CIA mission together. Believing his apartment might be bugged. Maybe getting his head cracked hadn't screwed up just his memory.

Still, for some reason he didn't want to finish this conversation here, and given what had happened outside, he wasn't eager to take it anywhere else. He crooked his index finger, indicating she should follow him. She hesitated a second or two before she got up, slipping her feet back into her shoes.

He led the way down the hallway to his bedroom and its attached bath. He walked into the room and was halfway across it before he realized she wasn't behind him. He looked back and found her standing just outside the door, her eyes on the bed. When she realized he was watching her, her gaze came back to his face. Her lips moved, tightening minutely, and then she stepped through the door and began to cross the room. He turned and walked on into the bathroom.

He turned the faucet on at the sink and then reached inside the enclosure to turn on the one in the shower, running only the cold water to keep from steaming up the place. He also flipped the switch for the ventilator in the ceiling. Its fan made enough noise to cover anything.

"Close the door," he ordered, when he found her hovering outside it, just as she had in the bedroom.

She obeyed, stepping inside and shutting the door behind her. She leaned against it, her hand on the knob. As if she didn't want to be in here with him. As if she didn't trust him? If they had really been partners, as she claimed, that didn't seem to make a lot sense.

Something was definitely going on, however. She wasn't comfortable being in this small, enclosed space with him. There was a tension about her that hadn't been there before.

He could only deal with one unknown at a time, he reminded himself. First he'd figure out what was going on with the men who'd been taping them, and then he'd worry about why being this close to him made Paige Daniels uneasy.

"Suppose it's not the CIA," he said, picking up the thread of their interrupted conversation. Some of the tightness in her face relaxed, making him wonder what the hell she'd been expecting when she had followed him here.

"That's possible. The toxin would be worth a lot of money on the black market. When I found that the CIA had set you up with a new identity, I assumed you had already told them where it is. Maybe everyone else hasn't made that assumption."

"Say that again," he ordered, trying to make sure he understood what she had just implied.

"That I assumed you must have already told them where the nerve agent is hidden? Or that someone else may not have?"

"Are you saying no one knows where that stuff is?"

"It disappeared when you did. And as far as I know, it hasn't turned up since."

"DEFINITELY FOLLOWING YOU," she whispered, her eyes on the bedroom's television, where the videotape that had been in the camera he had taken was playing. They were sitting together on the foot of his bed, watching it.

There was no arguing with her conclusion. And seeing those images unfold on the screen was almost as strange as reading the material the cops had given him on his supposed biography. The tape covered everything he'd done in the last few days except the time he'd spent sleeping or at the office. Most of what they'd filmed had been exits and arrivals. At work or at home.

Of course, that's all they would have needed to tape if they also had his apartment bugged. Given that possibility, he had turned the bedroom stereo up, letting Vivaldi bounce off the walls as they watched.

And as he looked at those images, his outrage grew. The long weeks of rehab had eroded any sense of privacy he might once have had. In the hospital he hadn't felt like a person. Not just because of the amnesia, but because it had never seemed as if he were really a person to the people who cared for him.

He had been a patient. A slab of broken flesh and bones, something to be tended to. Mended. A damaged mind to be probed. He had never felt as if he were a man in their eyes.

Only in the last couple of months, since his release, had he begun to regain any sense of privacy. And now, with a few minutes of tape, someone had destroyed that.

"Any idea what they were looking for?" he whispered back, trying to control his anger at the invasion. The violation.

"I think they're looking for you to make a wrong move," Paige Daniels said, her eyes still on the screen.

"A wrong move?"

"You show up after all this time, the only person who knows the location of something that's worth millions, and you can't tell them a thing about it. You've conveniently forgotten everything that happened. Wouldn't you be suspicious?"

"Maybe," he said, bringing his eyes back to the tape as he thought about what she had said. "But if they're suspicious of the amnesia, why didn't they ever question me about the nerve agent? Or about this mission?"

"Maybe thcy did," she suggested. "Maybe it didn't mean anything to you, so you just…"

"Forgot they'd asked?" He thought about the possibility and then he shook his head. "Nobody mentioned nerve agents. Or the CIA. Or Vladistan." *Or you.* "No matter what kind of shape I was in, I would have remembered that."

"You said you'd been researched. Because of the amnesia. Maybe the researchers weren't really interested in the amnesia. Other than seeing if they could break through it."

None of the questions they had asked him, however, had been about the mission she'd described. The doctor doing the questioning had only talked in very general terms about reclaiming his past. About ways to reconnect with it.

"He asked for permission to have someone hypnotize me," he said, suddenly remembering the single session he'd agreed to.

"They hypnotized you?"

Paige Daniels sounded shocked. He hadn't been. At the time, it had even seemed like a good idea. A way, maybe, to get into the part of his mind that was locked.

There was no question, however, that he had been bothered by that session. Afterwards, for almost a week, there had been a lot of disturbing dreams. Without even being able to remember what those dreams had contained, he shivered.

"A therapist," he said. "Someone the hospital recommended."

"How many times?"

"Just once. I wouldn't let him do it again."

"Why not? I would think you'd be as eager to recover your memory as they would be to help you do it."

"They said—"

He paused, still not convinced the CIA had been behind that attempt to dredge up something from his past. It had been presented to him as pure research, and he had bought that story. Of course, at the time he had still been weak from his injuries and trying to come to terms with the fact that his mind seemed to be a clean slate with nothing written on it.

"They said what?" she prodded.

"They said nothing had surfaced during the session," he said, thinking about what he'd been told. Wondering if it had all been a lie. "They said that wasn't unusual, especially with a brain injury as severe as mine."

"You didn't believe them," she said softly, obviously reading that in his face or in his voice.

"I did then. I couldn't imagine any reason for them to lie. But then there were those dreams..." His voice had dropped, little more than a whisper now, and again his flesh crawled.

"About what?"

"I don't know," he said. "I don't ever remember dreams. I don't think I ever did. Even before the wreck. Occasionally, I'll have bits and pieces of them stuck in my head when I wake up. Most of those as ordinary as anyone else's dreams. The ones after that session, however... There was something wrong with them. They were...just *wrong*."

Although he knew how simplistic it sounded, that was the best description he could come up with for what he had felt.

The dreams that single session had created had just been very wrong.

"But, despite those dreams, the therapist told you that nothing about your past had surfaced?"

He hadn't wanted any more sessions, and the therapist hadn't pushed it. Nobody had. He had assumed that was because the one they had done had been unproductive. What if it hadn't been? What if they had gotten all they needed in that single session?

"Maybe I told them what they wanted to know," he said. "Maybe I told them where the nerve agent was."

"Then...why are they following you?"

"For the same reason they're bugging your apartment."

Her eyes searched his. "Which is?"

"I don't know," he said, turning back to the images on the TV. Trying to think.

If he had told them the information they wanted, they should be through with him. And if he hadn't told them where the toxin was, then why had there been no more sessions with the hypnotist? Why hadn't they insisted on more of those?

"It doesn't make any sense," he said finally.

"None of it does," she said, sounding tired. "And this is getting us nowhere."

He turned to face her again. For some reason his now-uncertain temper had been sparked by those words, which he took to be accusatory. "Where do you want it to get us? What the hell do you want from me?"

He had had enough to deal with without all this cloak-and-dagger stuff. And he didn't even know whether he believed what she had told him.

"I want Steiner off my back," she said. "I don't want my apartment bugged. I don't want someone filming me."

"You think I do? About something I can't even remember?"

"I know," she said, taking a breath. "You didn't ask for this either, but...like it or not, it seems we're in this together. At least until we find out what's going on."

"So who else knew about the nerve agent?"

If that missing toxin was as valuable as she had said, then there probably were a lot of people who would like to get their hands on it. Most of the terrorist groups in the world would be interested in its potential.

"I don't know. Special Ops, of course. The rebels knew we had taken it. They were actively looking for it. Looking for us. I'm not sure they had any idea who we were working for."

"And the Russians?"

"I don't know if they even knew the rebels had stolen it. It had been taken from one of their weapons facilities, but given the instability of the situation at that time..."

"There's no proof that the Russians knew the CIA had been sent in to bring it out?"

She shook her head. "I don't know what they knew, but it seems to me that if they had known it was missing, they would have recovered it as soon as they put down the rebellion."

"What makes you think they didn't."

"If it's back in Russian hands, why would Steiner want to talk to me about that mission?"

"Maybe he wanted you to do exactly what you did."

Her eyes widened. "He wanted me to come looking for you?"

"That's what you did, isn't it?"

He could see she was thinking about it. The thoughts moved behind those dark, intelligent eyes. And looking into them, he again had a fleeting sense of déjà vu.

"That's why it was so damn easy," she said. "They intended for me to find you. They think I can make you remember."

Chapter Five

She had forgotten how intuitive Joshua Stone could be. He had taken everything she had told him and had arrived at the one conclusion that made sense of all of it. Which made her feel stupid. And as if she had been betrayed by her own agency.

"They're using me," she said.

"Obviously. *My* question is why they believed they could."

She refused to let her eyes fall before the intensity in his. They were exactly as she remembered them. Almost the only thing about his face that hadn't changed.

She hadn't told Steiner what had happened between her and Joshua Stone. Her reluctance to do so was probably ridiculous, considering the way people viewed sexual encounters these days. Maybe she had been unwilling to expose the events of that night because she wanted to think that in their case what had happened had been something more than a "sexual encounter."

She and Josh hadn't had time to discuss what it was or what it had meant. Or, more importantly to her, what it might lead to. In the long, dark hours they had spent together, they hadn't *discussed* anything. And the next morning, when those questions might have been answered, Joshua Stone had been gone.

That's when she had begun creating the myth. It had been so tempting to imagine that night had meant the same thing to him it had meant to her. Tempting and, given those circumstances, it had also been possible.

There had been no dulling of the passion that had exploded between them. No slow and painful realization that the person she had chosen to love wasn't the person she had imagined him to be. There had been none of the disillusionments that were an inevitable part of any ongoing relationship.

Joshua Stone had never become anything less to her than what he had been that night. A man she had fallen in love with during the course of a long and difficult mission. A patient and skillful lover who had exceeded every fantasy she had ever had.

And for three years, she had held onto those memories. Savoring them. Embellishing them, perhaps. Knowing that what she had felt for him then would always be the same. Dead men don't change.

Except Joshua Stone was alive. Alive, and demanding that she tell him exactly what had been between them. And from a distance of those long years, she found she was no longer sure.

"We were partners," she said.

"On that mission or before?"

"Only on that one mission."

"You said you hadn't been with the team very long. So why would the CIA choose you to try to make me remember? Why not an agent I knew better. Someone with whom I shared more memories."

She knew the answer to that, but she wasn't ready to admit it to him. They had sent her because there were different kinds of memories. Things the senses remembered that the mind might not, at least not consciously.

Smells were the most evocative of those sensual memories, but there were other kinds as well. Sight. Feel. Tactile, physical memories, which were not dependent on the mind.

That was not very scientific, she supposed. Simply noticing the shape of Josh's hands, however, had triggered for her the clear memory of how they had felt moving over her body.

That had happened before she had even approached him. Maybe Steiner had been hoping for those same kinds of remembrances to occur for Josh when he saw her again.

''Because I'm the only one still at the agency,'' she offered.

That wasn't the reason Steiner had chosen her, and she understood that. But it made sense, and it might very well have played a part in his decision. As her superior, Steiner knew she wouldn't have a choice about coming into his office for that interview, the one where he had casually dropped the hint that something new had surfaced about Stone's disappearance.

With her access to the computers, it had been easy for her to find the newly created file for Jack Thompson. Too easy, she realized. They had *meant* for her to find it. They had *wanted* her to know exactly where Joshua Stone was.

And there was another reason she had been chosen, of course. She understood that as well. Despite the fact that Josh had had closer friends on the team, she was the person who was the most vulnerable to Steiner's treachery. She was the one who needed most desperately to know what had happened to him. And if, as she now believed, Griff had put everything she had told him into his original report, Steiner would understand that need.

''I was the one who was with you in Vladistan,'' she continued, as all the real reasons ran though her head. ''Maybe they thought our association would trigger memories of that particular mission, which is what they're looking for.''

He nodded, still holding her eyes. "Nothing else?" he asked as the tension stretched, thin and brittle, between them.

"I can't think of any other reason. Unless you think my inexperience made them believe I would be the easiest to manipulate."

And that was the most humiliating aspect. She had been. She had done exactly what Steiner had hoped she would do. As soon as she found that file, she had applied for leave and headed straight to Atlanta. Straight for Joshua Stone.

She shouldn't have to explain that part of the equation to him. Not until he remembered more than he had about their relationship. *If* he ever remembered. And it seemed that was still a big if.

She was surprised when Josh used the remote to stop the VCR. He didn't even bother to rewind the tape. He stood up, walked over to the machine, and ejected it from the recorder. When he turned around, he held the tape in his hand.

His eyes, however, were focused on her face. She tried to control her expression, unwilling to give him any clue about what she was feeling. She probably did, because she was totally unprepared for his next question.

"There was something between us, wasn't there?" he asked, his voice very low, despite the volume of the music reverberating around them. "Something physical."

One part of her wanted to agree. Just to confess what had happened and get it over. But she knew the dynamics of that sexual relationship would complicate everything. She had already experienced some residue of it during the confrontation with the two men in the street.

The way she felt about Josh had affected her judgment out there. If he hadn't managed to kick that gun away, she might have been forced to shoot a fellow agent. And she would have if it had been necessary to protect Josh's life.

She would have made that decision, even though she hadn't understood what was going on. She would have made it despite the fact that Steiner was suspicious about Josh's disappearance. And about his loyalty.

She had started on this quest because she felt someone should defend Joshua Stone's reputation. And until she had something more to go on than Steiner's distrust, that was still what she intended to do.

But dredging up old emotions wouldn't help them deal with what was happening now. Especially since they didn't really *know* what was happening. All they knew was that there was a strong possibility the CIA had deliberately put them back together.

"We were partners," she said. "That's all we were."

"Strictly a professional relationship," Josh said. It wasn't a question, and the tone was mocking.

"We were trying to prevent a limited nuclear war. That was our assignment. That's what we were doing in Vladistan. Not whatever you're imagining."

"Then tell me why being alone with me makes you nervous."

"A lot has happened tonight. I wasn't—"

"You weren't nervous in the street. You weren't nervous in the living room. That tension didn't start until we came back here. *Toward* the bedroom. And it peaked when I asked you to close that door."

"Whatever you're imagining—"

"I didn't imagine it," he said sharply. "Being close to me made you uneasy. And I want to know why."

"Because I can't be absolutely sure you're Joshua Stone." She had been sure almost from the first. She couldn't prove it, perhaps, but she didn't doubt what her senses were telling her. "Any more than I can be sure I understand what the agency is doing. Or even sure they're the ones who are doing it."

"You seemed sure of everything a minute ago," he said.

She had been. She still was. But there *were* a lot of un-answered questions. Questions that anyone with a couple of functioning brain cells would ask.

"Why would they turn you loose? Why listen to your objections about the hypnosis? If they thought that was the only way to find out what you know, they would have done a hundred sessions, whether you objected or not. And if that didn't work, there are always drugs."

There were drugs for everything, including ones for making someone talk, even if he didn't want to. They weren't perfect, but very few people were able to resist. Why hadn't the agency shot Joshua Stone full of one of the most powerful of those so-called truth serums and found out everything he knew?

"If you're cynical enough to believe they would manipulate you to get you to come here," he said, "what makes you think they haven't already used those."

"You don't remember anything like that, do you?"

"I was in the hospital for a couple of months. In a coma. At least that's what they told me. I don't have any recollection at all of that time."

She was almost nauseated at the thought of what he was suggesting. A drug-induced coma? Resulting in a drug-induced amnesia? Had the CIA destroyed part of Joshua Stone's brain in trying to retrieve information only he could give them?

"You said they wouldn't have any moral compunction in going after what they wanted," he reminded her. "Maybe they've already tried every trick in the book. Maybe you're their last resort."

"And maybe we're way off base with what we're think-ing," she said. "Because none of it explains where you've been for the last three years. We know where you were the last few months. Where were you the rest of the time you were missing, Josh? And who was trying to learn what you know then?''

"I NEED TO GO," Paige said, after they had kicked the possibilities around a few more fruitless minutes.

She needed to get some distance, both from him and from the questions that had been raised. Distance also from the bitter disillusionment of what Steiner had done to her. And from the humiliation of how easy it had been for him to do it.

Josh followed her back to the living room, turning on the radio on the kitchen counter as he entered the room. She didn't see any reason for that precaution. After all, they hadn't discussed anything Steiner and the agency didn't already know. Nothing had changed. Joshua Stone couldn't remember anything about that mission. Or about the nerve agent. Or about her.

She walked across the room toward the couch where she'd left her things. Her nearly untouched glass of scotch, which was still sitting on the coffee table, looked a lot more appealing now than it had when she had left it there.

It wouldn't clear up any of those circling questions, but it might help her sleep. Which was something she hadn't done too well since this had started. That was something else that made her angry. A self-directed anger.

She had slept with a man. Once. Three years ago. And she hadn't seen him since. And then when she had, the memories of that one night, of that mission, had haunted her, almost as much as they had during the first few months after Josh disappeared.

She didn't understand the hold this man had over her emotions. She hadn't understood her fascination with him then. She didn't now. She knew, however, that the more time she spent in his company, the more confused those emotions would be. And the more vulnerable she would be, which was the last thing she wanted. Or needed.

"I don't think your leaving is a good idea," he said.

"Why not?" she asked. "They don't want to interfere with what they've set up. Steiner worked too hard to bring this off."

Actually, it hadn't been hard at all. The head of special operations had simply dangled the possibility that Joshua Stone was alive in front of her nose, and she had been more than eager to do his dirty work. She had jumped at the chance.

"The guy in the street pulled a gun. Not exactly what I'd call non-interference," Josh reminded her.

She thought about it for half a second. "Window dressing," she said, picking up her coat from off the couch. "He wouldn't have used it. Not with you out there. He wouldn't have dared."

"There's no doubt in your mind that the company is behind this?"

Either Josh Stone was a very quick study, or the familiar vocabulary was all still in his head, ready when he needed it. When she had used the word "company" the first time, he had thought she was talking about Debolt. Now he was using the CIA nickname himself, seemingly comfortable with the terminology.

"It fits," she said. "It all fits, from Steiner telling me just enough to make me start wondering again about what had happened to you to the fact that the new folder was right there, waiting for me to find it. The hidden microphone in my apartment was icing on the cake. Personal involvement. Personal threat."

"I still don't like it," he said.

"That I'm not spending the night here? I have a hotel room, reserved and paid for, which I intend to use. It's the same one I slept in the past two nights. Nobody bothered me.''

"They didn't have you on tape then," he said.

"*You* have the tape. Remember?"

"Those men saw you."

"What does that matter? Steiner knows I'm here. He *wanted* me here. That's what this is all about. Besides, I'm *not* the one carrying invaluable information around in my head."

"Information I can't get to," he said, an edge of bitterness in his voice she hadn't heard before.

Josh didn't know what had happened to him. Or whether the agency had done it. Whatever it was, however, had left him damaged. Maybe permanently damaged.

"We'll figure out a way," she said softly. Right now she didn't have a clue what that might be, but her natural inclination was to offer comfort. "In the meantime, don't worry about me. I'll be careful, I promise. But…I don't have anything they want. That much we can be sure of."

He nodded, obviously reluctant to let it go. Or maybe, she thought, reluctant to let her go? And that was certainly wishful thinking. "Could you get me a cab?"

While he made the call, she shrugged into her coat and slung her purse over her shoulder. Then she watched him. He was standing at the kitchen counter, his back to her, the phone to his ear. He nodded once, and then hung up the receiver, turning to look at her again.

"A couple of minutes," he said.

"Thanks."

She walked over to the front door, and he followed. When she reached it, she stopped and turned, looking up into his face, trying to find the man who had made love to her that night. So much had changed about their lives. And he had no memory of her.

Or did he? She remembered his question, triggered, or so

he had said, by her tension at the thought of being alone with him. *There was something between us, wasn't there? Something physical.* Maybe he hadn't just read her body language to arrive at that conclusion. Maybe...

Josh reached above her head, leaning across her in order to slide the latch the safety chain was attached to out of its slot. He was near enough that for the first time she was aware of the scent of his body.

Soap. The cotton dress shirt, which, despite the long day, still carried a hint of laundry starch. Maybe cologne, but if so, it was something very natural, pleasant and understated. And underlying them all was the subtle fragrance of his skin. Warm. Salt-touched. Masculine in a way she couldn't begin to explain. And as hauntingly evocative as a half-remembered snatch of an old melody. Once known. Dearly familiar. And then forgotten.

Almost forgotten, she amended. Because the sensations moving through her body were even more evocative of the memory of his lovemaking than his mere proximity was. He leaned back, and that shattering sense of déjà vu was gone.

Dangerous physical memories. And they, of course, were why she had been nervous about being alone with him. About being close to him. Alone and close. Just as they had been that night when he had unexpectedly slipped his hand into the opening of her parka and cupped her breast.

"Tell me where you're staying," he said, breaking the spell of those memories.

She hesitated, and wasn't sure why she would. Mistrust? If so, it made no sense. This was Josh, and no matter what Steiner had suggested about his disappearance, she was as certain as Griff Cabot had been that there had been no criminal or traitorous intent behind it.

"The Towers on Peachtree," she said.

"Under what name?"

She smiled, thinking again that he really was much better at this than she was.

"My own. I didn't see any need not to use it."

"Paige Daniels," he said.

Because he had forgotten what she had told him? Or was he saying it aloud for some other reason she couldn't fathom?

"That's right."

"Is that the name you were using then?"

She laughed, a little surprised by his persistence. "That's the only name I've ever used. I told you I didn't have much to do with those other missions, the clandestine ones the EST carried out. The kind where you had to use another identity."

"It doesn't ring any bells," he said unnecessarily.

"I know. Neither did Griff's. Or Steiner's. I didn't expect mine to."

"For some reason *I* did," he said.

"There's no reason it should. I told you. There were other people on the team who were closer to you than I was. Jordan Cross for one."

He shook his head.

"Hawk?" she suggested.

"Nothing."

"Maybe..."

"Maybe what?"

"Maybe you ought to think about trying hypnosis again."

He held her eyes, studying them. His seemed shuttered and opaque. Because he was remembering the dreams he had told her about? The dreams that were so *wrong?*

"You won't be free of this until you remember," she warned.

He nodded, the movement very small. Not agreement perhaps, but an indication that he was thinking about it?

''I better go. The cab may be down there,'' she said when the silence grew strained.

She didn't feel as if she could push that idea any more tonight. Or push Josh. Let him think about it. And she would, too. Was this what Steiner had wanted her to do? she wondered. Had he hoped she'd urge Josh to try to recover those memories, despite how painful that might be for him?

Even if it were, and as much as she hated the thought of doing Steiner's dirty work, she knew that what she'd said was the truth. Josh would never be free until he remembered. And, she acknowledged, neither would she.

As soon as the door closed behind Paige Daniels, he walked across the room and turned the radio off. The stereo was still blaring from the bedroom, but it was distant enough that it didn't impact on the pounding in his head.

The aspirin he'd taken earlier didn't seem to be making a dent in the growing headache. If he took the stronger stuff, it would knock him out for the next eight hours. Something he wasn't sure he could afford.

The sense of foreboding he had felt as he watched Paige Daniels gather up her things and prepare to leave the apartment hadn't lessened. Actually, it had intensified during the few minutes she'd been gone.

He couldn't imagine what he was worried about. If he believed what she was telling him, then he was the one who held the dangerous secrets. She was just a tool, a key, the CIA was using to try to unlock them, so there shouldn't be any risk to her from what was lost in the dark, broken maze of his memory.

So why did he feel as if there might be? Why was his stomach tight with anxiety?

Try as he might, he couldn't come up with a reasonable

explanation for what he felt. All he knew was he wasn't comfortable with this. Daniels shouldn't be out there alone.

Did he feel that way because she had once been his partner? Or because he was right about what he had felt in the bathroom. And he had felt it again as they had stood together by the door. *Something physical.*

He had known her body. He had touched her. His mouth had once lowered to meet hers, which had opened, welcoming his tongue's invasion. He knew that as surely as he now knew that he wasn't Jack Thompson.

And he had wanted to kiss her again a few minutes ago, the urge so strong it was almost a compulsion. A compulsion like this one. He had done nothing about the other, but his mind wouldn't let this go.

The strength of those endlessly circling thoughts that wouldn't leave him alone were another lingering result of his injury. Or so he had been told. Something that would go away in time, they'd assured him.

He had learned during the last few months, however, that fighting against them didn't help. And he also knew, even as he walked across the room to the door and lifted the safety lock to slip it back into place, that it would cause him nothing but problems to fight this one.

Chapter Six

The cab ride wouldn't be nearly long enough to begin thinking about all that had happened, Paige thought. And especially not long enough to deal with the feelings that had resurfaced. If only Joshua Stone's memory could be brought back to life as easily as those long-buried emotions had been.

She ducked her head, trying to determine through the front windshield how close to her hotel they were. She wasn't familiar enough with the landmarks to know for sure, and finally she gave up the effort, sitting back and looking out the side window instead.

She wasn't really aware of the darkened streets they passed. Instead, her thoughts went back to what had happened at Josh's apartment. And then, inevitably, back to three years ago. Back to a small Eastern European country on the verge of a revolution. To the cellar of a bombed-out building.

Her consciousness lingered there, no longer denied access by her will to the memories she had fought so long. And fighting them hadn't done much good. They were intact. As powerful as they had ever been. More powerful now, perhaps, because she had seen Josh again, something she had never expected to happen.

When she realized the cab was pulling into the semicircular drive in front of the hotel, she slipped her billfold out of her purse, shifting her weapon out of the way to reach it. That was something she didn't think she had ever had to do before. Of course, she could count on the fingers of one hand the times she'd even held her weapon, other than on the firing range.

She eased up on the edge of the seat, opening her billfold in preparation for paying the fare. She glanced at the meter, mentally calculating the tip. She had taken the bills out of her wallet and was in the process of handing them to the driver when the door beside her opened.

She didn't even look around, confident it was the doorman. Then a hand closed around her upper arm. Surprised at the familiarity of the gesture, she turned her head, and for the first time realized something was going on.

The man who had taken her arm wasn't wearing a uniform. He had apparently gotten out of a black Mercedes, its windows tinted so darkly that she couldn't see inside, which had pulled into the semicircle before the hotel's entrance, stopping beside her cab. It looked just like the cars favored by the diplomatic corps. She had made that identification automatically. Government car, which meant...

She tried to pull her elbow out of the man's grip as her eyes rose to his face. Not anyone she had ever seen before. And not one of the two men who had been filming Josh.

This man's complexion was olive, his features heavy, with a wide nose and fleshy, beard-shadowed jowls. His face matched the bulk of his body, which was clad in a dark suit and a white shirt. His eyes were deep set, almost black, as was his hair, except for the sweep of gray at the temples.

Instead of releasing her when she began to struggle against his hold, he increased the pressure, urging her out of the cab. Again Paige tried to pull her arm away, but his grip was too firm. And the first stirring of fear moved in her stomach.

With the force he was exerting, her arm was raised almost at a right angle to her body, the beefy fingers digging into her flesh. She hadn't been aware of the pain before, shock maybe, but she was aware of it now. It infuriated her that she was being manhandled by one of Steiner's goons.

Suddenly the strain on her arm increased. The man was using it to drag her across the slick vinyl of the back seat. She slid a few inches toward him before she realized what was happening. She put her foot on the pavement outside, bracing to keep from being pulled out of the cab.

"Hey," she said sharply.

Obviously Steiner had something else to say to her. *Like an apology?* she wondered. *Yeah, right.*

She leaned away from the man holding her arm, using the foot she had planted on the asphalt to give her leverage. It allowed her to resist, at least temporarily, the force he was applying. With her free hand, she pried at his fingers.

Even as she fought him, she never considered screaming or appealing to the cabbie or the hotel doorman for help. This was an agency matter. Not something to get outsiders involved in.

"Let me go, you bastard," she said, each word separate and distinct, punctuated by a strong jerk of her arm.

During the long seconds she'd been resisting, the driver had apparently verified that the money she'd given him was correct. Only when she had demanded her release, had he realized what was going on in his back seat. He began to yell.

Distracted by the noise, Paige looked up. The driver was peering over the back of the bench-type front seat, his eyes widened with shock. She shot a glance to her left, toward the entrance of the hotel, and found that the noise the cab driver was making had attracted attention. The doorman, interrupted in the middle of giving directions to a couple on their way out for the evening, was looking in this direction.

No one seemed to be moving toward the cab, but people were definitely beginning to take notice of what was happening. And drawing a crowd would be the last thing the men in that big, black government car would want to do.

Her advantage, Paige thought with a sense of satisfaction. They would be forced to realize they couldn't get away with this. The adrenaline was surging, roaring through her veins in a flood that lent strength to her indignation.

Screw Steiner, she thought. *And screw the guys doing his dirty work.*

Sensing victory, she kicked out with the foot that had been anchoring her in the seat. Her heel connected with a solid thunk against the man's shin. It took her assailant off guard. Pain loosened his fingers as none of her struggling had done. Paige didn't have a chance to take advantage of that success, however.

In order to kick him, she had been forced to lean further into the interior of the cab, unbalancing the delicate equilibrium that had kept the man from dragging her out. When he had suddenly released his hold, she had still been pulling against it. As a result, she fell forward, so that she was lying on her side across the back seat, propped up by her left elbow.

Her assailant reacted more quickly than she did to their altered positions. He reached into the cab, wrapping sausage-like fingers in her hair. Then he jerked it, dragging her upright before she could begin to resist. Eyes stinging from the agony, she raised both hands to try to pry his fingers apart.

She didn't stand a chance. Her stabilizing foot, the one that had been planted on the asphalt drive, had found no purchase there after the kick. Virtually without resistance, she was dragged out of the cab and onto the pavement outside. She landed on her right knee. The pain was enough this time to make her cry out. Ignoring her, the man began trying to get her to her feet, still using the hand wound through her hair for leverage.

By this time the cabbie was yelling nonstop in a language she didn't understand. She could no longer see the doorman, so she didn't know if he might be coming to help her or if he had gone inside to call the cops.

Actually, all she could see from the ground between the two cars were the tires of the Mercedes and the legs of the man trying to force her into it. Her hands beat at his fingers, which were still entangled in her hair, but the blows seemed to have no effect as he relentlessly pulled her along behind him.

The roughness of the asphalt ripped skin from her knees. And it seemed there wasn't a damn thing she could do about it. He outweighed her by more than a hundred pounds. This was a battle she was going to lose. No matter how much she fought, she was being inexorably drawn toward that open door.

She heard another door slam, but the cabbie's shouts hadn't changed in volume or pitch, so she knew he wasn't clambering out to rush to her rescue. A more likely explanation was that the driver had gotten out on the other side of the Mercedes and was coming to help get her into it. Coming to put an end to something that, from their point of view, had gotten out of hand.

In desperation, she threw herself down onto her left hip, swiveling her body so she could kick out again, trying to connect once more with the guy's shins.

He jumped back, adroitly avoiding her feet. It might be satisfying as hell to think he didn't want a repeat of the first time she'd kicked him, but since he hadn't loosened his hold as he'd dodged away, it wasn't very helpful.

Her attempt seemed to infuriate him. He jerked her hair hard enough that it felt as if the handful he held would be torn out by the roots. She yelled, not words, but an inarticulate expression of pain and rage.

Even as she did, she realized she was being dragged nearer and nearer to the open door of the black car, her efforts to get his fingers out of her hair grew more frantic. He would have to turn it loose in order to lift her inside, she told herself, and when he did—

Suddenly, like a miracle, his hand unclenched. She looked up in time to see his body fly backward into the door he'd been dragging her toward. He fell into the back seat of the black car, almost disappearing.

An arm fastened around Paige's midsection, pulling her onto her knees and then to her feet. As she stood, trembling and swaying, she turned her head and looked straight into the furious blue eyes of Joshua Stone.

"Get in the cab. Get the hell in the cab."

His voice brooked no argument, even if she'd been inclined to make one. She wasn't. She scrambled across the back seat, assuming he would follow.

Instead, he turned in time to meet the advance of the driver of the Mercedes, coming around the back of his car like a berserker. Coming until he encountered the edge of Josh Stone's flattened and rigid right hand. Moving almost too fast for the eye to follow, it had connected with the driver's nose. Paige knew by the sound bone had broken under the impact.

Then the driver, too, disappeared from sight, staggering backward before he lost his balance and went down. Josh spun around, putting his palm flat against the window of the open door of the back seat. The man he had pushed inside had been attempting to crawl out. He didn't make it because Josh slammed the door on him.

Since the guy's legs were hanging out of the car, it wouldn't close completely. It closed far enough, however.

The resulting scream competed with the cab driver's unintelligible diatribe.

Josh didn't follow up on his advantage. Instead, he grabbed her purse from where it had fallen on the pavement and flung it into the cab. It hit her in the shoulder and fell onto the floorboard as Josh jumped into the seat beside her.

"Drive," he ordered.

The word wasn't loud, but his tone of command broke through the cabbie's hysteria. He pressed the accelerator to the floor, sending the cab squealing out of the driveway and onto the street. Luckily, there was no approaching traffic.

A shot rang out behind them, striking the back window and cracking it. Although the safety glass didn't shatter, Paige ducked, hands over her head. Joshua Stone turned, however, looking out through the starred glass at the gunman running behind them.

"Window dressing, huh?" he said sarcastically, but at least he didn't look at her as he said it.

They ran the red light at the corner, tires still squealing. The driver hadn't asked Josh where he wanted to go.

And neither did Paige.

"NOT EXACTLY The Peachtree Towers."

She couldn't detect any note of apology or regret in Josh's tone, despite how far this motel, located in one of the city's seedier suburbs, was from the elegance of her downtown hotel. And Josh had asked for one room, which came equipped with only one bed.

If being alone with him in the bathroom of his apartment made her nervous, she wondered how she was going to feel, cooped up all night with him in a motel room. And then she realized she didn't seem capable of feeling anything right now except glad to be alive. Barely alive, she amended, hobbling stiffly to the bed and sitting down wearily on the end of it.

She looked down at her battered knees. This was the first time she had seen them in the light, and the sight made her ill. Her skirt and panty hose had been no protection from the roughness of the driveway's surface. The hose were a torn and bloodstained mess. As was the skin they covered.

Considering how they looked, it was a wonder her knees didn't hurt any more than they did. Bruises and abrasions, she told herself. If there had been anything more serious, she wouldn't have been able to walk the long blocks from where they had gotten out of the cab. She hadn't argued with Josh about that precaution, and he hadn't apologized for taking it, but it must have been obvious by her limp that the trek hadn't been easy.

She heard water running and realized that he had disappeared into the bathroom. After a minute or two he came back out, carrying a wet washcloth.

"Take those off and clean away the blood," he instructed, handing her the cloth. "I'll go for some ice."

Ice for her knees. And suddenly she realized that she'd rather have him here than have the ice. Because, despite her silly bravado at the door of his apartment, Josh had been right. What had happened in front of the hotel hadn't felt at all like window dressing. The bullet that had hit the back window might have struck either one of them. There was no way the man shooting at the cab could be certain it wouldn't.

Without asking permission, Josh picked her purse up off the bed and took her gun out of it. He checked the clip as he headed for the door. He looked through the peephole before he unfastened the night latch. Finally he eased the door open slightly and surveyed the hall. Only then did he slip the semiautomatic into the pocket of his slacks and step outside.

He had been that careful after they left the hotel, too. They had seen the lights of a car following close only once, but under Josh's direction, the cabbie had lost it. Then they had wandered through a dark maze of streets, well off the main thoroughfares, until Josh was sure no one was tailing them. No matter what else he had forgotten, all the old skills seemed intact.

Paige realized suddenly that she hadn't made any move to do what he'd told her. She didn't know how far away the ice machine was, but given the size of the motel complex, it couldn't be far.

She stood, hitching up her skirt, and hooked her thumbs into the top of her panty hose, easing them down over her hips. That was the easy part. The rest was going to be more difficult and probably a lot more painful. The hose were stuck to the torn and bloody abrasions on her knees, and she had never been a fan of the rip-off-the-bloody-bandage school of masochism.

She sat back down on the edge of the bed and carefully began to peel the nylon away from what was left of her skin, easing them down as she worked. She had just succeeded in getting the panty hose off when Josh opened the door.

She looked up and found his eyes focused not on her face but on her knees. She held the ruined hose away from her as if they were contaminated and dropped them ceremoniously on the floor. Then she stretched her legs out in front of her, looking down at them. Without the laddered and bloody hose, her knees didn't look quite as bad, she decided.

She took the washcloth Josh had brought her and began to dab tentatively at the left one. Bearable, she decided, rubbing a little harder and beginning to have more success in removing the dirt and gore. Bits of paving material had been ground in so that the top layer of skin was pretty well shredded. However, none of the abrasions seemed deep.

After a few seconds, she heard Josh set the plastic ice bucket down on the heater/air-conditioning console. Then he put the night latch back on the door.

Identifying those actions by sound, she didn't even look

up from what she was doing, deliberately keeping her concentration on the task at hand. She didn't need any visual reminders that they were now locked in a motel room together.

Josh went back into the bathroom and returned this time with a couple of towels and another dampened washcloth. He walked over to the bed and stood watching her try to remove the embedded debris without taking any more skin off with it.

"Slide back," he suggested after a few seconds.

She looked up, not sure she would be comfortable doing that or sure why he would want her to.

"That's as clean as you're going to get them with that," he explained, nodding toward the dirty and bloodstained cloth. "Lean back against the headboard, and I'll finish up."

Remembering how grateful she had been when he had shown up tonight, she decided not to argue. She wasn't about to try sliding backwards on the bed to reach that headboard, however. Not as short as her skirt was and minus panty hose.

She stood up, dropping the washcloth she'd been using on top of the ruined hose. She limped around the side of the bed and pulled the thin quilted spread far enough down to expose a couple of cheap foam pillows. She stacked them in front of the headboard before she crawled onto the bed, leaning against them.

When she looked up, she realized Josh had been watching her again. She resisted the urge to tug at her skirt, which had ridden up midthigh. Of course, the damaged legs it exposed couldn't be very appealing, so he probably hadn't noticed how much of them were revealed.

He walked around to the side of the bed, his eyes on her knees. "Looks like mostly bruises and scrapes," he said, "but I'd like to take a closer look to be sure."

His gaze lifted to her face, and she wondered if he were

waiting for permission. And then wondered if she wanted to give it. Finally, she took a fortifying breath and nodded. She wasn't sure which she dreaded more, the touch of his hands against her bare skin or the pain of his examination.

He sat down beside her, slipping his palm behind her left knee and lifting it to give him better access to the damage. He looked everything over, occasionally applying the damp cloth to an area she'd missed.

Not too bad, she thought in relief. His touch was impersonal, almost professional. And she managed not to allow any outward reaction to the occasional twinge it caused.

When Josh started on the right knee, the one she had landed on as she'd been dragged from the cab, she knew it was going to be a different story. That one had already begun to swell and turn blue, and it was a lot more sensitive to the pressure he was using to get the last of the ground-in flecks of asphalt out of the cuts.

The sound she made when he touched a particularly tender spot was low, originating in her throat. She hadn't intended to allow her discomfort expression, but the severity of the pain had surprised her. His hand hesitated, and his eyes came up to her face, questioning.

"Just bruised," she said. "It hurts more to the touch than it did to walk on it."

He nodded, again looking at her leg. He laid the cloth down and using his other hand to cup under her heel, he bent her knee. He twisted her leg a little so that he could look at the outside and then turned it the other way. There was some pain with each movement, but not enough to elicit any further sound. She was prepared now, her lips compressed.

Finally he put her foot down on the bed, her leg still bent. His hand, the one that had been cupped behind her knee, began to move. She thought he was going to manipulate the joint in a different way, and anticipating that it might hurt, she had braced herself.

It was probably a good thing she had, because what Josh did next was not at all what she'd been expecting. His hand smoothed down the back of her calf. His palm was calloused, slightly abrasive as it moved over her skin, its slow glide incredibly pleasant.

Her body reacted, a small tremor of sensation deep inside. Shocked by the familiarity, and even more surprised by her involuntary response to it, her eyes flew up and found his intent on her face.

Getting to be a habit, she thought, but she didn't pull her gaze from his. She probably couldn't have, even if she had wanted to. And she didn't.

Josh held her eyes for a long time without saying anything. The movement of his hand had stilled. Finally he leaned forward, almost exactly as he had earlier when he had reached to unlatch the chain on his apartment door.

She held her breath, having no doubt this time what he intended. When his face was inches away, blue eyes still examining hers, he hesitated. Her mouth had already opened, anticipating the kiss.

It never came. His gaze fell to her parted lips, and she closed them, embarrassed that it must be obvious what she'd been expecting. His mouth tightened, and then he leaned back. Putting distance between his mouth and hers. Putting distance between their bodies.

After a moment he stood up, taking a step away from the bed. Her eyes followed, reading quite clearly what was in his face, just as she had only a moment before. He had wanted to kiss her. That had been apparent. And yet he had backed away.

Because there was nothing in the relationship that existed between them now that should have created that desire? *Nothing that existed now,* she repeated mentally.

Which must mean that on some level, Joshua Stone remembered that once there had been. Had he just remembered her? Perhaps even remembered what had happened between them?

If *that* particular memory had emerged enough to almost be translated into action, then it was an absolute certainty that the rest of his memories were there as well. However deeply buried in his subconscious they were, they were there. Still intact. And still incredibly dangerous.

Chapter Seven

"You take the bed," Josh said.

Despite a couple of hours spent holding an ice-filled towel over her right knee and a long hot soak in the tub, Paige had still been limping when she came out of the bathroom.

Josh had gone out to the vending machines, but there hadn't been much conversation to accompany the snacks. The near-kiss seemed to have destroyed any urge they had to talk, even about what had happened tonight. And she had expected Josh to have other questions about the things she had told him. About the team or about that mission. If he did, he hadn't asked them.

After she'd eaten, she had pretended to read the newspaper Josh brought back with the food, but she couldn't help remembering the last time they had been together. Her attempts to banish those memories weren't helped by his nearness. Or by the fact that occasionally when she glanced up, she would find his eyes on her.

By ten o'clock, she had decided that the uncomfortable silence might be better used for sleeping. Discarding the ice, she had gone into the bathroom to get ready for bed. After she climbed out of the tub, she had stood in front of the mirror, studying the familiar features of the woman reflected there.

More than a little worse for wear, she acknowledged, but

nothing that rest wouldn't help. She debated whether or not to sleep in her clothes and decided she didn't have a choice. She couldn't see herself parading into the other room in her underwear, as distasteful as putting back on that stained skirt and the blouse she had worn all day might be.

Despite the fact that she was fully dressed when she came out of the bathroom, something must have indicated she was ready to turn in, which had prompted Josh's offer of the bed. She thought about being noble, but it took only a second to realize what a bad idea offering to share the bed would be.

For one thing, Josh hadn't made the same decision in the matter of sleeping attire she had. He had taken off his jacket and shirt, draping them along with his tie over the chair. A white T-shirt stretched across his chest and shoulders, and for a man who had recently spent several weeks in the hospital, he seemed to be in surprisingly good shape.

As a means of comparison, Paige allowed herself to visualize his body as it had looked that night in Vladistan. Suddenly, what had begun as a harmless, intellectual exercise became something very different. Highly disturbing. Although his chest was covered now, for a moment it seemed she could again feel the coarse dark hair that covered it moving against her breasts.

She turned her head, contemplating the solitary bed. And knew she wasn't going to offer to share it with Josh Stone. After all, he'd endured far worse than a night spent on the floor of a warm, carpeted room. As a matter of fact, so had she.

"Thanks," she said simply, making no disclaimer.

She did limp over to the closet to see what kind of extra bedding the motel provided. There was a thin blanket on the shelf, but nothing else. She took it down and walked back to the bed to remove one of the two pillows she had leaned against as she iced her knee. She held the items out to him and watched amusement touch the blue eyes.

Heat crept under the thin skin of her throat and moved upward into her cheeks. The blush made her feel silly. Sixteen and virginal. And she couldn't imagine why she was embarrassed.

She had slept with this man. He had made love to her for hours, in ways no one else ever had. He knew her body more intimately than anyone else on earth, so why should being alone with him be so difficult?

"Shouldn't we put a chair under the door?" she asked. Any topic other than the one occupying far too much of her thoughts.

"We weren't followed," he said, taking the blanket and pillow out of her hands.

As careful as Josh had been, there really was no way anyone could find them. Still, she wanted that chair under the knob before she closed her eyes. And if he wouldn't do it...

She limped around the bed and transferred Josh's discarded clothing onto the table that held the tourist information booklets. Then she lifted the chair and carried it across the room, fitting it under the knob.

When she turned around, Josh was watching her, still holding the blanket and pillow she had handed him. The corners of his mouth moved slightly, almost a smile, before he turned away. He took the bedding into the short hallway that led to the bathroom. He tossed the pillow on the floor and wrapped the blanket around his shoulders, serape style.

"You don't sleep walk, do you, Daniels?" he asked.

Before she could formulate an answer, he took her 9-mm out of the pocket of his slacks. Stooping, he laid it on the floor beside the pillow, and then he looked up at her again. There was no amusement in his eyes now.

She knew what must be in hers, considering what was

suddenly in her head. The sequence he had just enacted was the same as the night they had spent making love. Laying his gun down on the cellar floor had been the first step of all that had followed.

Coincidence? Or something else? Something deliberately provocative. Which would mean... She shook her head, thinking about what that would mean.

"Don't worry," she said. "If I ever did, I can promise you I won't tonight."

THE SOUND WAS LOW at first, not enough to bring her fully awake. It nibbled at the edge of her consciousness, so that her tired mind tried to fit it into the context of her dream. When that didn't work, she attempted to ignore it, to fall back into the comforting escape of a sleep where she didn't have to think. Not about Steiner. Or the men in the Mercedes. Or anything else. Especially not about Joshua Stone.

After a while, however, the noise grew loud enough that she was unable to block it. Awake now, her eyes opened in the dimness. The patterns of faint light and heavy darkness represented by doors and windows didn't correspond to the familiar ones of her bedroom. It took a few seconds for her to realize that was because she wasn't there. Another few to remember exactly where she was. With whom and why.

And a far longer time to recognize what had awakened her. Someone was moaning. Maybe the reason it had taken her so long to identify that sound was because it was non-verbal. Almost bestial. It was certainly inarticulate, but more than that, it was the essence of something in pain. Some *thing*.

She examined her conclusion, wondering how she had reached it. Because a man would have words to express his suffering, she realized. This was an agony without any means of expression. And as the moaning grew in volume, a chill invaded her body.

"Josh?" she whispered, and then she waited. For a second or two after she spoke his name, the noise had ceased. She held her breath, expecting him to answer her. Instead, into the silence the sound came again, starting low and then gradually increasing.

For a breathless eternity, she fought her inclination to go to him. To throw off the covers and run across the room and wake him. To offer Josh an escape from this nightmare, just as she would have offered it to anyone in such anguish. Instead, she lay as if paralyzed, hardly daring to breathe, and listened to the sounds the man lying on the floor was making.

Her ears strained, trying to distinguish words or phrases within them. There were none. If Joshua Stone were dreaming, there was no dialogue involved in his nightmare. There was only raw agony. And finally she could not listen to it any longer.

She pushed the sheet and the thin velour blanket back and slipped out of bed. There was barely enough light to make out his form, still lying in the hallway that led to the bathroom. She hurried across the room and stooped beside him. Only when she was so close did she realize that his head was thrashing from side to side, the motion as frantically and emphatically negative as the inarticulate noise had been.

"Josh," she said aloud, leaning over him.

There was no response. He was so deeply enmeshed in the net of the dream that the sound of her voice couldn't free him.

Hesitantly, she put her hand on his chest. With her touch the restless motion of his head stopped. His chest expanded as he took a breath, filling his lungs as if they had been deprived of oxygen. She could hear it, air drawn shudderingly through parted lips as if in preparation for some exertion.

"Josh," she said again, louder this time. And then, using the hand that had been resting on his chest, she shook him.

The body beneath her fingers exploded into motion. His right arm came up under hers, throwing it off. The movement continued, propelling her backward, pushing her violently away from him. If she had been kneeling instead of stooping, she might have managed to maintain her balance. Instead, the blow rocked her enough that she fell against the wall behind her.

She wasn't hurt, but she lay against the wall, stunned, as Joshua Stone crouched before her like a wild animal. And the same deadly hand that had broken her assailant's nose last night was again poised to strike, this time at her.

That blow that would have crushed her windpipe, exposed and vulnerable because of her position, was never delivered. Despite the lack of light in the hallway, she could gauge the return of awareness, of blessed sanity, to those pale blue eyes, still locked on her face.

"Josh?" she whispered again.

This time the name she spoke was tentative. Inquiring. This wasn't the Joshua Stone she had known. This man was a stranger. A cold-eyed, snarling stranger, whose hand had been raised against her in anger.

"It's me, Josh. It's Daniels."

That's what he had always called her. And perhaps she used that name in hope that something would connect in his trauma-damaged brain before he could deliver a blow that would kill her.

His hand fell. She could hear him panting, the sound ragged, as if he had been running. Even when he had fought those men in front of her hotel tonight, his breathing hadn't been like this.

"What's wrong?" he asked, as if she were the one who needed help. As if she were the one in distress.

"You were dreaming," she said.

Now that the threat was past, her heart rate began to slow. She hadn't realized until it did how fast her pulse had been racing. Flight or fight. Except in this case, she had been unprepared to do either.

After a moment, she could see the tension begin to seep out of Josh's body. He slumped against the opposite wall, and he seemed to be trying to control his breathing, taking deep, calming breaths. She could still hear them in the darkness, but the sounds of these were not nearly so harsh as the ones before had been.

"You were dreaming," she said. "Do you remember it?"

Was it possible there was something in that nightmare which might offer a clue about what had happened to him in Vladistan? Perhaps even a clue to the information Steiner wanted? If she could give them the location of the toxin, this might finally be over, and the real healing of Joshua Stone could begin.

"I don't know," Josh said. "I can never remember dreams."

"It sounded as if whatever was happening might have been painful," she said. *And if ever there had been an understatement in the history of the world...*

"The wreck, maybe," he suggested.

His back still against the wall, he brought his knees up and rested his forearms on them. Finally he put his head in his hands as if it hurt. She could no longer see his face, and she knew she would do this better if she could. At least she would have had some way to gauge his reactions.

"There wasn't any wreck, Josh," she said softly.

There was silence for several long heartbeats. Slowly he lifted his head until he was looking at her again.

"That was just something they told you to explain your injuries."

More silence. She let it stretch, knowing that he had to participate in this. He had to want to know what had happened to him or they would never be able to unlock the barriers that were so firmly in place.

"How would *you* explain them?" he asked.

She was surprised at the lucidity of the question, given his confusion only seconds ago.

"I don't know," she said truthfully. "But...I think something happened to you during the time you were missing. Something so terrible that you don't *want* to remember it. In spite of what you want, however, sometimes you do. You remember it when you dream. And it terrifies you."

He put his head back against the wall and closed his eyes. Maybe he was thinking about what she had said. Or maybe he didn't want to think about that possibility any more than he wanted to remember. And judging by the sounds she had listened to, she couldn't blame him.

"I think you have to try again," she said after a long time.

"Try again?" He didn't lower his head to look at her.

"I think you have to undergo hypnosis again. I think that might be the only way to ever get your memory back."

"I'm not sure I want it back," he said.

Which made perfect sense, if what she had just been thinking was correct. Except he didn't really have all that many options. There were too many people interested in the information Joshua Stone possessed, including the CIA and the State Department.

And judging by their encounter with the men in the Mercedes tonight, someone else wanted it as well. A threat that might be much more serious than the one represented by Steiner's games.

WHILE JOSH was in the bathroom getting dressed the next morning, Paige had been straightening the bed, limping around it from one side to the other. Although her knee was as stiff as she had anticipated, she had decided that being in a motel room with Josh Stone and an unmade bed was a little more intimacy than she wanted to deal with right now.

As she was turning away after pulling the spread up over the pillows, she noticed numbers scrawled across the top sheet of the pad the motel furnished for messages. Josh must have written them there some time after they'd come into the room last night.

"What's this number?" she called. "The one by the phone."

"Part of the license plate on the Mercedes. I'm going to get someone to check it out."

Paige looked back down at the pad, wondering why he hadn't mentioned this last night. Apparently, since there were just four digits on the sheet, he had caught only a glimpse of the tag. Since they knew the make and color of the car those four belonged to, however, the national computer could probably match them to the owner.

"Why take that risk?" she asked.

"Because we might find out who the car belongs to?"

Surprised that his voice was so close, she glanced up and saw that Josh was standing in the hall. He had put his shirt and jacket back on, but not the tie. Apparently he had also managed to put the dreams from last night into some kind of light-of-day perspective. He sounded just as he always had. Confident. Almost arrogant.

"You think it's a good idea to run this through the agency?"

She didn't want Steiner to be able to find them, and she couldn't believe Josh would either. Maybe he wasn't as back-to-normal as she thought.

"I didn't say I was going to run it through the agency."

"Then how?"

"The cop who helped uncover my background might do it as a favor. With the drunk driving charge, we weren't what

I'd call friends, but he was pretty fascinated by the amnesia."

"And you think that's going to make him willing to run a tag through the computers for you?"

"Why not? Cops do it all the time for friends. He might if I tell him I saw that car and thought I recognized the person driving it. And that I'm hoping that hearing the name will trigger something. I can make up a story he'll buy."

"And if it turns out the car belongs to Uncle Sam?"

"You really think those guys last night were from the company, Daniels?"

"I think it's a possibility," she hedged.

"Do you believe Steiner would order somebody to shoot at you?"

"Heat of the moment," she suggested. "You did a number on them. Pain, anger or even humiliation can do funny things to logic, even with trained agents."

"So they just decide to shoot at us when what they'd been ordered to do was to take you in? Is that the kind of operatives they have at the CIA these days? A bunch of loose cannons."

"Why would anyone come after me? I'm not carrying secrets in my head."

"Maybe *they* don't know that."

And Steiner did, of course.

"Besides," Josh went on, "We both know the why of whatever is going on. The why is several million dollars worth of a missing nerve agent. What we need to worry about is the who."

"I'VE BEEN THINKING about your suggestion," Josh said. He had been. More than he had wanted to, actually.

They were waiting for Detective Rombart to return his call about the numbers from the tag. He had used Paige's cell phone, which couldn't be traced back to their location.

And he thought the detective had bought the story he had woven.

"My suggestion?" Paige asked, looking up from the paper.

She was leaning back against the headboard again, an ice-filled towel resting over her right knee. He had brought both the ice and the newspaper back to the room with their breakfast. And he hadn't been surprised to find there was nothing in it about the attack at the hotel last night.

"About trying hypnosis again."

"Are you sure?" she asked.

Probably not the response Steiner would have wanted her to make, he thought. If he was right about the motives of whoever had tried to kidnap her, however, the secret he carried was endangering Paige as well. She should be encouraging him to submit to hypnosis again, not questioning whether he wanted to.

And he didn't, he admitted. For one thing, he wasn't interested in a replay of last night.

"At least it had some result. In comparison to everything else..." He shrugged.

Of course, there had also been some result from her reintroduction into his life. Actually, the same one the hypnosis had created—those terrible dreams he couldn't remember.

She didn't remind him of that, and she didn't argue with his decision. After all, she was the one who had told him he'd never be free until he'd regained his memory. If he were ever going to reclaim his life, he needed to get to the bottom of what had happened to him three years ago. And he needed to do it as much as the CIA needed him to.

"But not with the same therapist as before," he said. He was sitting in the chair, his feet propped on the foot of the bed, ankles crossed. "I'm pretty sure where his loyalties lie."

Paige laid the paper on her lap, leaning back against the

pillows stacked behind her. "I'd be willing to bet a transcript of that session landed on Steiner's desk."

"At least this time I'll know the outcome before they do. Bastards," he said, the word under his breath.

It was almost drowned out by the ringing of Paige's cell phone. Her eyes widened and met his. She let it ring one more time before she picked it up and handed it to him. He took his feet off the bed and sat up in the chair, feeling anxiety stir.

"Jack Thompson," he said after he flipped open the case. Despite the smoothness with which his call to the detective had gone, he found he was far more nervous about hearing his response than he'd let on to Daniels.

"Rombart here. We found that vehicle you asked about."

"And the registration?" Josh asked, signaling Paige to hand him the pad and pen from the table beside the bed.

"You said the driver was somebody you thought you knew?"

"That's right," Josh said. He didn't like the tone of the question. It had a cop feel to it that the detective's voice hadn't held when he had made his request.

"I think you might want to come in and talk to us then."

Josh hesitated, thinking about all the things a suggestion to come in and talk to the Atlanta police might mean. In this case there were way too many possibilities, none of which he particularly liked.

"Is something wrong?" he asked noncommittally.

Maybe Daniels had been right. Maybe the cops had traced the car back to the CIA, and now they were wondering why Jack Thompson, average Joe citizen, would be interested in a vehicle that belonged to that particular government agency.

"The registration didn't lead us anywhere," the detective said. "We're still trying to follow up on it, however, because hitting a dead end like that usually means the vehicle has been involved in some kind of criminal activity."

Or that the registration information is being protected, Josh thought. Not something he was going to suggest to Andy Rombart. "I thought you said you'd found the car," he said instead.

"Literally found it. Somebody pushed it into Lake Lanier last night. A fisherman noticed tire tracks leading down to the water at dawn this morning. The county just got it out."

"And you have no idea who owns the car?"

"Maybe the guy in the passenger seat," Rombart said.

It took a heartbeat for that to register. *Maybe the guy in the passenger seat.* Suddenly Josh realized he was in deeper than he'd intended. And he needed to be very careful. Andy Rombart was sharp enough that finding a dead body and at the same time getting a request for the registration information about the car it was in would set off bells.

"There was somebody *in* the car?" Josh asked, infusing shock into the question.

"No ID. Nothing on the body. We're running the prints. I just thought you might give us a head start on who he is."

Josh wasn't sure whether Rombart was beginning to doubt his amnesia or if he was only wondering why Jack Thompson would know someone who had ended up dead in a lake. Neither line of thinking was anything Josh wanted the detective to pursue.

"The name of the guy in that car was what I was hoping to get from *you*," he said. "I've got no information to share. I don't mind telling you, however, that it makes me uneasy that I thought some guy looked familiar and then his car ends up in a lake with a body inside."

There was a small silence on the other end of the line.

"I thought it was worth a shot," Rombart said. "You still interested in the name when we get it?"

"The name of the dead guy?"

"Yeah," Rombart said, "the name of the dead guy." He sounded almost amused.

"He may not be the man I thought looked familiar."

"No guarantee."

"One body?"

"You think there ought to be more?" The tone of that question seemed sharp, more interested.

"There were two men in the car when I saw it," Josh said. "If that's helpful."

"It might be. I'll have the sheriff's boys look around in the lake. You gonna be at this number a while? I'll let you know what we turn up."

Josh wasn't sure staying in touch with the Atlanta police department was smart. However, this was the only lead they had to whoever had made Paige a target last night. And with the addition of a dead man to the equation, everything about what had happened had suddenly become a lot more urgent.

"I'd appreciate that," Josh said.

"We'll be in touch," Rombart agreed before he broke the connection.

"Body?" Paige repeated as he snapped the cell phone closed.

"They pulled the Mercedes out of a lake this morning. Dead end on the registration. They're running prints on the guy who was inside."

"One of the two from last night?"

She sounded shocked that someone she had encountered so recently was dead. And that was probably a normal response to that kind of news.

Josh realized that shock hadn't been what he'd felt when he'd heard it. His response had been more like a sense of vindication. A sense that what had happened to the guy was just. Because they'd hurt Paige? Or because their sheer ineptness deserved some kind of punishment?

"Maybe his job performance wasn't up to standard," he said.

It took a second, but she got it right on the first try.

"You think they killed him because he didn't succeed in getting me into that car."

"You have a better explanation?" he asked.

Apparently, for whoever was behind whatever was going on, failure wasn't an option. The people who had tried to kidnap Paige were playing for keeps. And in this particular game, Josh suspected she was in way over her head. Given the fact that he was operating almost completely in the dark, maybe they both were.

Chapter Eight

"You're the one who was so certain no one could have followed us," Paige said. "So I ought to be able to do this without attracting attention. You need to stay here and wait for Rombart's call. Maybe the guy's name will give us something to go on. Until we know it, however..."

"I don't think splitting up is smart," Josh said.

"You don't think I'm capable of looking out for myself."

Maybe that *was* it, Josh admitted. All his protective instincts seemed to come into play where Daniels was concerned. After she'd left his apartment last night, he hadn't been able to deny the conviction that she was in danger.

And when he'd arrived at the hotel and found her being manhandled, he'd been ready to kill. He remembered how sick he'd felt when he'd gotten his first look at what they'd done to her knees. Then later, when he'd sat down on the bed beside her, it had been so damn tempting to lean forward and cover her mouth with his own. It had felt as if doing that would have been the most natural thing in the world. Natural and familiar.

"I don't *know* whether you're capable of looking after yourself. Frankly, I don't know a damn thing about you," he said, frustration making his voice sharper than he'd intended. "You show up and tell me we were partners, and then all hell breaks loose. In case you didn't notice, Daniels, those were real bullets they were using last night.''

"And one of the men who fired them is dead," she said, as if his death had destroyed the threat. "We agreed that we need to find the name of a good hypnotherapist. There's probably someone qualified right here in Atlanta, but it's going to be tough to find them using only the phone book."

"Tough maybe, but safe," he said.

"I think the risk is minimal. And it *is* my risk."

She was right. He wasn't in charge of Paige Daniels. She claimed to be a CIA operative, and he didn't know what the hell he was, Josh admitted. Or who he was. All he knew were the stories he'd been told. Directly conflicting stories.

"Stay in touch," he ordered her, just as if he had the right. She nodded, the tension that had been in her face as she'd argued relaxing minutely. "And be *damned* careful."

"I DON'T WORK that way, Ms. Daniels."

Paige had made every appeal she could think of, including patriotism and a not-so-subtle hint of a threat to national security, to get Dr. Helen Culbertson to agree to see Josh. She wasn't about to let something like methodology stand in the way.

She had used the computers at the branch of the public library nearest the motel to search out hypnotherapists in the area and to research their standing in the medical community. There weren't all that many who had the right credentials, but Culbertson had been at the top of every list that had come up.

Remarkably, the psychologist had agreed to this impromptu meeting with Paige during her lunch hour. After she had listened to Paige's story, she had asked for her identification. And then she had insisted on calling the CIA for verification. Reluctantly, Paige had given her Pete Logan's extension.

And as long as Pete didn't connect the therapist's request for a reference to the summons Paige had gotten from Special Ops last week, there should be no way for Steiner to tie her to an Atlanta psychologist. It didn't seem to occur to Dr. Culbertson that what Paige was asking her to do was a little out of the purview of Sector Analysis. Logan's acknowledgment that Paige Daniels did indeed work in his department had done the trick. The only roadblock now seemed to be Paige's insistence that she be allowed to be present during the session.

"In this case, I'm afraid that's the way we'll have to do it," Paige said. "I need to sit in because I might pick up on a minor detail, something you could miss, that could have some significance to the location of what we're looking for."

"And you don't intend to tell me what that is," the psychologist said, looking at Paige over her half glasses, the expression in her gray eyes skeptical.

Paige smiled at her, disarmingly she hoped. "Not yet. There's really no point in revealing classified information until we determine if you can take this subject back to the time when what we need to find went missing. And I feel it only fair to warn you. Hypnosis has been tried before."

"Unsuccessfully, I assume."

"I'm afraid so."

"Whoever tried it didn't know what they were doing."

A statement that definite should probably be reassuring, Paige thought. Instead it made her wonder if she'd come to the right person. Her understanding of hypnosis was that it was far from being an exact science.

"You think anyone with amnesia can be made to recall his or her past?" she asked, trying to keep her sudden doubt from being reflected in that question.

"Not in a case where the critical part of the brain which is responsible for memory is damaged. And there are always clear physical indications if that's happened. If, however, as you've indicated, the subject can remember skills, but not events, and if he shows no evidence of motor or cognitive impairment—''

''There's no evidence of any of that,'' Paige assured her. ''He remembers everything he's ever learned, but not how or when he learned it. He can't recall any personal information about himself, however. Not even his name. I was told that kind of amnesia is very rare.''

The therapist's lips pursed as if she might be thinking about that. ''So rare that I don't believe what you've described could be the result of any kind of physical trauma.''

''Then... I'm not sure what you're suggesting, Dr. Culbertson. Or where it leaves us as far as the possibility of recovering the information we need.''

''I won't know where it leaves us until we get more deeply into this. Based strictly on what you've said, however, this sounds more like the *repression* of certain memories rather than a true loss of them.''

''You're saying he doesn't want to remember who he is?''

''If what you've told me is true, for some reason this man has deliberately destroyed or repressed any sense of self— and that's all he's repressed. And I don't think that in all my years of practice I've ever seen anything like that before.''

PAIGE DIDN'T HAVE the cab drop her off as far from the motel as Josh had last night. Although her knee has loosened up during the course of the day, it was still sore, and by the time she reached the room, she was ready to stretch out on the bed and rest it for a while.

Which wouldn't be long, she realized, glancing at her watch. They were to meet Dr. Culbertson at her home at seven. She was still a little surprised that the therapist had agreed to that, but she had seemed to be interested in the professional challenge Josh's amnesia represented.

Although Paige had one of the plastic room keys, she assumed Josh would have the night latch on. She knocked on the door and waited for him to open it.

There were a couple of people unloading luggage in the parking lot, and she watched them as the slow seconds ticked by. She began to feel a little too exposed, so she knocked again. Maybe during her absence Josh had decided to take advantage of the vacant bed and make up for the sleep he'd missed.

When there was no response to her second knock, she fitted the key into the slot and turned the knob. The door opened, exposing an empty room. The covers on the bed were exactly as she had left them this morning, pulled up over the pillows rather than tucked under them. If the maids had come to clean, Josh must have turned them away.

She hesitated on the threshold, feeling a prickle of unease skate along her spine. Josh was supposed to stay here and wait for Rombart's call. The memory of the morning she had awakened alone in the cellar of the bombed-out building where they had taken refuge was suddenly in her head. Josh was supposed to have been there as well. And he hadn't been.

One of the people who had been unloading luggage was now coming along the sidewalk, looking at numbers on doors, obviously trying to match the key card he held. Paige stepped inside the room, closing the door behind her.

As she did, shutting out the noise of traffic on the nearby interstate, she heard the sound of the shower. She released the breath she'd been holding and set her purse and the shopping bag she was carrying down on the console. She slipped off her shoes and limped across the carpet to the closed bathroom door.

She raised her hand to tap on it, but hesitated, debating

whether it would be better not to disturb him. Of course, if Josh finished his shower and thought he was still alone in the room, it might prove embarrassing to both of them. She rapped the back of her knuckles lightly against the wooden panel.

"Josh?" she called, pitching her voice so that she thought it would carry over the sound of the water. "I'm back."

She listened for a moment, ear to the door, but there was no response. Finally, she decided she was too beat to stand around knocking on doors. She walked back to the bed and lay down on it, sighing in relief as she stretched out her aching knee.

She wondered if she would have time for a shower before they left to meet Dr. Culbertson. Shower or grab a bite of real food somewhere? Right now, listening to the sounds coming from the bathroom, she had to admit the prospect of standing under a cascade of hot water came out way ahead of a meal.

She closed her eyes, consciously trying to relax the tension she had felt all day. Despite her assurances to Josh that what she was going out to do wouldn't be dangerous, she had felt the constant urge to look over her shoulder.

She burrowed more deeply into the pillow, turning on her side and pulling the spread from the other half of the bed around her shoulders. She wondered if Rombart had called. Wondered if what they had found out about the dead man had been helpful.

Her thoughts returned to Dr. Culbertson's office, remembering the hypnotist's opinion that Josh's amnesia was the result of repressed memories rather than injury. The idea had been one Paige herself had considered. It made sense, given the strange parameters of what Josh could remember. Of course, the therapist had made it clear she couldn't reach any firm conclusions about that until she met with Josh.

The sound of the shower beat on soothingly in the background. Gradually, so gradually that she wasn't aware it was happening, the present faded away. Paige drifted into sleep, making up for some of what she had missed last night.

AS SOON AS he opened the door, letting the steam that had accumulated in the bathroom escape, he knew Daniels was back. Despite the fact that he was wearing only briefs, he stepped out into the hall, his eyes searching the darkened bedroom for her.

She was asleep on the bed, the quilted spread pulled around her. She had left her shoes by the door. Which was unlocked, he realized uneasily. He walked back into the bathroom and pulled on his slacks, zipping them as he came out again. He crossed the room on bare feet and slipped on the night latch, automatically looking out through the peep-hole in the center of the door.

The parking lot was practically deserted, just as it had been all day. It was dark enough that the halogen lights were coming on, illuminating the cars parked under them. There was nothing out there that looked the least bit suspicious.

He turned around, expecting that the metallic click of the lock being thrown might have awakened Paige. It hadn't. She was still asleep, dark lashes resting motionless against her cheeks.

Watching her, her face as unguarded as a child's, something stirred in his chest. It wasn't the same instinct to protect that he had felt outside her hotel last night. He might have felt that for any woman who was being attacked.

Nor was it whatever had made him want to lean forward and cover her mouth with his. That, too, might have been simply a natural response to an attractive woman. After all, it wasn't as if there had been all that many women in his life lately, he acknowledged, crossing the room again to stand beside the bed.

Paige turned restlessly, her lips parting and a small breath sighing out between them. It had been a long twenty-four hours, he thought, remembering all she'd been through.

And that's all it had been, he realized with a sense of wonder. That's all the time he had known her. Twenty-four hours. She had shown up in the restaurant where he was having dinner last night at about this time.

Before that, he had had no idea Paige Daniels existed. And since then... Since then, his life and everything he had believed about it had been turned upside down.

Turned upside down *again.* Just as he had been coming to terms with what they had told him after the wreck, she had shown up and destroyed everything he thought he knew about himself.

He couldn't begin to explain why he had believed her. There was no explanation for it except that what she had told him had felt right. As nothing had since he'd awakened from that coma.

He had nothing else to go on but that feeling and the fact that somewhere inside he knew with absolute certainty he had known this woman. Known her in every sense of the word, even the Biblical one. Without his volition, his hand reached out, the back of his fingers barely making contact with a dark strand of hair that lay against her cheek.

He didn't allow them to touch her skin, however. He didn't want to awaken her. He wanted to look at her. To allow his mind to examine what looking down on her as she slept made him feel.

Something inexplicably powerful. And as if she were his. His to keep safe. To guard. *Standing guard over those we love.*

The phrase echoed in his brain. He knew it was supposed to mean something, and then, as suddenly as it had appeared within his consciousness, it was gone.

He lifted his fingers from her hair, but he stood in the

shadows a long time. Unmoving. Watching Paige Daniels sleep.

SHE WASN'T SURE what had awakened her. She lay in the darkness a moment, trying to remember what she had been listening to. Water. Somewhere in the background there had been the sound of running water.

As awareness of where she was gradually returned, she turned her head, looking around the shadowed room. The plastic-backed drapes had been pulled across the windows, but there was a faint light shining out into the hallway.

From the bathroom. As she made that identification, she remembered that the sound she had listened to as she drifted off to sleep had been the shower. Josh had been taking a shower. And she had been planning to take one before—

Before they met Dr. Culbertson. There was a moment of panic as she thought about that appointment. Her eyes found the bedside clock, and she was relieved to see that it was only a little after five-thirty. It would have been hard to explain to the therapist why they hadn't shown up after all her talk about national security and the importance of re- covering this information as quickly as possible.

"Josh?" she called.

Only when he moved did she realize that he was sitting in the chair she had put under the door last night. Sitting in the darkness beside the curtained windows. Which seemed pretty strange. She let the thought of its strangeness go, how- ever, the importance of keeping the appointment foremost in her mind now.

"We have to meet Dr. Culbertson at seven," she said.

"That's the hypnotist?"

"She's supposed to be one of the best."

"What did you tell her?"

"Enough to give her some appropriate questions to ask

when she puts you under." There was another silence, which lasted until she broke it. "Did Rombart call?"

"There was no match for the guy's prints."

"Damn it," she said softly. She hadn't realized how much she had been hoping the identification of the dead man would lead them somewhere. And apparently it wouldn't.

"They did discover something interesting," Josh said.

It didn't sound as if interesting were the right word, not the way he said it. She wasn't sure she wanted to hear what they'd found, but she didn't suppose she had much choice.

"What was that?" she asked.

"His clothing was made in Russia."

"Russia?" she repeated disbelievingly.

The thought had never crossed her mind. Of course, now that she knew, it even fit. Both his features and the style of the dark suit were consistent with his being Russian. That and the fact that he had never spoken a word to her during the time they had struggled. He hadn't issued any orders or threats or warnings. All his communicating had been done with the hand that gripped her arm and then her hair.

"Not one of Steiner's, it seems," Josh said.

Which put an end to what had been the almost comforting possibility that everything that had happened was Steiner-inspired and CIA-instituted. If not the agency, then who the hell had tried to abduct her last night? And more importantly, why?

"IF YOU HAVE any questions—" Dr. Culbertson had begun, only to be cut off by Josh's abrupt denial.

"We don't have any questions. Just get on with it."

The therapist's eyes touched on Paige's, but she didn't comment on Josh's animosity. Having heard the sounds elicited by the dreams he could probably expect to be reproduced as a result of this session, Paige understood his anger.

As she listened to the hypnotist's soothing instructions,

Paige found her own mind returning to that mission three years ago. Perhaps she, too, was preparing for what she would hear. But for her, of course, the deepest trauma of those events wouldn't come up tonight.

She had given Dr. Culbertson only enough information to take Josh back to that time, but not anything about the specifics of the mission or what they'd been sent to recover. And, of course, no information about what had occurred between them.

She knew, because Dr. Culbertson had told her, that the therapist would begin by trying to get Josh to remember their arrival in the country, something that would surely be less stressful than those last critical days. And the psychologist had warned that, depending on Josh's response, they might not even reach the crucial period for several sessions.

That was always the likelihood when one tried something like this, Culbertson had explained. The more deeply suppressed the memories, the more difficult it was to unlock them and bring them out into the open.

After the doctor had put Josh under, she began asking him questions concerning his identity: name, birth date, height, weight, and current address. Paige had been surprised that the name he gave was Jack Thompson.

Apparently the therapist was confused as well. She looked at Paige, brows raised in inquiry above the reading glasses. Paige shook her head and pointed to the pad Dr. Culbertson held, which contained the series of questions they had formulated this afternoon. After a moment, the hypnotist shrugged.

As the psychologist began to try to take Josh back, Paige found that she was reliving those early days as well. Remembering her first impressions of the man on the couch. Remembering how quickly her initial wariness, based on his reputation, had changed to something else. And then eventually to those feelings which had led to their making love.

Josh made no response to the questions they'd prepared, no matter how many times the doctor repeated or rephrased them. Finally, the hypnotist tried a couple of parlor-trick-type requests to make sure he was in a trance.

He readily complied with those, but whenever she attempted to shift back to anything that had happened in Vlad-istan, he shut down. Even his face altered, assuming a rigid and strained alignment if the questions touched on that last mission.

After more than a fruitless half an hour of questioning, the hypnotist looked at Paige. "I'd like to ask him what he remembers about you. Maybe those memories are not as closely guarded as the rest."

Paige's name had already been introduced, although following the instructions she'd been given, the doctor had referred to her as Daniels. Paige wasn't sure what the woman was asking permission to do now, but given the lack of success they had had so far, whatever it was, it seemed worth a chance.

"Paige is here," Dr. Culbertson said softly. "She's been very concerned about you. She wants to know why you left her. She needs to understand why you left her there alone."

In the silence that fell after those words, Paige found she was holding her breath. Why he had left her alone wasn't really the important part of what they needed to know, of course, but it came very close to the heart of it. Maybe too close.

Suddenly Josh's head began to thrash back and forth. There were no sounds to accompany that movement, but his face contorted and his chest heaved, air shuddering in and out, just as it had during his dream.

"I'm not sure this is a good idea," Paige said.

"Shhh," Dr. Culbertson cautioned, watching Josh. She didn't seem to be bothered by his reaction, and because of that, Paige didn't protest again. Her eyes, too, focused on Josh's face.

"Tell me about Paige," the therapist urged. "Weren't you concerned for her? Weren't you afraid that something would happen to her if you left her alone?"

Those were questions Paige had asked a thousand times. And the answers, in the face of how tenderly Josh had made love to her before he'd disappeared, had led her to think that something beyond his control had happened to him that night.

She had never believed he would voluntarily have left her alone. Something had drawn him away from the cellar where they had slept. And whatever it was had prevented him from returning. That was the conclusion she had reached long ago, independent of anything anyone else might suggest about the reasons behind Joshua Stone's disappearance. And nothing had changed about it.

The sounds had begun again. Hearing them grow in volume, she fought the urge to cover her ears. She felt Dr. Culbertson's gaze on her face, and she looked up to find in it a reflection of the same horror she had felt last night.

"I'm going to bring him out," the hypnotist said.

Helpless before the force of that anguish, Paige nodded. They had learned nothing of what they needed to know, but she, too, knew that they couldn't do this to him any more. It was wrong. *Just wrong*.

"Jack?" Dr. Culbertson said loudly, speaking above the sounds. "You're going to wake up in a moment. When you do, you will feel very calm. Totally relaxed. Nothing of what we talked about tonight will trouble you. You'll know that it happened a long time ago, and you'll know that none of it can hurt you now."

Not exactly the truth, Paige thought. Not in their situation. Considering what she *hadn't* revealed to the doctor, however, that probably seemed logical to Culbertson. Something that had happened a long time ago, even something so horrible that it had deliberately been wiped from Josh's mind, shouldn't be able to harm him now.

"I'm going to count backwards from five. When I reach one, you'll awaken, completely refreshed and totally relaxed. Five, four, three, two, one."

The blue eyes opened. Perhaps it was a trick of the lighting in the doctor's study, but it seemed that Josh looked straight at Paige, holding her eyes before he deliberately turned to the hypnotist.

"Did you succeed?" he asked. The tone was dispassionate, as if he were discussing someone else's memories.

"Not tonight. But…I think we saw some progress. Perhaps tomorrow night we can try this again," Culbertson said. "If you're willing, of course."

"Willing?" Josh repeated harshly. "Whether I'm willing or not doesn't matter. I don't have any choice but to try again."

Dr. Culbertson looked at Paige for an explanation, but there was none she could give. Not without giving everything away. And the less the hypnotist knew, the better.

"Can you come back tomorrow night?" the doctor asked.

"Of course," Paige answered for both of them. "Then… You do think you'll eventually be able to make him remember?"

"Help him remember," Culbertson corrected, turning to smile at Josh. "I think he wants to, but there's too much in the way."

"Too much what?" Josh asked.

The doctor hesitated a second or two before she told him. "Too much fear, Mr. Thompson. I think that for some reason, you're absolutely terrified you *might* remember what happened to you three years ago."

Chapter Nine

Paige didn't know how many hours she had lain awake, dreading a replay of the sounds she had heard the night before. She had lost enough sleep, however, that there had been a dull ache behind her eyes when she crawled out of bed the next morning.

And there was a lingering tightness in her neck and across her shoulders, despite the fact that she had stood under the pounding spray of the shower as long as she dared. She didn't want to appear to be hiding out in the bathroom, although there was an undeniable appeal in not having to face Josh this morning.

He had been quiet on the way home last night, even after they had left the cab and walked together through the cold and empty streets to the motel. Paige hadn't pressed him to talk. She wasn't sure she wanted to know what he was feeling. And she wasn't sure what he would remember about the questions he'd been asked. If he remembered anything.

She wished she had asked Dr. Culbertson that. Actually, she wished she had asked Dr. Culbertson at lot of things *before* they had started this, but it was too late now for that regret.

She wiped steam off the mirror, her eyes studying her reflection as it swam out of the fog. Her hair was still damp, her skin flushed from the heat, and her eyes clearly revealed her lack of sleep. Despite her vigil of dread, however, she hadn't heard a sound from Josh last night.

So much for Dr. Culbertson's surety that she could break through whatever barriers were keeping him from remembering. To be fair, the therapist had warned her that memories buried so deeply would probably require more than one session, but still Paige had been hopeful that there would be some result.

She knew her eagerness to have Josh remember was not the result of any loyalty to her employer or even a concern over what might happen if that nerve agent did surface. Hers was an anticipation that was much more personal.

From the very beginning this had been personal. She had wanted Joshua Stone to remember her. To acknowledge what had happened between them. And she had needed to know what would have happened if he hadn't disappeared. She still did.

She turned away from the mirror and began to dress in the clothes she'd bought yesterday. While she had been out, she had thought longingly about her suitcase, sitting in that empty room at the Peachtree Towers. In the end, however, Josh's command echoing in her head, she had decided it would be safer to indulge in a shopping expedition at one of the local malls.

She had bought toiletries for both of them, a nightgown, which she'd worn last night, and underwear, slacks and a sweater for herself. She had also purchased a package of T-shirts and another of briefs for Josh, guessing at his size. She had briefly considered adding a change of clothes for him and had finally decided that would be beyond her estimating skills.

The slacks she was putting on would hide the damage to her knees, which had solicited sympathetic comments from the people who had waited on her. As she pulled the white sweater over her head, she caught another glimpse of her reflection in the mirror. The shower and a change of clothes definitely helped, she thought, brushing her hair off her face.

They even helped her outlook, she realized. She felt more optimistic that they would figure everything out than she had last night. She knew Josh's frustration with the session had been partially responsible for her mood.

And she couldn't blame him for being disappointed. It must be hell not to know who you were or to remember what you had done. Especially if what you couldn't remember put you in danger. Despite what Culbertson had said about his fears, Paige couldn't imagine that Josh *didn't* want his memory back.

She picked up her comb, running it through the disordered strands. Her hair's darkness only accentuated the winter paleness of her skin, which in turn emphasized the smudged circles of sleeplessness under her eyes. Maybe she should have bought some foundation while she was at it. Of course, the way she looked had been pretty far down her list of priorities.

She opened the bathroom door and stepped out into the hall. While she had showered, Josh, who had already been up and dressed when she'd awakened, had gone out for coffee. She could tell by the smell permeating the bedroom that he was back.

"Coffee's on the dresser," he directed, without looking up from the newspaper he was reading.

"Thanks." She peeled the cardboard top off the container and blew on the steaming liquid, unobtrusively considering what she could see of Josh's face.

"No identification as of this morning," he said.

The Russian. Obviously he was reading what the local papers had to say about the car and body that had been pulled from the lake. "Anything there we didn't know?"

"There was no second body," he offered, noisily turning

pages from the front to wherever the story had been continued.

"They know yet how he died?"

"No wounds or visible marks on the body."

"Maybe he drowned," she suggested, taking her first sip. The coffee was still too hot, but she took another, larger swallow. Despite the fact that it burned her tongue, she imagined she could feel the caffeine begin to kick in, stirring her sleep-deprived brain into action.

"Or maybe they just knocked him out and then pushed the car into the lake with him in it," she added.

"Until the medical examiner gets through, any speculating we do on the cause of death is just that."

Which effectively puts an end to that conversation, she thought. She continued to drink her coffee, letting the silence build. If Josh didn't want to talk, then they could just sit here. *Fine by me,* she thought.

After a couple of minutes, however, she realized he really had no intention of instituting another topic. His attention on the paper, he seemed to be deliberately ignoring her. And she wasn't sure what she'd done to deserve that.

"Are you angry with me about something?" she asked, disgusted, even as she did it, at her lack of willpower.

That brought his eyes up, at least. They touched on her face, considered the sweater, and then traced down the gray herringbone slacks. After a few seconds his gaze returned to the paper. He hadn't even bothered to answer her question, which had definitely been deliberate. And it annoyed the hell out of her.

"If you have something to say to me, Josh, why don't you just say it?"

There was no response for maybe twenty seconds. "What makes you think I have something to say?"

She laughed, short and hard, and his eyes came up again.

"Are you angry because I bought a change of clothes?" she asked, allowing her voice to express her disbelief.

Another small silence, but at least he was still looking at her. "I don't like being lied to, Daniels."

"Because I didn't tell you I was going shopping? That's not lying."

"That's not the only thing you didn't tell me. Not even when I asked you directly."

He *was* angry. Beneath the surface calm of his blue eyes was a simmering fury she had seen only once or twice when they had worked together. And she knew he had meant for her to see it now, or she wouldn't have.

That's not the only thing you didn't tell me. Not even when I asked you directly. Which didn't sound as if he were talking about her shopping expedition. And the only other thing she hadn't told him...

Something about her face must have betrayed that sudden realization. In response, his head tilted mockingly.

Fishing, she told herself. Griff Cabot had been particularly skilled at that. At drawing out information he didn't have by making you believe he already knew it.

"I don't have a clue what you're talking about," she lied.

"I had another dream last night, Daniels."

Obviously not the kind he had had the night before. Having lain awake half the night in anticipation of a reoccurrence of one of those, she was absolutely sure of that.

"A dream about what?" she asked, working to control her tone. She wanted it to be as impersonal as his eyes had been when they had traveled dispassionately over her body.

"You *know* what about, Daniels."

She shook her head. "I don't know—"

"I asked you if there had been anything between us, anything physical, and you denied it," Josh interrupted.

There was another silence, prolonged.

"Dreams don't necessarily reflect past events," she said.

"Then what did this one reflect? Our present relationship?"

She said nothing, forcing her eyes to remain on his.

"No?" he said. "We can at least agree on that. So explain to me why I would dream about making love to you."

"That's what you dreamed about?"

"Right down to the thermal underwear," he said softly.

The significance of what he had just said stopped any possibility of denial. If he remembered a minor detail like that underwear, what else could he remember or, more importantly, be brought to remember about that night?

"What else do you remember?"

"That it was dark."

It had been, of course, but considering the situation, and what she had told him before, that was not exactly a meaningful disclosure. It could even have been an assumption. It was certainly not something as concrete and indisputably accurate as his memory of her thermal underwear.

"That's all you remember? Those two things?"

"That's all that was left in my head when I woke up. Trying to get that damned underwear off. Are you telling me that didn't happen? That what I dreamed was some kind of...wishful thinking?"

It made no sense to lie to him now. When he had first asked this question, she had been trying to figure out what Steiner was doing. And wondering whether Josh's amnesia was real or whether something else was going on. Now they had gone beyond any of those questions.

"It happened. The last night we were in Vladistan."

"The night I disappeared."

She nodded.

"We made love and then..."

We made love and then... Through how many sleepless nights had she tried to fill in that blank? For her, that explanation had always been as hidden as it apparently was for him.

"When I woke up, a little before dawn, you weren't there. I thought at first you'd gone out to make sure the rebels hadn't left someone behind in the village. That made sense to me because you were always so careful."

"I never came back," he said flatly, again ignoring what could only be speculation.

"I waited a long time before I started searching, but…" She shook her head. "No one ever knew what happened to you."

"Then that's where we start," Josh said, his eyes on hers.

With their lovemaking? She examined the phrase he had used and decided that had to be what he meant.

"Do you mean that's where Dr. Culbertson should start?" she asked. "She tried to make you remember me last night, but you didn't respond. At least not verbally."

"Not *verbally?* Then…how did I respond?"

"You seemed disturbed by hearing my name. Your reaction was…a little like those dreams, I guess. The other kind," she clarified. "To a lesser degree, maybe, but still, it was obvious that something about hearing my name bothered you."

"She mentions your name during the session and I get upset. And then I come back here and dream about making love to you." That wasn't a question. It sounded as if he were simply repeating the sequence of what had happened, trying to make sure he had it straight. "Was that the only night?"

For some reason, she was finding it hard to discuss this with that kind of detachment. Maybe because it had meant too much to her. Maybe it still did.

"The only night," she said, her voice too low.

"So the memory of that particular night is obviously still

there. At least in my subconscious. Something the therapist said made me recall enough about you to trigger the dream.''

She nodded.

"So it stands to reason if *that* memory is intact, the rest of that last night we spent in Vladistan is retrievable as well.''

"That makes sense," she said carefully.

Obviously, Josh was more interested in the other things that had happened that night than in their lovemaking. The things that had major international implications, she reminded herself, mocking her own tunnel vision.

She had built their lovemaking into something more significant than it had been. Given the circumstances surrounding it and her feelings for him, that wasn't surprising. Nor should it be surprising to realize that for Joshua Stone she had been nothing but a quick, end-of-a-successful-mission lay.

"So we start from there," he said again. "Did you tell Culbertson about the relationship?"

"No," she said.

"You don't think that might have been helpful?"

She had known it might be, and yet she had deliberately withheld the information, just as she'd withheld it from Steiner.

"Dr. Culbertson didn't think it was time to remind you of that particular night. And after all, the very first time she mentioned my name…"

She needed to rephrase that, she realized when she had reached midsentence. What she'd been about to say sounded as if she thought she had played a larger role in what happened to Josh than she really had.

"I reacted to it," Josh said.

"But…you don't remember that, do you? Your reaction during the session?"

"I remember the anxiety. Pounding heart. Adrenaline

rush. The fear. And she's obviously right about that," he added. "For some reason I'm afraid to remember what happened."

"And that bothers you," she said, hearing it in his voice.

Joshua Stone hadn't been afraid of the devil himself. That had been his reputation, part of the mystique. And even if this man didn't remember being Joshua Stone, he was. The same psychological profile, the same risk-taking personality that had made Stone one of Griff Cabot's top operatives, still underlay this very different persona the CIA had created.

"My life is missing, Daniels. *That* bothers me. And then some self-proclaimed expert tells me I've lost those years because I'm afraid to remember them. Wouldn't that bother you?"

"I'm sure it would," she said.

But not nearly as much as it would bother a man like Stone. Women were allowed fears. Men weren't. Not even in a situation where someone would have to be a fool not to be afraid. She was convinced something like that, something utterly terrible, had happened to Josh. And he *wasn't* a fool.

"And it bothers me that you lied to me," he said.

Full circle. Back to where this had begun.

"I didn't know if you'd ever remember. That night or me," she said. It didn't sound like reason enough, but it was the ultimate truth behind what she'd done.

Maybe there had also been fear on her part that he wouldn't believe her if she told him they'd made love on that mission. Somehow she found it hard to believe that the controlled, self-contained, and highly experienced agent she had worked with for four months had broken his own hard and fast rules that night.

"I don't think that explains why you didn't tell me," Josh

said. "Especially when you knew that might be the key to breaking through this...blankness."

"I didn't know that. I couldn't have. No one could."

He ignored her excuse, obviously considering it as unworthy as it was. And his accusations beat at her conscience.

"We were *partners,* Daniels. A relationship that, by necessity, is based on absolute trust. Our lives rested in each other's hands. Of all the people who might try to keep something from me, I would never have expected it from you."

What *had* been her reason for doing that? she wondered. Nothing that seemed to make much sense now.

"I wanted you to remember me on your own. If you didn't, I wasn't sure you'd ever believe me."

"Why the hell wouldn't I?"

"Because what we did..." She hesitated, unsure how to explain her own fears. "I know we probably weren't the first operatives to...have sex on a mission. I'd be a fool to believe that, considering the stresses. But you were always so damned hard-line about personal involvement."

"Until that night," he concluded for her.

"Until that night."

"Why would I have changed my mind?"

She had wondered that a thousand times. At least once for every day he'd been missing. Because she had always remembered what had been in his eyes when he laid his gun on the ground and looked up at her. She had always known there was some connection between that look and his subsequent disappearance. And the most obvious was that he had known he would never see her again.

If she believed that, however, then she would have to believe that Joshua Stone had planned or participated in his own disappearance. And that particular explanation was one she hadn't been psychologically able to contemplate.

"That was the one thing Griff kept asking me. I never had an answer for him. I could never imagine why you would leave. Not without saying something to me. Not after..."

The unfinished phrase hung in the air between them. *Not after we'd made love.* That would have been too revealing of how much that night had meant to her.

"And what did Griff think about that particular aspect?"

"He never told me what he thought. I know he trusted you implicitly. He trusted all of us. Even me," she added, again feeling that she had been unworthy of that trust.

"And what did Steiner think?"

She shook her head. "I never told him," she said, remembering their conversation. "He didn't ask. He called me in and suggested there were some unanswered questions about your disappearance. About your... motives."

"My motives?"

"He suggested you had left that night in order to keep an appointment. A lucrative appointment. Maybe he just said that to make me angry enough or curious enough to do some backtracking. To try to discover what he meant. To prove him wrong."

"What did you think, Daniels?"

"About what Steiner said?"

"About why I made love to you that night, something you thought was against my professional ethics, my personal code of conduct. Why do you think I made love to you that night and then vanished?"

He had demanded the truth. He had claimed it was an absolute necessity between partners. And maybe if they were ever to discover the whole truth about that night, she would have to tell him the one thing she had never admitted aloud. Certainly not to Steiner. Not to Griff. Not even willingly to herself.

"I think you knew you were leaving," she said softly. "And I think you thought you'd never see me again."

Chapter Ten

The silence after her accusation stretched unbroken for a long time. His eyes held on her face. The fury she had seen in their blue depths was gone, but she couldn't identify the emotion that had taken its place. Maybe it was better she couldn't.

His lips parted, and she held her breath, pulse hammering. And then, into that waiting stillness, came the intrusive ring of her cell phone. Neither of them moved until it rang again.

"Rombart," she said.

Josh's face was still set, almost rigid with the control he was exerting. He nodded, however. Then he laid down the paper and walked over to the bedside table to pick up the unit before it could ring a third time.

"Jack Thompson," he said, his voice remarkably normal.

Now that his gaze wasn't pinning her, Paige swallowed against the knot in her throat. She had told him the truth, which was what he'd demanded, but it had felt like betrayal.

Joshua Stone had been her partner as well as her lover. And she had just confessed that for the last three years, she had wondered if he'd committed treason.

"No problem," Josh said, still speaking into the receiver. "What time?"

Dr. Culbertson, rather than the detective. Paige had given the therapist her cell phone number in case anything went wrong with the arrangement to meet tonight for another session.

"You mind if I bring a friend?"

Not the hypnotist, then. Apparently Josh had just agreed to meet with Rombart and was asking permission to bring Paige with him. And she wasn't sure she was comfortable with that.

For one thing, it didn't seem like something Joshua Stone would have done. The Atlanta police didn't know anything about Paige's involvement in all this. She couldn't understand why Josh would want them to.

"Rombart wants me to come down and take a look at the body," he said, after he'd closed the phone.

"He wants you to take a look at the *Russian?*"

"I *did* tell him I thought I knew the guy."

"Do you think that's smart? Going down there?"

"Refusing to would make him suspicious. Especially since the police are still operating under the assumption that the man they pulled out of the lake was involved in something criminal."

"They haven't been able to trace the car?"

"Not yet."

"Probably stolen," Paige said.

"Or a diplomatic vehicle."

He meant one of theirs. The Russians. She had no idea how those were licensed, but Josh seemed to be suggesting that a car owned by the Russian embassy might be untraceable, which didn't sound logical. Diplomatic vehicles surely had to be registered, at least with the State Department.

"In either case," he continued, "I don't think I have any choice but to look at the body. After all, I approached the cops. Besides, Rombart's our only source of information. Without him, we have no way of knowing what the police find out about this guy. And if I refuse to go to the morgue, or seem uncooperative, it may make Rombart dig deeper into my past.''

"You think he might discover something there that could trace back to the agency?''

"Not if they did a good job of erasing Joshua Stone. There is, however, the occasional loose thread in that kind of switch. And there's no one more likely to find it than a good cop with an unsolved case. If the file on this murder isn't closed, you can bet Rombart will do some more digging into Jack Thompson.''

"You think he suspects that there's something phony about the background he helped uncover?''

"He doesn't seem to. Not yet. But with an unsolved homicide on his hands, the homicide of a guy I asked about right before he turned up dead, he may become suspicious.''

"Even if he does, what could that matter to you?''

After all, Josh was no longer an agent. He felt no loyalty to the CIA. According to him, he didn't even remember that he'd worked for them. Even as she thought that, she realized that he had just been particularly adamant about the rules of partnership. Did it make sense that Josh would remember the unwritten code that had governed relationships within the External Security Team and not remember being a member of it?

"Maybe old habits die harder than we know," he said. "All I'm sure of, call it instinct if you want, is that we need to lull Rombart's suspicions about my phone call. The only way I know to do that is to make him believe I have nothing to hide.''

"I don't understand why you asked if you could bring me.''

"You're the one with the intact memory, Daniels. I can look at that guy until I'm blue in the face, and I won't remember if I ever saw him before.''

"But...'' She shook her head, not following the logic.

"We both saw him. We saw him that night. And trust me, Josh, I had never seen him before in my life."

"Did you get a good look at the driver?"

"Not really," she admitted.

"Then now may be your chance."

Josh was right. She had been assuming the dead Russian was the one who had failed to force her into the Mercedes. It could be the other one. The driver she hadn't seen.

"Besides," Josh continued, "what if this is *not* one of the men who attacked you? What if this is someone else? Someone *they* killed and dumped in that lake. Until we see who's on that slab in the morgue, we can't rule anything out. And you're the only one of us who could possibly tie the dead man to what happened in Vladistan. No option about your going, Daniels."

He sounded the same as she remembered from their one mission together. Patient, a little amused, as he explained something he thought she should already have figured out. And what he said, as always, made sense. She nodded reluctantly.

"We go take a look at this guy together," Josh said, sounding almost coaxing now, "and then maybe we'll be one step closer to figuring out what really happened that night."

"And maybe not," she said, almost defiantly.

"And maybe not," he agreed. This time there was no trace of the amusement that had colored his voice before.

"THIS THE GUY you saw?" Rombart asked after the technician pulled the drawer out and left them alone with the corpse.

The ensuing silence lasted so long Paige's eyes lifted from the man lying on the morgue tray, whom she knew she had never seen before, to Josh's face. He was still contemplating the body, his features cold and composed.

"I think that's the man I saw," he said. "Looking at him now, however…" He shook his head, the movement very slight, as if he were doubtful. "I'm not sure why I ever felt I might have known him."

"Sometimes it's hard to tell, seeing them this way," the detective said. "The face changes when the animation's gone. I've had witnesses who couldn't identify their own family."

"I can understand that," Josh said, his eyes on the body.

"How about you?" Rombart asked, and it took a second or two for Paige to realize he must be talking to her. "You think this is the guy you saw in the Mercedes?"

That had been the elaboration Josh had added to his story when they'd met the detective. He had told Rombart that Paige had been with him when he thought he had recognized the man in the Mercedes and that he wanted her to help him make sure it was the same guy. And Paige had to hand it to him. Josh had even made that sound plausible.

So far, she hadn't said a word beyond her response to Josh's introduction. She didn't want to make an impression on the cop, hoping to fade into the background instead. Josh might have been right about the need for her to be here, but the less Rombart thought about her after they left, the better she'd like it.

"I'm not sure," she said. "I just caught a glimpse of the guy. *After* Josh said he looked familiar. I guess this *could* be the same man." She shrugged, looking back up at the detective.

Rombart nodded, but his dark eyes held on hers a fraction of a second longer than she was comfortable with.

"Still no ID?" Josh asked.

"Not a thing. Realistically, we may never get one now. Not unless somebody reports him missing. Nobody's done that yet."

"How'd he die?"

"Funny you should ask," Rombart said, sounding interested in the discussion for the first time. "He didn't drown, which would be the natural assumption. Before he went into that lake, somebody shoved a thin blade, barely wider than an ice pick, into the base of his skull. Penetrated the brain stem at a critical juncture. Very little blood, of course, and what there was had been cleaned up or was washed away by his submersion in the lake. The wound was hidden by his hair, so it went unnoticed."

"In other words, an execution," Josh said, his voice flat.

Paige found she was uncomfortable with his contribution. It made Josh sound too knowledgeable about something Jack Thompson probably shouldn't know a damn thing about.

"Looks that way. You know who does something like that?"

The question seemed casual, but Paige knew it wasn't. To paraphrase what Josh had said, there was nothing more dangerous to keeping a secret than a good cop grown suspicious. And apparently Andy Rombart had, although he was hiding it well.

Josh shook his head, his hands lifting a little from their position at his sides. "Don't have a clue," he said disarmingly. It really sounded as if he didn't.

"Worth a try," Rombart said with a smile, not seeming surprised or annoyed by that confession.

"Sorry we couldn't be more help. I was really hoping that seeing this guy again might set off some kind of recollection. I'm not even sure what made me think he looked familiar."

"He doesn't now?"

Josh shook his head, his lips tightening. "Sorry."

"Worth taking a shot," Rombart said again. And then he flipped the sheet over the corpse's face and pushed the drawer in. After the hollow, metallic echo of its closing died away, he asked, "Still no luck remembering stuff from before that wreck?"

"When I'm dreaming maybe. I wake up thinking that whatever I dreamed about might really have happened, but...I can't even be sure of that," Josh said. "That's the hell of it, I guess. Not being sure of anything."

Paige wondered if that were directed at her, although he hadn't looked at her when he said it. *I wake up thinking that whatever I dreamed about might really have happened, but...I can't even be sure of that.* A reference to what he had dreamed about last night? About making love to her? And if so, did he mean that he couldn't be sure it had really happened, despite her confirmation? So much for trust between partners.

"That *must* be hell," the detective agreed. "I've thought about you a lot since we did that background search. Wondering what it would have been like if we'd turned up a wife and a couple of kids. Wondering how anyone would make the adjustment."

"I guess I was lucky," Josh said.

Rombart's eyes focused on Paige's face for a second before he grinned. "I guess you were at that."

"Was that the driver?" Paige asked as the door closed behind them, and they started down the steps of the precinct house.

"You sound surprised," Josh said.

"I was positive it was going to be the one who tried to drag me into the Mercedes. I thought they killed him because he'd botched it."

"He may turn up later, and then Rombart will have two interesting unsolved homicides on his hands."

"You think he believed us?"

"Not enough to let it go," Josh said.

He didn't. There had been a slightly speculative gleam in the detective's eye, especially when he had looked at Paige. Which wasn't good, of course. Josh had felt he had to bring her, just in case she recognized anyone from their shared past. He had known that would be a long shot. Maybe it had been a costly one if it made Rombart suspicious.

"There isn't much he can do about it, however," he said aloud. "Nothing other than dig a little deeper into my past."

He hadn't used Paige's real name when he'd introduced them. And no one had asked her for identification. To them she was just someone along to take a quick peek at a dead man.

"Do you think it was smart to let him know you recognized that as an execution?"

"Anybody who's seen a movie in the last few years would have known that was an execution. Playing dumb about things in the popular culture is a dead giveaway you have something to hide."

"You *do*," she reminded him.

"A lot of things to hide," he said. "None of which we want Rombart to figure out."

"He's smart," she said. "He didn't buy what you told him about why I was there."

"Even if he didn't, there isn't much he can do about that either," Josh said. "He doesn't know your real name. He's got nowhere to go with it, even if he didn't believe me."

"He does have *your* name," she reminded him. "At least he has Jack Thompson's name."

"Then we'll just have to hope Steiner and his boys did their jobs," Josh said.

"I'D LIKE TO TRY it tonight without you in the room," Dr. Culbertson suggested. She had sent Josh into her study, but she had caught Paige's arm, holding her back a moment as she lowered her voice to a whisper. "I think your presence may have prevented Mr. Thompson from going under completely during last night's session. He seemed resistant from the first, and you saw his agitation when I introduced your name.''

"I've explained why I need to be there, especially when you start asking questions about those last critical days.''

"I understand that. But until we make some progress in taking your friend back to that particular time and place, I can't see any value in your being in the room. It disturbs him. Why don't you let me try it my way tonight and see if I can get him under more deeply? I understood from what you told me that you need a resolution rather urgently.''

Remembering the ghastly face of the man on the morgue tray this afternoon, Paige couldn't deny that urgency. One man was already dead. Maybe two. And if the Russian who had tried to force her into the car wasn't dead, then he was still out there somewhere, probably looking for another opportunity.

She couldn't imagine what they thought they would have to gain by taking her. Unless they intended to use her to force Josh to tell them where he'd hidden the toxin. Maybe they didn't realize he couldn't do that, even if he wanted to. Or maybe they didn't realize that he didn't even remember her.

"We do," she agreed, "but I'm not sure that without me in there you'll know if he's remembered anything significant.''

"At this point, I'm just hoping to get him to remember *anything*,'' the psychologist said, her own frustration surfacing. "When he does, when I think I've broken through whatever is keeping him from remembering being in Vladistan, I can bring you in. I really believe that until he's more deeply into a hypnotic state, he's going to be distracted by your presence.''

Paige wondered how far she could push her insistence. After all, she had begged for Dr. Culbertson's help, and the woman did have an excellent reputation. What did they have to gain by not listening to her advice in her area of expertise?

"All right, we'll try it your way. But please, as soon as you feel you've made that breakthrough and he's ready to talk about those last few days, please call me in."

"Of course," the therapist said, as if surprised by Paige's tone. "You can write down any questions you want me to ask him and hold them up for me to read. I'll hand you a pad and pen as soon as I bring you in."

Still reluctant, but feeling forced to bow before the hypnotist's certainty, Paige nodded.

AND THAT had been more than forty-five minutes ago, Paige realized, looking at her watch. Surely long enough for the therapist to have worked through the series of simple questions she had used last night to make Josh comfortable. And long enough to gauge how deeply he was under. By now, she must have broached the subject they had come here to explore—those critical hours just before Joshua Stone's disappearance.

Paige had waited all day for Josh to bring up what she had said to him this morning. She had virtually accused him of staging that vanishing act. And they both understood the only reason for him to do that was if he were planning to put the nerve agent in the hands of someone besides the CIA, which would amount to treason.

The Joshua Stone she had known three years ago would never have let her get away with making that allegation. Not even with suggesting it. Not without forcing her to give some logical rationale for making it. This Joshua Stone had simply ignored what she'd said. And the uneasy feeling that had begun when Steiner sent for her had only grown stronger as Josh let her indictment go unchallenged, hour after hour.

He hadn't even bothered to deny it, she thought, again pacing over to the closed door of the doctor's study and leaning her ear against it. She had thought she caught the sound of voices a couple of times before when she had done this. They had been so low, however, that she couldn't distinguish which of them had been talking. And if it were only Dr. Culbertson—

Suddenly the door opened. Paige backed away from it guiltily, but not before Dr. Culbertson was aware of what she'd been doing. Although there was a brief flash of amusement in the therapist's eyes, she didn't comment on Paige's eavesdropping. Instead, finger over her lips, the doctor motioned her inside.

As soon as Paige stepped into the room, she realized why she had been caught with her ear against the door. The carpet was thick enough to sleep on. Her footsteps made absolutely no sound as she crossed the room. That muting that was probably necessary to maintain an atmosphere that allowed the subject of the hypnosis to relax, undisturbed by what was happening around him.

That was the first place Paige's gaze focused as she crossed the room. On Dr. Culbertson's current subject. Josh appeared to be sleeping, and he displayed no signs of the agitation he had demonstrated last night.

There was virtually no noise in the room except for a nearly subliminal buzz, which was coming from a tape recorder on the doctor's desk. As soon as she made that identification, Paige whirled to confront the hypnotherapist, who had lagged a few feet behind her. Culbertson had taken time to ease the door closed after they had come through it. She looked up, appearing to be startled by Paige's sudden about-face.

Paige jabbed her finger toward the recorder, which was large and very professional looking. The doctor's eyes followed the gesture and then came back to her face. Her brows were raised above them inquiringly.

"Why?" Paige mouthed.

"It's standard procedure," Dr. Culbertson said aloud, her voice reflecting neither anger or concern at being questioned. It was as calm and soothing as it had been last night when she had been trying to put Josh under. As she spoke, her eyes assessed her patient before they came back to focus again on Paige's. "I *always* record sessions. It verifies the accuracy of my notes and my impressions. It's an important diagnostic tool."

Paige shook her head. "Not this time," she said adamantly.

Dr. Culbertson's mouth pursed and her amusement at finding Paige listening outside the door seemed to have returned. However, she walked across to her desk and punched a button on the machine. The nearly soundless whir stopped abruptly.

"Better?" she asked into the silence, her voice pleasant.

Some of Paige's tension faded. She nodded, relieved this hadn't turned into a battle. She wished she knew more about the way regression hypnosis worked. Too much of her knowledge of it, like most of what she knew about amnesia, had been culled from movies and novels. From the popular culture as Josh had called it. All she could do, she supposed, was to trust what Dr. Culbertson told her and the therapist's reputation.

"Thanks," she said.

At the sound of the word, the therapist's gaze flicked again to Josh's face, and realizing that she had been speaking out loud, Paige's eyes followed. There seemed to have been no change. Josh appeared to be sound asleep. And totally relaxed.

When she looked back at Culbertson, there was neither anger nor annoyance in the psychologist's expression. She was patiently holding out a pad and pen, just as she'd promised.

As Paige took them, the hypnotist motioned to a chair on

the opposite side of the leather chaise on which Josh was lying. As soon as Paige was seated, the doctor took her own chair, leaning close to her patient.

"Now I want you to think about the last day of your mission in Vladistan," she said, as if there had been no interruption in the session. "The day you were supposed to leave the country. Thinking about that day will cause you no distress. The memories will be clear, but uncolored by whatever emotions you were feeling then. Do you understand?"

"Yes," Josh said. His voice sounded hoarse, but not tense.

"Tell me about that day."

"We were hiding," Josh said.

For some reason, the readiness with which he responded surprised Paige. Despite the doctor's confidence, she realized she had been expecting a replay of last night. Agitation. Refusal to return. Something other than this placid recounting.

"Where were you?"

Paige realized the therapist's eyes were on her face, even as she had asked that question. They lowered briefly to the pad Culbertson had given her, obviously prompting Paige to write down whatever questions she needed Josh to answer.

"A village a few miles from the border."

"Why were you hiding there?"

The doctor's voice hadn't changed, the tones as soothing as Paige remembered them. There was no evidence in it of the excitement that churned in Paige's stomach. No evidence that the doctor realized the significance of what they were doing.

"Waiting," Josh said, his voice very low.

"Waiting for what?"

"Until it was time to meet our contact. Time to leave."

While that exchange had been taking place, Paige had

written her first question, holding her pad up for the psychologist.

"Had you completed your mission?" Dr. Culbertson read.

There was only silence. Surprised, Paige looked up from the question she had been scribbling. There had been no hesitation before. She didn't see why that particular question should elicit any more anxiety than the ones Josh had just answered. As she watched, Josh's chest rose, his breathing no longer steady.

And then he said, "Mission accomplished."

For some reason that, too, struck a wrong note. She couldn't imagine Joshua Stone saying anything like that. It sounded like the dialogue in a spy movie.

Acting on impulse, she struck through the question she had been writing, and substituted another. One that had been in the back of her mind, unacknowledged. Unacceptable. In her haste, the block letters were lopsided and uneven, but as soon as she had completed the last one, she held up the pad.

The therapist glanced at the question, and then her eyes lifted to examine Paige's face. Her brows rose as they had before, questioning. Still holding the pad in the air in front of her, Paige pushed it closer to the doctor, demanding by her gesture that she read it.

"Who are you?" Culbertson read, her voice emotionless.

Josh's chest rose again, the intake of air as he breathed in this time shuddering. And he didn't answer. Hands trembling, Paige shook the pad, drawing the therapist's gaze back to it.

"Read it again," she mouthed.

The doctor's mouth tightened. Paige held her eyes, forcing determination into hers, until finally Culbertson broke off the staring duel to look down into her patient's face.

During the few seconds their standoff had occupied, Josh's breathing had become audible. His mouth was open, and behind the fragile skin of his eyelids, his eyes were moving as if he were caught in the throes of some nightmare.

"Who are you?" the therapist asked again. "You need to tell me your name, please."

Josh's head began to move, thrashing back and forth. Suddenly, his lips clamped together so tightly that they whitened from the pressure. The doctor put her hand on his arm, and he threw it off, the gesture violent.

"It's all right. There's nothing to be anxious about. Nothing can hurt you," Culbertson said, her voice crooning. "All of what you're remembering happened a long time ago. You're safe now. Nothing about that time can harm you. It's only a memory."

It seemed that the soft reassurances were having some effect. Josh's breathing was less gasping. The motion of his eyes slowed, then stopped. Paige pushed the pad forward again.

"I need to hear your name," Culbertson said, her eyes reflecting anger, although her voice was still calm. "Just tell me who you are. There's no reason to be anxious."

There was a long silence as they waited, watching the tautness of his muscles gradually lessen until Josh again looked almost as relaxed as he had when Paige had come into the room.

"Who are you?" Culbertson said again, the question very soft. And the answer, when it came, seemed almost anticlimactic.

"My name is Jack Thompson," the man on the couch said.

Chapter Eleven

"How did it go?" Josh asked as soon as the cab pulled away from Culbertson's house.

His internal radar had picked up on some kind of strain between Paige and the hypnotist. It bothered him, but he hadn't wanted to mention it until they were alone.

For one thing, he wasn't sure he was reading the atmosphere right. Both last night and tonight, he had felt strangely disoriented after the sessions. It wasn't that he was particularly anxious about whatever had gone on. And yet, given what was riding on the outcome, he knew he should be.

At his question, Paige had turned her head, her eyes leaving their contemplation of the passing scenery to consider his face.

"It didn't," she said succinctly.

"Nothing?"

"According to Dr. Culbertson, everything was progressing well until she brought me into the room."

He wasn't sure how to answer that. He wasn't even sure what it meant. "She succeeded in carrying me back to the mission?"

"She had gotten you to the village. The one where we hid that last afternoon and night."

"And then?" he prodded as the silence lengthened.

''When we got to the critical point, to what happened that night, you became so agitated she had to bring you out.''

Agitated. That hot edge of temper, which he had fought to control since emerging from the coma, made him want to hit something. Or someone. The only problem was there was no one to take his sudden fury out on. Apparently *he* was the obstacle that stood in the way of putting this behind him. His reluctance to face whatever was in those memories. His fear.

''There are other therapists,'' he said. The alternative— that he would never get his life back—was unthinkable. Besides, it would mean he had given up. It would be another failure. Like the mission in Vladistan. ''At least I remembered being in the village.''

''Dr. Culbertson thinks I'm keeping you from remembering.''

''What?''

''She thinks *I* make you agitated rather than the memories. She took you back to the village while I was out of the room, and when she called me back in...'' She shook her head. ''Even after she banished me, she couldn't get you back there.''

''Are you saying I was alone with her?'' Being under someone else's control made him feel vulnerable and exposed in a way he didn't understand. Somehow the thought that Paige would be there had kept that at bay, despite how much he hated the idea of someone like Culbertson probing his brain.

''She's convinced my being there kept you from going completely under last night. And judging by what happened tonight, she may be right.''

''How long were you out of the room?'' he asked.

His uneasiness about being alone with the hypnotist must have been revealed in his tone. The small crease that formed between Paige's brows when she was puzzled was there again.

"You *knew* I wasn't there. She made me stay outside from the first."

"She told me to go in and lie down. To try to relax. I never looked up when I heard the door. I just assumed... How long?" he demanded again, fighting anxiety he didn't understand.

"Less than an hour the first time. Maybe...fifteen minutes the second. Why are you so upset?"

"I don't know," he said truthfully. "I thought you'd be there. I thought you'd be there the whole time. How would she know if she stumbled onto something important with you out of the room? How would we know?"

"I have the tape," Paige said.

"She *taped* it?"

"Just the earlier part. Before she let me come in. I hadn't known she was going to, but the recorder was on when I entered the room. She said the taping was standard procedure, but..." She shook her head. "For some reason, I wasn't comfortable leaving whatever was on that tape with her, so I asked for it."

"And she gave it to you?"

"Maybe she felt she didn't have a choice. She knew this was a CIA investigation when she agreed to see you."

"You're sure it's the same tape?"

It took a couple of seconds for her to answer, either because his question had surprised her or because she was considering that it might not be.

"I saw her take it out of the machine," she said finally.

Which didn't exclude the possibility that the doctor had made a switch while Paige was out of the room. Apparently the same thought had occurred to her.

"There's no reason for her to try anything like what you're suggesting." Her tone was defensive.

"I'm not suggesting *anything,* Daniels. I'm trying to get straight on what happened," he said.

"If you think she's up to something, then say so."

"I don't necessarily think anything. You got the tape."

"But you still believe I shouldn't have left you alone with her," she said. "You think I screwed up."

"I'm not criticizing you."

"Really?" she asked. "Well, that would be a change, wouldn't it. *You* were the agency's hotshot," she said, turning back to look out on the darkened streets they were crossing. "You figure out where the hell we go from here, Josh. *You* tell me what we do next."

The words were bitter, and Josh realized that whatever their personal relationship had been three years ago, there must have been a certain antagonism in their professional one. An antagonism which had resurfaced.

The hell of it was that he knew, even if she didn't, how ill-equipped he was to do what needed to be done. He couldn't even remember Paige Daniels, except when he was asleep. How the hell could she expect him to remember things that must have meant far less to him, even three years ago, than she did?

STICKING THE TAPE Culbertson had handed over into the player they bought on the way back to the motel was the first thing they did when they reached the room. Hopefully, there would be something significant on it. Something that had been revealed during those minutes Paige had not been in the room.

Maybe just hearing what he had said while he was under hypnosis might trigger a remembrance now. They sat there as the minutes of tape whirled by, producing nothing but a slight static. Josh even tried the other side, just to be sure.

"She gave me a blank tape," Paige said, long after that had become obvious. "I can't believe this."

"You're sure the machine was recording?"

"I heard it when I came in. That damn study is as quiet as a tomb, and the recorder was a big sucker. It was recording. Or at least...the tape was turning," she amended.

"Then she must have exchanged it while you were out of the room the second time. She anticipated that you'd want it."

"I'm supposed to believe she changed tapes and lied to me *just* so she could have it on hand to verify her notes?" Paige said, the question mocking. "God, I can't believe she did this."

"I doubt her notes had anything to do with it," Josh said.

Paige knew that as well as he did, of course. And she was feeling guilty for agreeing to wait outside, especially after his questions in the cab. But considering the doctor's insistence and her reasoning, he might have gone along with it, too.

Culbertson must have arranged the whole thing so she could ask him questions outside Paige's control. And she must have succeeded in getting some answers because there had been something on the tape she didn't want them to hear. The real question was whether or not she had another intended audience for whatever he'd revealed. And he knew they couldn't take the chance that she might.

"We have to go back to Culbertson's house," he said. "We have to find that tape."

EVERYTHING WAS DARK. Since it was after ten-thirty by the time they got back to the house, there was the possibility that the therapist had simply turned in. Her car was no longer in the drive, but the house did have an attached garage. Maybe she had pulled it inside after they'd left.

Actually, Josh thought, almost anything was possible. Including that there was absolutely nothing sinister about the hypnotist's actions.

That wasn't what his gut was telling him, however. And if there was one thing he had learned since Daniels had shown up to turn his life upside down again, it was that his instincts were as reliable as any other information he'd been receiving.

"Those are the windows of her study," Paige said.

Josh turned his head and found her standing at his shoulder, her eyes on the right side of the doctor's house.

"Are you suggesting breaking and entering, Daniels?"

"I suppose *you're* planning to knock on the front door?"

"Actually, I was. I think that's considered the polite thing to do," he said, amused by her cloak-and-dagger suggestion.

"We're the CIA," she said as she moved purposefully past him. "Being polite isn't a requirement."

She crossed the lawn, staying in the shadows formed by numerous trees and bushes. Josh caught up with her just as she reached the two large windows she had pointed out as belonging to the room they'd been in earlier tonight.

Both displayed prominent notices that the property was guarded by a well-known home surveillance company. He pointed to them and gestured toward the front door. Even in the darkness, he could tell by her expression that she wasn't convinced.

CIA or not, Josh wasn't anxious to bring the cops and their inevitable questions out here. Either they'd be hauled in for breaking and entering, or Paige would be forced to produce her identification to get them out of it.

If tonight's escapade got back to Rombart, then their connection to the Russian's death would suddenly become a *lot* more interesting to him. And if Paige had to show her ID, someone in the department might also feel the need to check with the agency. Josh was uncomfortable with the thought of Steiner or his cameramen back on their tails, even though it seemed they probably had essentially the same goals. For him, finding out what had happened that night in Vladistan.

And for Steiner and the CIA, finding the nerve agent he'd been carrying.

"We can't chance the alarm bringing the cops," he whispered. "We go in and ask the doctor for the tape. I didn't sign anything that gave her permission to record these sessions. Legally, she doesn't have a leg to stand on. And while we're at it, we ask her why she withheld the tape when you asked for it. I think her answer may be as important as whatever's on it."

Paige didn't say anything for a few seconds. Josh heard the breath she took before she nodded, giving in, if not gracefully.

He led the way to the front door, sticking close to the house, where the shadows were deepest. There was no traffic on the quiet, tree-shaded street. Most of Dr. Culbertson's neighbors seemed to have also turned in for the night.

Josh's hand had already reached out to press the bell when Paige grabbed his wrist. She lifted her chin in the direction of the door, which was open a crack. A sickening surge of anxiety crawled through his stomach.

Even in this neighborhood, he doubted anyone would knowingly go to bed and leave the front door open. And the doctor had definitely closed it behind them when she had seen them out.

If the alarms had been set, they would already have gone off. Judging by the depth of the silence that had surrounded them since they'd been here, they hadn't. Which meant the system hadn't been turned on or that someone had turned it off.

In either case, it seemed an open invitation to push the door inward and make their own search of the therapist's study. Maybe too obvious an invitation? Josh wondered.

"Weapon," he whispered, holding out his hand.

There was a hesitation before he heard the soft noises that indicated things were being rearranged in the interior of

Paige's purse. "Okay," she said after a moment, ignoring his outstretched palm.

"If I go in first, Daniels, I'd like to be the one carrying," he said reasonably, almost amused by her reluctance to surrender control to him. However, he acknowledged, that was an issue he could understand better now than he ever had before.

"I'm the one with the ID," she said.

"And I'm the one who's supposed to have all this experience."

"Which, just in case you've forgotten, you don't remember."

"I remember how to shoot the damn thing."

A few heartbeats of silence ticked off, and then, with a force that was audible, probably too audible, she slapped the pistol into his palm. His fingers closed around it, feeling a sense of comfort he hadn't expected.

He put his shoulder against the door and pushed it farther inward, the opening just wide enough that he could look around it. The house was as dark as the yard. Light from the streetlamp lay in broken patterns across the foyer and the living room, which was off to his right. Beyond that was the study.

He started across the marble-tiled flooring, walking on tiptoe. He could sense rather than hear Daniels moving behind him. There seemed to be no other sound but his footsteps as they crossed the expanse of stone in the stillness.

When he was far enough into the living room, Josh could see that the study door was closed. When Dr. Culbertson had sent him there ahead of her and Paige tonight, the door had already been open. And she had left it open when she had seen them out.

Maybe she'd come back there to work after they'd gone. Maybe she'd come back to get the tape and put it in a safe place. Maybe she'd anticipated that they'd be back for it.

His fingers tightened around the pistol as his left hand closed around the knob of the study door. He found himself holding his breath as he turned it. Then he pushed open the door, far enough to reveal the interior of the room.

The drapes had been pulled over the windows behind the desk, and it was darker inside than in the living room where he was standing. Josh waited a moment, giving his eyes time to adjust. From this perspective everything looked just as it had when they'd been here before. He examined the perimeters of the room, eyes probing the areas with the blackest shadows.

He could see nothing out of the ordinary, but apprehension was building again. Something was wrong here.

Paige put her hand against his back, urging him forward, but he was as resistant to entering as he apparently was to retrieving those lost memories. It was as if he knew some threat lurked in those shadows, just as in the shadowed recesses of his mind.

"What's wrong?" Paige whispered.

He shook his head, trying to shake off that sense of dread as well. He could see the tape recorder sitting on the corner of the desk, and he was certain it hadn't been there when he'd entered the room the first time tonight.

As Paige said, it was a big one. Nothing remotely clandestine about it. If it had been there when they'd left, he couldn't imagine why he hadn't noticed it. That strange sense of disorientation the hypnosis had left behind?

Paige's hand pressed against his spine again, and he forced his feet to move, walking across the expanse of carpeting. He could again sense Paige following him.

When he reached the desk, he pushed the first button on the recorder. The empty tape slot popped open obediently. His eyes moved over the surface of the desk, but he couldn't see a tape or anything that looked as if it might contain one.

There was an opened laptop in the center. Did the therapist keep her records in the computer? Had she come back here after they were gone to listen to the tape and type up her notes?

Paige was moving. It took a couple of seconds to realize she was going around the desk to pull the draperies and let in the glow from the streetlamp that had lightened the living room. She reached out to push the doctor's chair out of her way. When it wouldn't move, Paige leaned over, bending closer to the desk to see what was holding it.

"Oh, my God," she breathed.

And Josh knew what was on the floor behind the desk even before she said it.

"It's Culbertson. I think she's dead." Paige's voice had been flat and emotionless, a control he knew was being rigidly imposed. He was fighting for his own. "Josh?"

He forced his legs to carry him forward, struggling against an incredibly powerful reluctance to face what he knew would be back there. Culbertson's body was in the cramped space between the desk and windows. She was lying on her side, curled into a fetal position, a wheel of the desk chair wedged against her hip.

In the dimness, the pool of blood beneath her head seemed to have turned the pale cream carpet black. And there was a lot of blood. All Josh could think of was that this one hadn't been the neat, execution-style murder Rombart had described.

"I think she's been shot," Paige said.

They should attempt to verify the therapist was dead before they speculated on the cause, but somehow, even in the darkness it was obvious she was. He reached over Paige, who was still stooping beside the body, and pulled the draperies back.

Suddenly there was enough light to see the small hole in the therapist's right temple, almost covered by bloodied wisps of gray hair. The damage the bullet had done when it exited was mercifully hidden by the position of the other side of her head against the carpet.

"The gun's down here," Paige said.

"It's probably hers."

"*What?*" She looked up at him, her face very pale in the dim illumination of the streetlamp.

"We're supposed to believe the doctor committed suicide," he said, pleased that his voice was beginning to sound normal.

"But…"

Now that the shock was over, Josh's brain was starting to function. He knew this was what he had sensed when he'd pushed open the door. This was the wrongness he had known awaited them in this room. Maybe the scent of all that blood had subconsciously triggered that response.

He had taken note of the laptop. Now he realized that the top side drawer of Culbertson's desk was not completely closed. Staging for the suicide? Was that where she normally kept the gun? Or was it possible someone had searched the desk after they'd killed her, leaving that drawer partially open?

"Why would someone like Culbertson have a gun?" Paige asked.

"Protection, maybe," he said absently, studying the scene.

"It didn't work," Paige said. She put her hand on the corner of the desk and rose slowly, as if it were an effort.

"Wipe it," he ordered.

She met his eyes and then she nodded, rubbing the sleeve of her coat over the surface. "We need to find that tape."

"I think somebody beat us to it," he said, nodding to the open drawer. Her eyes followed the movement.

"If it had been in the recorder, if it had been anywhere obvious, they wouldn't be searching drawers. Maybe they looked for it, but couldn't find it."

"Then what makes you think we can?" he asked, his eyes still examining the surface of the desk. "Can you read those?" He pointed to a stack of papers beside the laptop.

Stepping gingerly around the body, Paige scanned the top one. "Patient files. Looks like she might have been putting her notes into the computer."

"You have gloves?"

She fumbled a pair of brown leather driving gloves out of her coat pocket and held them up for him to see. Not ideal as far as flexibility was concerned, but they would prevent her from leaving fingerprints. He nodded.

As Paige pulled them on, Josh's visual search expanded to the area around the desk. He was looking for anything that might have spilled out of the drawers if they had been searched. Of course, chances were that whoever killed the doctor had simply found the tape in the recorder and looked no further, but the opened drawer nagged at him. Stage setting or significant?

"Nothing about you," Paige said, laying the stack of papers she had gone through back on the desk.

"I'd like to know the name of the last file she pulled up on the computer," he said.

Paige bent over the laptop. Because of the position of the body at her feet, getting to the keyboard was awkward. Josh almost urged her to be careful not to step in the blood, but decided that she wouldn't appreciate any more indications that he thought she wasn't capable of doing this.

Daniels seemed to be a competent investigator. After all, she was the one who had located him. And she *was* the one still working for the agency, he reminded himself.

While Paige woke the computer and began to pull up a listing of files by date and time, he walked back around the front of the desk and to the other side, looking down into the waste basket that sat beside it. There was nothing there. Not even a scrap of paper. Good housekeeping or had the murderer taken everything that had been there with him to examine at his leisure?

"Something called 'Report,'" Paige said, her eyes still focused on the screen. Her fingers were poised over the keyboard, ready to pull up that file, the last Culbertson had worked on tonight, when suddenly she turned, looking over her shoulder and through the windows behind her.

Josh's gaze followed hers. He could see nothing on the shadowed lawn that might have drawn her attention. And then far in the distance he heard what she had heard—the wail of a siren.

Her eyes came back to his. Together they listened for a few shocked seconds longer than they should have. It was as if they had gotten complacent about what they were doing. The possibility that Atlanta's finest were on the way, however, served as a reminder of the seriousness of their situation. They were in a house where the owner lay dead, shot through the head.

"Bring it," Josh ordered.

He turned and started across the room toward the door that led back to the living room. Behind him, he could hear Paige closing the laptop. He didn't wait, knowing that they would need to find the way to the back of the house and then out through the yard, which he hoped wasn't fenced.

The front door, he remembered suddenly. It would give them a few seconds if he locked it. He had made it almost across the study, his mind occupied with the process of getting them out of here, when something hit the back of his neck and the top of his shoulder.

For a split second he thought he'd been shot. He fell to his knees, struggling to remain conscious, struggling to do something. And then he was struck again. The blow this time had the desired effect as the world went black around him.

Chapter Twelve

After she grabbed the laptop, Paige had turned back to drag the draperies across the window. There was no reason for doing that, but her first panicked thought when she heard the siren was that they had to put everything back exactly as they'd found it.

As she started around the desk, she heard another sound. She didn't identify it immediately, but it drew her eyes across the room in time to watch Josh fall to his knees. Although she had just shut out most of the light in the room, he was recognizable because of the light gray slacks he was wearing.

The dark, formless shape behind him had already raised an arm to strike a second blow before she fully understood what was happening. Someone was in the room with them. Someone, and it was not the cops. She could hear the sirens, growing louder, but still in the distance.

Hampered by the laptop, she had already started fumbling in her purse before she remembered she had given Josh her weapon. By then the second blow struck the back of Josh's bowed, defenseless head. He pitched forward onto the carpet, and the man raised whatever he had in his hand to hit him again.

"Hey!" Paige shouted.

A ridiculous response to that viciousness. It stopped the

downward motion of his arm, however, and without any thought of her own safety, she began to run toward Josh's assailant.

He had turned toward her, but she could tell nothing about his face or build. He was dressed completely in black and was wearing a ski mask, which left an eerie rim of white skin showing around the eyes and mouth. Better prepared for this kind of night visit than she and Josh had been, she thought, but then they hadn't come to commit murder.

She realized he was rushing to meet her charge. They ran toward one another, the silent sequence as terrifying as any horror movie she had screamed her way through as a teenager. Screamed bloody murder, her grandmother used to say. *Bloody murder.* She was in the same room with a murderer.

As those erratic thoughts rushed through her brain, Paige lifted the laptop and began to swing it in a wide arc. Thank God, it wasn't one of the newer models. This one had enough weight to do some damage if it connected.

And it did, only not where she'd intended. The man who had knocked Josh down must have caught a glimpse of it coming at him out of the shadows. He half turned, putting up his arm, and the computer caught him on the back of it instead of the side of his head as she'd intended.

His grunt of pain was satisfying, but the blow hadn't been enough to disable him. She began pulling the laptop back, trying desperately to get it far enough around to swing at him again. She didn't stand a chance.

He punched her in the stomach hard enough to send her staggering backwards. She stumbled a couple of steps, trying to regain her balance, before she hit the arm of the chair she had been sitting in during the session. She fell into it with enough force that the chair overturned, and she went down on top of it.

She had tried to get her hands behind her, automatically

attempting to break her fall. As she did, she released the laptop, which bounced a couple of times on the thick carpet.

The man in the ski mask snatched it up and started toward the door. Still entangled in the chair, Paige struggled to right herself. By the time she did, the murderer had disappeared.

Nauseated and holding her stomach with both hands, she ran over to see about Josh. As she reached him, she heard a door slam somewhere in the back of the house. And in the background was the wail of the sirens, which sounded now as if they were pulling onto the street outside.

"Josh," she whispered, as she shook his shoulder. He was out cold, and her urgency couldn't reach him.

She sat back on her heels and tried to think if she could change what was about to happen. There didn't seem anything she could do but stay with Josh and show her identification to the police when they arrived. That should offer them protection from arrest, at least. And they both bore evidence that there had been someone else in this room.

As the sirens ground to a halt outside, the flashing colors of the lights played against the closed drapes. She listened to footsteps running up the walk and wondered if anything she could say would convince the cops that she and Josh weren't responsible for the dead body they were about to find.

"AND I'M SUPPOSED TO BUY this cock-and-bull story about missing nerve agents and aborted missions to Russia? All of that on *top* of a very convenient amnesia?" Detective Andy Rombart leaned across the table, putting both hands on its surface, his flushed face only inches from hers. "You're going to have to do a whole lot better than that, lady. I've got two dead bodies on my hands, and you and Thompson are involved with both of them."

"I know it must sound unbelievable—" Paige began tiredly, trying to think what else she could tell him. She ran her fingers through her hair in an effort to push it off her face.

"You're damned right it does," Rombart snapped.

"I'm telling you the absolute truth," she continued, ignoring the interruption. "And I'm probably breaching national security to do so."

"Oh, for Christ's sake, lady, gimme a break."

Disgustedly, Rombart pushed up off the table and took a couple of angry paces toward the other side of the coffee room. When he had asked for a private place where they could talk, a member of the harried emergency room staff had brought them here.

At least there was coffee, Paige thought. She took a sip of hers, watching Rombart over the rim and wondering if the doctors would be able to find her to tell her how Josh was doing.

He had regained consciousness before the paramedics arrived at Culbertson's house. Although he had seemed alert and aware, she had insisted on a more complete examination than could be given at the scene. Considering his history of head trauma, they couldn't take a chance that the blow to his skull might have done more damage than it had seemed to.

Her CIA identification had impressed the uniforms enough that they hadn't questioned letting the EMTs bring Josh here. Apparently it had impressed them a lot more than it did Rombart. She didn't know who had called the detective, but she hadn't been surprised when he'd shown up at the hospital.

"How come none of this CIA stuff surfaced when we ran Thompson's background?" he asked, pacing back over to the table.

As she had from the beginning, she balanced what she could tell him against her mistrust of Steiner and the need to keep Josh safe. There was too much of this she didn't understand.

"Because they had erased his real identity," she said.

"The CIA?"

She nodded.

"And after they did that, I suppose they put him in a car and drove it into a bridge," he said sarcastically.

Maybe, she thought. The technical people would have no trouble doing something like that. Somehow, however, she couldn't see the agency causing the injuries Josh had described.

"I don't think one necessarily has anything to do with the other," she said carefully. *And if you buy that, I have another bridge for you to consider. This one for sale.*

"Oh, you don't?" Rombart said, the sarcasm still strong in his voice. "I think you better level with me and you better do it fast. I don't like the feds playing in my backyard. I especially don't like them leaving dead bodies lying around when they get through. Tell me about the guy in the lake."

"He was probably after information about the nerve agent."

"The nerve agent the two of you kind of forgot and left over there in the former Soviet Union?"

"We didn't forget it. We couldn't get it out."

"This all happened… What? Three years ago? And people are just now noticing a highly toxic nerve agent is missing? Just now figuring out that it's ripe for the grabbing?"

"With the Russians in control no one could mount a search. Now that there's going to be a rebellion…" Even as she said it, she knew how weak it sounded.

"So maybe the Russians already found it."

That had always been a possibility. Steiner apparently didn't believe they had, which was good enough for her.

"That's always possible," she conceded.

"So how does some Russian looking for a nerve agent end up in a Georgia lake with a stiletto in his brain?"

"I don't know," she said.

"Did your boyfriend know him?"

Paige doubted Rombart would appreciate knowing that Josh had been using him to track down a registration. And he was pretty angry as it was. "He thought the guy looked familiar."

"And this is the same guy who can't remember nothing else?"

"Repressed memories are...tricky. Things surface."

"And that's what the two of you were doing at the doctor's tonight? Trying to make something surface by using hypnosis?"

"That's right."

"And then she gets murdered, and you go back and find the body and both of you get beat up by her murderer."

"I told you. She taped the session without permission. When I asked for the tape, she gave me a blank. We went back to ask her for the real one."

"To ask for? Or to take?"

"The door was open, and Dr. Culbertson was already dead when we got there. We surprised the murderer. He hit Jack, and then he went out the back just before the patrol cars arrived."

"Would it surprise you to know we got a call about a burglary in progress at that house?"

"From the security company?"

"A call from somebody who didn't leave his name."

What the hell did that mean? Paige wondered. Who would have called the cops? One of Culbertson's neighbors?

Just then the door opened, and a young man who didn't look old enough to be out of high school, much less med school, stuck his head into the room. "One of you Daniels?"

"I'm Daniels," Paige said. She got up from the table, mentally preparing herself for bad news.

The resident came into the room, nodded at the detective, and then turned back to her. "Everything looks good with your friend. Because of his history and the loss of consciousness, we did a CT scan. We didn't see anything to make us overly concerned. He's pretty adamant about not spending the night here, and frankly, he'll be just as well off at home, *if* someone can wake him and check his responses every couple of hours. That would be you, I suppose?" He smiled at her for the first time.

"That would be me," she said.

"Okay. Well, he's up and raring to go. I can take you to him if you want and show you what to look for. This place can seem like a maze unless you know your way around."

Paige glanced at Rombart, lifting her brows in question. She wasn't hopeful that he was going to let them go anywhere except downtown, but he surprised her.

"Where you staying?" he asked.

"The Peachtree Towers," she said. There *was* a room there with her name on it. "And you have the number of my phone."

He also had her identification number. She had no doubt he'd use it to verify with the CIA what she had told him tonight. Of course, since she had no intention of staying in that room at the Towers, she wouldn't have to face Rombart again if she didn't want to. So she didn't really care what the agency told him. She just wanted to get Josh and get the hell out of here before something else happened.

"I'll have somebody run you over there, but I want the two of you in my office in the morning." He glanced at his watch. "Hell, it *is* morning. Eleven o'clock."

"We'll be there," she said promptly.

She had no way of knowing whether Josh would agree to that meeting or not. It seemed they were pretty exposed as it was. Too many people knew they were together. And where they were. More than she was comfortable with.

"You damn well better be," Rombart said softly, "or somebody at the CIA is going to be hauling their ass down here to explain why you aren't. You understand me, *Agent* Daniels."

"Perfectly," she said.

And then she turned and followed the resident out of the room. The last thing she heard before the door closed behind them was the long, noisy breath Rombart expelled.

"How's THE HEAD?" she asked Josh, as she inserted the key in the motel room door. He looked as if he had the mother of all headaches.

Since it had been after one o'clock on a weeknight when they reached the Towers, there had been almost no traffic in front. The patrolman had let them off in the semicircular drive, exactly where the Russians had tried to abduct her. Thankfully, nothing like that had happened tonight.

They had entered the hotel and waited until the taillights of the patrol car disappeared. Then they'd stood inside the lobby until the cab she called arrived. This time there was no early departure from the taxi before they reached their destination. Paige doubted either of them was up to walking. Josh didn't even suggest it. The driver dropped them at the door of the motel room.

"They gave me something, but I'm not sure it's kicked in yet," he said.

She nodded, opening the door and following him inside. Despite everything that had happened in the intervening hours, the small room looked exactly as it had when they'd left it.

"You can have the bathroom first," she offered. "And you take the bed tonight."

Josh's mouth moved a fraction. She anticipated his refusal, but he didn't make one. "If I'd known that getting hit over the head would get me the bed, I might have tried it earlier."

"Earlier, and it wouldn't have worked."

She realized suddenly that this was the first night they'd be spending together when she wasn't constantly aware that this was a man to whom she had once made love. A man she had been in love with. And still was, she admitted.

Right now Josh was simply her partner again. And he was injured. Although he was trying to downplay the effects of that blow to the head, she could still hear the sound of it in her memory. She shivered.

"Cold?" he asked.

"Delayed reaction, I guess. I never believed I'd say this, but I'm very glad to be back here."

The movement of his mouth was more obvious, almost a smile.

"We've been in worse spots," he said.

"I've got a feeling Rombart's office tomorrow will be another one of those."

"We should probably try to get some sleep."

She nodded, waiting for him to avail himself of her offer of the bathroom. He didn't.

"You okay?" he asked instead.

"Am *I* okay?"

"It can't have been easy finding Culbertson's body."

It hadn't been. And it had been terrifying to watch Josh topple facedown onto that same thick carpeting. Terrifying to attack the guy in the ski mask with nothing but a laptop. And exhausting to walk the minefield of Rombart's questioning. Until Josh asked, however, that soft note of concern in his voice, she hadn't realized how exhausted she was, mentally and physically.

"I'm just tired," she said. "I feel like I could sleep for the next twenty-four hours, which isn't on the agenda."

"You don't have to go through that check-the-pupils routine, Daniels. Believe me, I've had enough experience to recognize a plain old garden-variety headache. Get some sleep, and in the morning, we'll figure out where we go from here. By then maybe I'll be able to think again."

She nodded, too wiped out to argue. She would wake him in a couple of hours, and if there had been no change, then she'd assume he was right that there was nothing to worry about. Besides, by the time the next pupil check rolled around, it would almost be time to be up and preparing for their meeting with Rombart. And if he had called the CIA in the meantime...

"And you can have the bathroom," Josh said. "All I need right now is about six uninterrupted hours of sleep."

"It's all yours," she said, her eyes moving involuntarily to that bed.

Then she turned and headed for the bathroom, remembering how good the pulse of the shower had felt pounding against the back of her neck this morning. A little water therapy and even the floor would feel good. She didn't think she would have any trouble sleeping tonight, no matter what kind of dreams the man sharing the room with her had.

WHEN THE ALARM went off less than three hours later, Paige opened eyes that felt dry and gritty, as if she couldn't possibly have closed them more than ten seconds ago. The room was still dark, and for a moment she hadn't been able to figure out what the unfamiliar buzzing was. It was irritating enough, however, that she didn't just roll over and put the pillow over her head.

After a second or two, she recognized it was the alarm. She reached out and with surprising accuracy hit the button on top of the motel's clock radio. She had moved it down on the floor beside her before she'd gone to sleep. And by the time its noise stopped, she had remembered where she was. And why she was sleeping on the floor.

She had to check on Josh. She was supposed to make sure his pupils were equal and reactive. Make sure he was still mentally alert. According to the resident's explanation, any change in status could indicate an epidural hematoma and require another trip to the ER. Of course, since she wasn't feeling terribly alert herself—and she wasn't the one who had been hit over the head—she could imagine how Josh was going to react when she woke him. Not that she had any choice, she decided regretfully.

She pushed the blanket off her legs and stood up. Every muscle protested both the hard surface she'd been lying on and the lack of sleep. *Check on Josh,* she told herself, the words like a promise, and when she had, she could go back to sleep.

She made it to the bed without stumbling over anything. She fumbled for the switch of the bedside lamp, and when her fingers finally found it, she hesitated a moment, listening in the darkness to the steady rhythm of Josh's breathing.

He didn't seem to be suffering any ill effects. She supposed that just knowing he was still breathing wasn't enough. The doctor had been very specific about what she should look for. Besides, the sound of the alarm hadn't disturbed him, which was troubling. She flicked on the switch and sat down on the edge of the bed. She put her hand on his shoulder and shook it gently.

"Josh? You need to wake up. I need to check your eyes."

There was a subtle change in the tone of the muscle she touched. Not a clench or a recoil, but something. After a moment, he rolled over, blinking against the glare.

She gave his eyes a few seconds to adjust, and then she took his chin in her hand and turned his face directly toward the light. The pupils shrank to pinpoints. Equal pinpoints.

"You know who I am?" she asked.

"*I'm* the only one I don't know, Daniels."

Given the circumstances, she supposed that was as co-herent an answer as she could hope for. "Any nausea?"

He shook his head, and she realized she was still holding his chin. She released it, but not his eyes. "Headache?"

He seemed to be evaluating. "My neck's stiff. The stuff seems to have worked against the headache."

She nodded, trying to remember if there was anything else she was supposed to look for. "You remember what we're going to do tomorrow?" she asked, just to make sure she hadn't misinterpreted his earlier response.

"Meet Rombart. Probably get taken into custody, if only the protective kind." He didn't sound as if he cared.

"You really believe that's what will happen?"

"I believe Steiner isn't going to be a happy camper when he hears what's been going on."

"Unless he's been orchestrating it."

Josh didn't say anything for a few seconds, and then he closed his eyes. "Mind if I try to figure that out when I've had a little more sleep?"

"No," she said. "I was just trying to decide if you're mentally alert."

"Not enough that I'm going solve any of this."

"Okay," she said. She cut off the light and stood up.

"There's no need for the other side of this bed to go to waste, Daniels."

Her eyes had not yet adjusted to the darkness, and she could no longer see Josh. His voice had sounded totally mat-ter-of-fact. She tried to decide if that invitation could have been as offhand as it sounded.

"It's up to you," he said, "but I know how hard that floor is. A good night's sleep will be your best defense against whatever gets thrown at us tomorrow."

A good night's sleep sounded innocuous enough. Some-where inside disappointment stirred. During the past three years she had never allowed herself to consider the possibility that what had happened between them had been nothing to him but a one-night stand. Now she was alone once more with Joshua Stone in the blackness of another midnight. And what she had been anticipating since she had found him had nothing to do with a good night's sleep.

"I'm not going to take advantage of you, Daniels, if that's what you're afraid of. Frankly, I doubt I could." That patient amusement was back in his voice, the almost patronizing hint of his experience making allowances for her inexperience.

"What makes you think I'm afraid of being taken advantage of?"

"The fact that you're still standing there. And the fact that we're both still awake."

He was right. Put up or shut up. And the floor was damned hard. She walked around to the other side of the bed and turned back the sheet and blanket, which were relatively undisturbed. Josh had practically passed out as soon as his head had touched the pillow. And he would probably be just that deeply asleep again in a matter of seconds.

She slipped under the cover, turning on her side and facing away from him. She lay unmoving as his breathing settled into the familiar rhythm she had disturbed when she'd awakened him.

She listened to it for a long time, remembering the last time she had gone to sleep beside Joshua Stone, sheltered in the warmth of his arms. Finally, despite those images, which played over and over in her brain, her eyelids drifted closed, lulled by the regularity of his breathing and by a sense of peace she hadn't felt anywhere else during the past three years.

Chapter Thirteen

Paige didn't know how long she had been asleep when she was again awakened by an unfamiliar noise. Not the alarm, although it took her several groggy seconds to realize she had forgotten to reset the clock when she'd climbed into bed with Josh.

Into bed with Josh. She was in bed with Joshua Stone. And it was the noise he was making that had awakened her. He was dreaming again. Or at least he seemed to be dreaming, she amended, because what she was hearing now was nothing like what she had listened to in frozen horror that first night.

This was no anguished, nonverbal plea for help. It was, rather, a stream of soft, unintelligible utterances, almost like someone in delirium.

Delirium? With the injury Josh had suffered tonight, she couldn't assume what she was hearing was part of a dream and just go back to sleep. Instead, she rolled over, automatically trying to make out the words he was muttering.

She half sat and, propping on one elbow, leaned closer. Most of what Josh was saying was indistinguishable, but one of the words, repeated several times, was her name. At least it sounded like Daniels, which was what he had always called her.

What he *still* called her, she realized. She had never before thought to question the strangeness of that. Even while claiming not to remember anything about his former life, Josh still called her exactly what he had called her then.

After a moment she heard another word that was recognizable, buried in the rest of that incoherent mumbling. Josh had said Griff. And since Griff Cabot had been dead for more than two years, it was obvious Josh must be reliving something from the past. Was it possible he was dreaming about those events that were buried so deeply in his subconscious he had never been able to retrieve them? Not even under hypnosis?

Whatever he was dreaming about, it was definitely not the agonizing experience he'd relived that first night. Listening to these almost soothing sounds whispered into the darkness, she knew he was remembering something very different. And if he were awakened in the middle of *these* memories…

The thought was incredibly tempting. If he were awakened now, would Josh remember what he had been dreaming? Would it be the breakthrough that might lead to the restoration of all the other memories? Something Josh had said at the beginning made her think the doctors had told him something like that. That once the barriers he had erected were broken, and the remembrances had begun…

Not a certainty, perhaps, but at least worth a try. And what could it hurt? she wondered. They had tried everything else and were no closer to a solution than when they'd started.

Her hand hovered hesitantly over his chest. She tried to think of any valid reason *not* to wake him. After all, she had awakened him when he was in the throes of that first terrible nightmare. He had been disoriented, but she hadn't been able to see any lasting effects from what she had done.

And this didn't seem to be a nightmare. It shouldn't be nearly so traumatic to be pulled out of this dream. Actually, she reasoned, this might represent their last chance to break through to whatever Josh had been repressing before Steiner and the agency stepped into the picture tomorrow.

Her hand touched Josh's chest. The murmur stopped, and he took a rapid breath, the jerk of the pectoral muscles under her palm discernible, almost a flinch.

"Josh," she said aloud.

His chest rose and fell again, more measured this time, and then his eyes opened, shining like sapphires in the dimness. They focused on her face. His mouth closed, the flow of inarticulate words cut off. And then he raised his hand. His fingers grazed the side of her neck. A feather touch, tentative and trembling, but his eyes never changed.

"I thought you were a dream," he said. And then his lips moved, tilting upward at the corners.

At the sight of that smile, something shifted, low and deep and hot, in the pit of her stomach. It was a little like reaching the top of a roller coaster and then beginning the swooping descent. That same bottom-dropping-out feeling.

Slowly she shook her head, feeling the slight abrasiveness of his fingertips against the sensitive skin of her throat.

"I'm not a dream," she said.

"Not this time," Josh whispered.

The anticipation that had already begun to simmer inside her destroyed any thought of tomorrow. Every doubt she had unwillingly entertained about Joshua Stone's disappearance evaporated. All that was left was the brush of his fingers over her throat and the unsettling intensity of that blue stare. The same intensity she remembered from a night three years ago.

The position of his hand changed, its movement so subtle she was unaware of it until his thumb was on one side of her jaw and his fingers arrayed on the other. The pressure they exerted wasn't great—no force involved—but they were definitely urging her head downward. She bent, and at the same time his upper body, supported by his elbows, rose to meet her.

At the last possible second, she closed her eyes, her head slanting to the side to align her mouth over his. As their lips touched, the feeling that had been building in her stomach released, as if she had reached the nadir of that long descent.

There was nothing tentative about his kiss. His tongue took possession with a surety she remembered. Hungrier now than she had been then, hers met its every movement, answering each tantalizing demand. It was as if the years between were washed away in the flood of emotion that swept her body. She knew now that she had wanted Joshua Stone to make love to her from the moment she had seen him again.

The kiss lengthened past exploration, and finally Josh shifted his weight, pushing her onto her back. Throughout the change in position, his lips never released hers. His fingers, their movement completely unhurried, found the buttons at the neck of her gown and began to unfasten them, one after the other.

This was the kind of lover he had been before. Skilled. Infinitely patient. The kind of lover he would be tonight, she thought, anticipation stirring again in her lower body.

She seemed drugged by the power of his kiss, any will to resist sapped by the slow, hungering caress of his mouth. She didn't want this to end, but she understood what the inevitable outcome would be if she allowed it to continue.

And there were so many unanswered questions, including the one that had haunted her for the last three years. Why had Joshua Stone made love to her that night and then vanished, leaving her alone in a hostile country on the verge of war?

She had never had a satisfactory answer. She still didn't. And now he was again making love to her. And she was again allowing it.

He had finished with the buttons. As his lips continued to move over hers, his hand found the bottom edge of her nightgown, which had, during the course of the restless night, rucked up around her thighs. Now the slight abrasion of his palm, sliding under the hem of it and moving against her hip, seemed to destroy the near paralysis in which she had existed since he had opened his eyes and touched her throat.

She put her hand, flattened, over his, stopping its motion. His tongue stilled, and then his mouth released hers, lifting only far enough to whisper, ''What's wrong?''

She couldn't think what to tell him. Why *was* she hesitant about letting him make love to her again? Her body wasn't. It was preparing for his entry, the sweet, heated wetness of desire making a mockery of the feeble protest her hand made.

''Do you remember?'' she asked. ''Do you remember me?''

Even as she whispered the words, she wondered why she bothered. What did that matter? Why would she care if what was happening between them now had nothing to do with the first time he had made love to her?

The hand she held captive under hers didn't move, and slowly Josh pushed up, again supported by his elbow. He looked down on her, his eyes moving over her features as if he were trying to decide the answer to that question.

''I remember this,'' he said softly. ''I remember making love to you.''

Again something shifted inside. The cold, hard knot of fear that had lodged in her chest dissolved at what was in his voice. It matched the darkness that surrounded them. Warm and comforting and tender, it soothed the raw and aching places his disappearance had left on her soul.

''I remember *you*,'' he said.

The hand that had captured his freed it. She lifted those

same trembling fingers to touch a whisker-roughened cheek. The texture of it was evocative. And dearly familiar. She closed her eyes as his mouth began to lower again.

"I remember the way your skin smells," he whispered. His face moved against her cheek, the slow breath he drew as he touched her audible. "I remember the way it feels moving against mine. The incredible softness of it."

Warm, hard fingers glided across her stomach, which was covered by the smooth fabric of her panties. He turned his hand, bending his wrist so that his knuckles dragged downward over the small indention of her navel and then lower still.

She held her breath as his fingers reached their destination. One knuckle traced along the cleft between her legs, which had fallen apart as if boneless. Despite the barrier of her panties, there was contact with that most sensitive area of her anatomy. The jolt sent shock waves spiraling upward.

"Still too many damn clothes, Daniels," Josh said, his voice touched with amusement as he began to struggle, one-handed, to peel off her panties. She lifted her hips, and let him tug them down over her knees. She finished the task with her feet and then kicked them away to be lost in the tangled sheets.

"Better," Josh whispered.

She waited for the return of his hand, wanting it again exactly where it had tantalized before. There was no barrier now, and she ached for his touch.

Instead, his mouth found hers. After a long time, his lips moved lower, trailing, slightly opened, against her throat. They explored the area exposed by the buttons he'd unfastened. His beard rasped gently over the beginning swell of her breasts. Another sensation evocative of their previous lovemaking.

He placed his palm under the weight of her left breast, cupping it through the fabric as his tongue and mouth caressed the valley between them. She put her hand over his again, lifting it this time and carrying it downward. She laid it over the protrusion of her hipbone, almost where it had been before. And then she waited.

His thumb moved slowly against the bone, tracing up and then down, the pressure seductive. That wasn't what she wanted. At least not all she wanted. Not nearly enough for her now.

She arched her back, lifting her lower body so that it came into closer contact with his left hip, which was resting against hers. The movement of his mouth stilled. When he opened it to speak, she felt the warmth of his breath turning to coolness the moisture he had left on her skin.

"In a hurry, Daniels?" he asked, amusement threaded through the husky whisper.

"Yes," she breathed. She guided his hand lower until it lay atop the bare skin of her thigh, and then she moved it upward, pushing his fingers under the hem of her gown.

Instead of obeying that unspoken command, Josh pushed himself up, propping on his elbow, so that he was half sitting, looking down at her. Her eyes opened, afraid of what she would see in his face. She found that he was smiling. That small, enigmatic smile she remembered so well.

Amused by her eagerness? she wondered. If so, she didn't care. There was very little she cared about tonight except the glide of his hand over her body. And what would follow.

"Let's get rid of this," Josh suggested, touching the soft flannel of her gown.

She nodded, sitting up as he had. She helped him pull it over her head, fingering her hair away from her face when it was done. He held the nightgown a moment, simply looking at her, before he threw it toward the foot of the bed.

And then they were sitting side by side, almost facing one another, their hips together. Only now, in contrast to Josh, who was still fully clothed, she was nude.

As she watched, his gaze left her face to travel downward. There was very little light in the room, but enough that she could see him. When his eyes came back to hers, she swallowed the thickness in her throat created by what was in them.

"I didn't see you before," he said. "Not enough. Not all that I wanted. My hands knew your body, every inch of it, every pore of your skin. Bone and muscle. But not my eyes…"

The words faded as his gaze again lowered. Hers were drawn downward, too, so that she watched long, dark fingers move against her skin. He touched the outside of her breast almost reverently. Then his fingers skimmed along the top of it, moving forward until they reached the rose-brown border that encircled the small, hardened bud.

His fingertips brushed against her nipple, and it seemed that every nerve ending in her body was centered there. Josh lowered his head, and with his tongue, he rimmed the distended nub with hot, wet heat. The breath she had been holding released again, sighing out into the darkness like a sob. Wanting this. Wanting so much more.

His mouth fastened over the peak of her breast, creating a deep suction, which was echoed by an answering one in her lower body. An aching emptiness that only he could fill. She had always known that.

Which was why there had been no one else. No one in the years since he had disappeared. She had known instinctively no one who could take Joshua Stone's place, not even when she had told herself that she was clinging to a memory. And to a ghost.

There was nothing spectral about the man who was again making love to her. Nothing insubstantial about the body she held, her hands gripping his shoulders now as if she were indeed on some dangerously exciting carnival ride.

His mouth shifted to the other breast, suckling so strongly

there was an edge of pain to the depth of her pleasure. A clamoring ecstasy grew within her body, so that she was impatient for what came next. Impatient for the feel of his bare skin sliding sweat-slick and hot against hers. Impatient for him.

And so her fingers slipped onto the front of his shoulders, pushing him away. He obeyed, moving back far enough that his eyes could examine her face, his question in them.

She began to work at the buttons on the front of the shirt he wore, hurrying over the task. When he realized what she was doing, his hands joined hers, ripping the tail of it out of his waistband. Then he began to undo buttons, working from the bottom up. When their hands met, just below his ribs, he stripped the shirt off impatiently, letting it fall to the bed behind him. The white undershirt followed, jerked over his head by one dark hand grasping its fabric at the back.

There was a second's hesitation when it fell. Neither of them moved. It was as if they were stunned by the fact that they were together again, nude from the waist up, a few scant inches between their bare bodies.

She could hear her own breathing, rapid and uneven. And then Josh's arms came around her, gathering her to him as if she were something fragile. Something infinitely precious. There was a gentleness in his touch she didn't remember from before. A gentleness which, given the shocks of the past few days, was surprisingly poignant.

He pulled her against his chest, his palm soothing over her spine. She closed her eyes, savoring the movement of her breasts against his hair-roughened chest as she breathed. He simply held her for a few long heartbeats, her cheek resting against his shoulder. After a moment, he put his lips against her hair, burying his face in the tangled strands.

"I remember this, too," he said. "Holding you. The feel of your hair against my face."

She nodded, unable to speak. Until he had said the words,

she hadn't been aware of how much she had wanted him to remember her. To remember what they shared.

They were together again in another darkness. Another night. And a thousand empty midnights stretched between the two.

"Make love to me," she said, turning her face so that the soft words whispered against his skin.

His hands on her upper arms, he held her away from him. She hadn't wanted to be separated from the strength of his body. From its safety. He looked down into her face for a long time, and then finally, he laid her on the mattress.

He shifted his position, putting one leg over her hips and easing down over her. The weight of his upper body rested on his elbows, his hands shaping either side of her face. With his thumbs he followed the line of her brows and then traced over her temples. His fingers spread, slipping into the disordered strands of hair that lay against the pillow. And then they moved beneath her head, lifting, bringing her mouth up to his.

Without her conscious volition, her legs opened again as she felt the strength of his erection straining through his clothing. Her hands lowered, working awkwardly between their bodies at the buckle of his belt. When he realized what she was doing, he lifted away from her. Off the bed.

Exposed to the cold air of the room after the warm, heavy weight of his body, she shivered, her eyes following the frenzied movement of his hands as he stripped off the rest of his clothes. And then he was with her again, his body over hers, his erection brushing erotically across her stomach as he positioned himself.

Her eyes held on his face as his body lowered to hers. There was another searing jolt, the sensation a hundredfold more powerful than the first time he had touched the narrow cleft between her legs. And then, using one hand, he guided himself into the heart of it. The slow exhalation was his.

After a few seconds, he pushed deeper. And then deeper still.

Her body reacted, recoiling slightly from the incredible sense of fullness. Comforting, his lips found her temple, the fine new hair there sweat-dampened.

"Shhh," he whispered, his breath feathering over the moisture, the gentle sibilance easing her small fear that the pressure was more than she could bear. He waited again, and then eased downward another millimeter. She took a breath, and in response he put his lips over hers, his tongue circling them.

"Shhh," he said again, his breath mingling with hers.

And then he pushed downward once more, one final thrust, strong and controlled. His mouth captured her gasp as he touched the bottom of her soul, filling her completely. He nibbled her lip with his teeth, substituting that small, teasing discomfort for the pressure she didn't want to fear.

And when he began to move above her, she closed her eyes, willing herself to relax. After all, there was no pain. There was simply a strength that dominated and controlled, calling for the ultimate submission. The ultimate trust.

This was the second time she had given that to Joshua Stone. The second time she had lain in his arms in a midnight darkness as his body moved above hers, creating sensations that began to vibrate outward, moving along nerve pathways designed only for this. Only for this purpose. For this pleasure.

Gradually, the tension she had felt at the beginning began to ease. As he sensed that slow relaxation, the movements that had been so careful and controlled began to change. To become more powerful. Demanding.

And just as she had answered his kiss, her body responded to the driving force of his. She sought to increase the pressure she had briefly feared, trying to hold him within her. Trying to draw him deeper inside with each measured thrust of his hips. Hers rose to meet his, their bodies straining together for something that shimmered before them, elusively out of reach.

Surprisingly, she was the first to feel the quaking tremors of it. They racked her even as he continued to drive into her body, deeper and faster, seeking his own release. And when it came, seconds after her own consciousness had shattered into a thousand broken shards of sensation, she found climax again, and this time hers joined his.

When it was finally over, they lay together, nerves and muscles trembling with exhaustion and exhilaration. Skin sliding against dampened skin as they gasped for breath.

"We ought to try that a little more often, Daniels."

"Once every three years not enough for you?"

Her lips curved in the darkness, as he began to push onto his elbows again, lifting his upper body away from hers.

"Maybe so," he said, his breathing still uneven. "Especially if it's going to be like that every time."

"I'm supposed to check your pupils," she said, her voice amused. "Can I take it that won't be necessary?"

"Check my heart rate instead."

"Your heart's fine," she whispered, lifting a little to touch his bottom lip with her teeth. "I can feel it." She could. It hammered with reassuring strength against her breasts.

"Me, too," he said. His lean cheeks puffed outward a little, and he expelled a small breath, strong enough that it made a whooshing noise. "If I had a hematoma, it would have exploded after that."

"Bite your tongue," she said. "I don't think this was what the doctor had in mind when he said I should wake you."

"Who knows?" Josh said, lowering his head to brush her nose with his lips. "You could probably wake the dead like that."

Wake the dead. For just a second those unthinking words were too graphic. To near reality.

She had just made love to a man who had supposedly been dead for the last three years. Despite the vitality of the body that had strained above hers, that macabre thought sent a finger of ice along her spine. She wasn't aware that her expression revealed that sudden, unwanted chill, but Josh's forehead creased, and one dark brow lifted in question.

"What's wrong?"

She shook her head, trying to ignore the mental imagery. After spending only three days with him, it was hard to imagine her life without Josh in it. She realized only now how *without life* her existence had been since he had disappeared. And that was something she would never admit to anyone else, probably not even to him.

"Nothing's wrong," she said. "Just…remembering."

He nodded, as if that made sense. Maybe it did. After all, he had been existing in an even greater vacuum than she had. And she wondered if finally that emptiness was over for Josh as it was for her.

"Do you…?" she began, but his mouth had already lowered to cover hers. And it was a long time before it lifted. Long enough that she no longer remembered the question. And long enough that she no longer cared about the answer.

Chapter Fourteen

When Paige opened her eyes, it was obvious, even with the rubber-backed drapes drawn across the double windows, that it was full daylight outside. She rolled over, reaching for the shrilling telephone. It didn't seem to be in its normal position on her bedside table, and by the time she had figured out why, she had also remembered where she was. And remembered that she shouldn't be alone in this bed.

She managed to wrap her fingers around the receiver by the third ring, wondering why Josh, who was already up, hadn't answered it. Maybe he'd gone out for coffee or maybe he was in the shower. In any case...

"Hello," she said into the mouthpiece.

It was only then that she realized she was holding the room phone and not her cell phone. And before she got a response to her hello, she had time to think that answering this call might not have been the smartest thing she'd ever done.

"We *said* eleven o'clock," Rombart said.

Her eyes searched for the clock radio, but it wasn't on the bedside table. She lifted her left wrist, checking the time as she pulled the sheet up over her breasts. It was a little late for modesty, but she found there was something very different about being nude in the middle of the night and being nude at eleven-twenty in the morning.

The cop Rombart had assigned to drive them to the hotel last night had apparently been given instructions to wait around to see if they left. He must have followed them back here and then reported their location to the detective.

As she was figuring out how Rombart had found them, her eyes examined the room. Josh's clothes were gone, which didn't explain where he was, of course. Nor did it eliminate the possibility that he might be in the shower.

"We overslept," she said finally, running the fingers of her free hand through her hair, pulling the disordered strands away from her face.

"How's Thompson?"

"He's okay," she said. *At least the last time I saw him.*

And then her lips tilted. The pleasant soreness in her body was a reminder of exactly how "okay" the man Rombart knew as Jack Thompson had been last night.

Her eyes circled the room again, which seemed empty. Surprisingly...sterile. She pushed up a little in bed, looking over the edge of the mattress. There was nothing down there. No shoes. No socks. Not a single stray article of clothing. If Josh had stepped out for coffee—

"I talked to Langley this morning," Rombart said, bringing her concentration back to him in a hurry.

She tried to interpret his tone. Fairly unemotional. Not screaming anger, at any rate. She closed her mouth, pressing her lips together against the questions she was tempted to ask.

That was another trick she had learned from Griff Cabot. *Listen, and don't talk.* Especially if you don't know the direction in which the conversation is headed.

"Your boss said to tell you he's looking forward to your return. *And* Thompson's."

That didn't sound like Pete Logan. "My boss?" she ventured.

"A guy named...Steiner?" From the hesitation, she

guessed Rombart was looking at notes he'd taken during that conversation. "He seemed pretty interested in what's been going on down here."

She would bet he had been. She would bet Steiner had been very interested in what Rombart had to tell him.

"It didn't sound as if you'd been keeping him informed," the detective went on. She had no trouble identifying the tone of that. Smug satisfaction.

"With highly sensitive information, it's sometimes hard to do that from a distance and still maintain the necessary security." *Another bridge up for sale.*

"Judging from his tone, I think you might want to lessen the distance," Rombart said, not buying it.

"Thank you for your advice, Detective Rombart. Anything new on the victims?"

There was nothing wrong with turning the tables, especially in an exchange like this, where it was obvious each party needed information. Rombart had been probing for some. It seemed that turnabout should be fair play.

"Funny, that's just what your deputy director asked."

She almost corrected Steiner's title, which was actually assistant deputy director, but again she compressed her lips. She wished Josh would get back. It had become more evident with each passing second that he wasn't in the shower.

"And I told him the same thing I'm gonna tell you," Rombart continued. "We've got nothing on those victims but a lot of publicity we don't want. Prominent psychologist gets killed in her own quiet, supposedly safe neighborhood is a headline that doesn't make us or the citizens we work for very happy. I told him I wanted an explanation of why his people were involved in two homicides in a forty-eight hour period down here."

"I've already told you why we were involved," she said.

"I suggest you use the flight back to Virginia to work up a better story than the one you gave me."

"The story I gave you happens to be the truth."

There was a beat of silence. "Maybe a version of it," the detective admitted. "But I don't think a *version* of what's been going on down here is going to satisfy your superiors. Who, by the way, seemed surprised to find out you were in Atlanta. It seems the CIA didn't send you here."

"I wouldn't be here if they hadn't sent me." And that, too, was a version of the truth.

"There are several afternoon flights. I'd be on one of them if I were you."

"Then we're free to leave?"

"I know where to find you," Rombart said, and the connection was broken.

I know where to find you. The words seemed to mock her as she looked around the empty room.

"Josh?" she called tentatively.

There was no answer. She pushed off the sheet she had pulled up over her breasts and crawled out of bed. She found her nightgown on the floor and pulled it over her head as she walked into the bathroom.

Which looked exactly as it had last night when she had gone to bed. The razor and can of shaving cream she'd bought for Josh were still out on the counter, as were the toothbrushes. She touched them and found they were dry. And then she touched the inside of the shower curtain, which was dry as well.

As she turned to go back to the bedroom, she caught a glimpse of her reflection in the mirror. The skin of her cheeks and throat were as red as if she were blushing. She leaned closer to the glass, touching the splotches of color before she realized what they were. Like the slight tenderness in her lower body, the beard-burned skin was a reminder of what had happened last night. Josh had made love to her through the long hours, and then...

The eyes of the woman in the mirror widened as her brain

automatically finished that phrase. Joshua Stone had made love to her all night and then, just as he had three years ago, he had disappeared.

PAIGE HURRIEDLY SHOWERED and dressed, trying to think what she should do. Rombart was the logical one to ask for help. He was local, and he already knew most of the story.

However, considering the international implications of Joshua Stone's second disappearance, it might be a good idea to lay everything out to someone in the agency. The only thing she was sure of was that someone wouldn't be Carl Steiner.

Maybe Pete Logan, she thought, as she threw clothing and toiletries into the same shopping bag in which she had brought them here. At least she had no qualms about Pete's loyalties.

There was a knock on the door, and her hands froze over the nightgown she had been folding. *Maids,* she thought in relief. It was midmorning, and they would be coming to clean the room.

She walked across to the door and looked through the peephole. Two men, wearing dark suits and overcoats, were standing outside the room. She didn't know their faces, but there was something instantly recognizable about them, maybe just that carefully nondescript persona.

The knock sounded again. She thought about not answering it, but she knew that if she didn't, they would show their identification and get the manager to let them in.

''Who is it?'' she called.

''Steiner wants to see you,'' the man nearer the door said. He held up his identification, peephole high, as his partner continued his vigilance over the deserted parking lot.

It certainly hadn't taken Steiner much time to get someone down here. And she supposed there wasn't much point in delaying the incvitable. She threw the night latch and turned the knob.

"I'd like to get my things together," she said.

The man nodded, folding the case that held his ID. He held the door open with one hand as she turned back inside, walking over to the table where she had been in the process of packing the shopping bag. She pushed the flannel nightgown into it and then looked around the room to see if she'd missed anything.

Her eyes touched on the unmade bed and lingered there a heartbeat. Her lips tightened, but she forced her gaze away. When she slipped her fingers into the handles of the shopping bag and turned back to the door, both men were watching her.

"I'm ready," she said.

She walked across the room, picking her purse up off the air-conditioning console. She wondered if Josh had taken her weapon with him. From the weight of the purse it seemed he must have.

He had taken the gun, but not the toothbrush or razor. *How damned typical,* she thought cynically. Of course, being played for a fool twice in one lifetime by the same guy would probably make anyone a cynic.

She walked through the door, which the agent allowed to close behind her. She followed them across the asphalt to a pale blue, midsize rental car, bland enough that she would have been able to pick it out of the parking lot as being CIA.

The one who had shown her his ID began to unlock the door. His partner had moved to the other side of the car and was waiting by the front passenger door. That meant she got the back seat to herself. At least they didn't seem to expect conversation, which she wasn't up to.

She heard the noise at the same time the agent unlocking the driver's side door fell against it. His hand clawed for purchase on the roof and then on the window as he slid down to his knees. It wasn't until she saw the smear of blood on the glass that she realized he'd been shot. That softly pneumatic *phut* had been a bullet fired through a silencer.

Her first instinct was to go to the downed agent, but as his partner began to return fire, Paige ducked, edging around the back of the car toward him and safety. A bullet struck metal somewhere near her, singing off into the sunshine.

Someone would call the cops. There must be dozens of people in those motel rooms. Someone would realize what was going on and get the authorities. If they could only hold on…

Still in a crouch, she made it to the other side in time to watch the second agent lift his head above the car's protection, either to squeeze off another shot or to check the position of whoever was firing at them. As soon as he did, he fell as if he'd been jerked backwards, his body landing almost in front of her. On the way down, his hand had released the gun it held. The weapon struck the pavement and skittered across it a few feet, coming to rest under another car.

She glanced down at the agent's face, an automatic assessment, despite the danger of her situation. His eyes were open, but it was obvious by the small bluing hole in his forehead that he was dead or would be very quickly. There was nothing she could do for him.

Dropping her purse and the shopping bag she hadn't been aware she was still clutching, she scrambled on her hands and knees around his body and toward the gun. She had already gotten her hand on it, when she heard someone behind her, the soles of his shoes slapping on the pavement as he ran.

She rolled over and sat up to face him, bringing the gun around with her. Her left hand slipped under the right, supporting it, as she began to raise the pistol to fire.

From her position on the ground she found she was looking up into the barrel of an Uzi 9-mm. And it was held by the man who had tried to drag her into the black Mercedes.

"Drop it," he ordered, the words unaccented.

The motion to bring the pistol she'd picked up into firing position halted. She wasn't sure she had consciously made the decision not to challenge him, but it had physically been made. After all, she had seen what the weapon he held could do. He could cut her in half before she could get off a shot.

Would he? They had killed two people, but if they intended to kill her, they already would have. For some reason they wanted her alive. *Window dressing* echoed in her head as she stared up into that cold, deadly black hole.

"Drop it," he said again.

Instead, finding a courage she didn't know she possessed, she begin to lift the pistol again. Whatever they were going to do to her, they would have to do it here. Here in the sunshine. If she was going to die, this was a far better place than wherever they might take her, and a quick death far preferable to a slow torture. If they intended to try to get information out of her, she reasoned, especially information she didn't have—

She never completed the motion or the thought. The back of her head seemed to explode. The weapon she held slipped from suddenly nerveless fingers. She thought she heard it hit the pavement, and then she heard nothing else for a very long time.

"SECOND GUY just died," Andy Rombart said. "I'm sorry."

Joshua Stone glanced up at the detective's face and realized that he really was. "Officer down" sent a wave of fury through any member of the law enforcement community.

Josh nodded, and then he looked down again, determined to finish the task he'd begun. He had gathered up the feminine garments that had spilled out of the shopping bag and was pushing them back into it. One corner of the paper bag was soaked with blood, as was the flannel gown.

Someone had stepped on the cloth as well, marking it with

a crinkle-patterned sole. Cop shoe, he realized, not evidence. Still, he resisted the impulse to brush the mark off. It was too late to worry about that. Too late. *Too late.* He picked up the bag and Paige's purse, and then he stood, moving as if he were tired or old, to face the detective.

"Anybody see anything?"

"We're checking. Door-to-door. Found somebody that heard the shots, but nobody's got a description. Not even of the car."

Josh nodded, his gaze sweeping the parking lot instead of looking again at the bloodstains on the asphalt. The crime scene people had come and gone, drawing their outlines and taking pictures. The blood all seemed to belong to the two agents, but he didn't suppose there was any guarantee of that. Not until the lab did the workup, and that could take days.

"Somebody saw something," he said, bringing his gaze back to the detective's face. Rombart's eyes seemed compassionate.

"If they did, we'll find them," the detective said, and then he added, "I talked to her not thirty minutes before this. She didn't mention you weren't here."

Josh wondered if Rombart thought he had had something to do with what had happened. Of course, whatever Rombart thought about him didn't matter. Not as long as it didn't prevent the detective from doing everything he could to find Paige.

"She was still asleep when I left the room."

Josh had debated waking her, but in the end, standing silently beside the bed, he'd decided there was no point. He didn't plan to be gone all that long.

The cop nodded. "Sounded like I woke her up. You want to tell me where you went?"

"I needed to make a phone call."

There was a small silence. "Why not do it from the room?"

"The cell phone was dead when I tried to use it. I didn't want to use the room phone in case they traced the call."

"They?"

"I called the CIA. I was trying to reach a man named Steiner there if you need to check that out."

"That's funny," Rombart said. "A man named Steiner didn't know Jack Thompson when *I* talked to him this morning."

"If you talk to him again, ask him if he knows Joshua Stone. And if he tells you he doesn't, tell him that he's about to."

JOSH HADN'T WANTED to leave Atlanta, but he knew none of the answers were there. And unless he could get a handle on what was going on, he'd never be able to find Paige.

They didn't kill her, he told himself a hundred times, both on the flight and after he had arrived in Virginia. They had killed the others, but they had taken Paige with them, just as they had tried to do before. He repeated that over and over as he had waited for the slow bureaucratic red tape to untangle. And then he repeated it again as he sat in Steiner's outer office at Langley, waiting for the head of Special Operations to acknowledge that a man name Joshua Stone had a right to be here.

There was no logical reason for them to harm Paige. Of course, he was finding it difficult to be logical. Or rational. And if he didn't get some answers pretty soon from Carl Steiner—

"Mr. Steiner will see you now."

The assistant deputy director's secretary opened the door to the inner office. And for some reason, Josh found he was almost reluctant to enter. Reluctant to finally confront the man who had been pulling the strings, as if they were puppets dancing to his commands? Or reluctant because nothing here had felt familiar, and from what Paige had told him, it should have?

He stood up and walked across the room to the door. "Thank you," he said to the secretary before he stepped through it. And as he got his first look at the man behind the desk, he heard the door close, leaving him alone with the head of Special Ops.

"You wanted to see me?" Carl Steiner said. The inflection wasn't questioning. It was flat and hard.

"I want an explanation," Josh said.

The dark eyes studied his face, letting the silence build. Then Steiner leaned back in his chair, putting his hands together, index fingers tapping reflectively against his chin.

"An explanation for what?"

"We'll start with something simple. Like how I ended up in a hospital in Atlanta, Georgia. And not the official version. That one I've heard."

"I thought it rather creative."

"*I* thought it a bunch of crap," Josh said, mocking his tone.

Steiner hadn't asked him to sit down, but he walked across the room and sat in the leather chair situated opposite the one on the other side of the gleaming mahogany desk. The cold, dark stare of the man behind it didn't lighten.

"Carefully designed crap in any case," Steiner said. "And rather costly. It was intended to hide you until we could determine exactly what *had* happened to you."

"Not a wreck," Josh said. It was no more a question than Steiner's comment had been.

Steiner's lips pursed, and the movement of his fingers stopped. They rested against his chin as he spoke.

"You were dumped in the vestibule of a Russian Orthodox church, naked and suffering from a variety of injuries, the most life-threatening of which was a fractured skull. That

was in New York City almost six months ago. No one on
the emergency room team who worked on you that night
thought you'd live. You surprised them. And the next morning someone at the hospital finally thought to call the number that had been written with a black permanent marker
across your chest.''

The narrative stopped, but Steiner's eyes held on his face.

''I'll bite,'' Josh said. ''Whose number?''

''The main switchboard number here, as a matter of fact.
We asked NYPD to provide us with fingerprints of their
John Doe. When we got them, we discovered that one of
Griff Cabot's people had managed to rise from the dead.
Quite a feat, I'm sure you'll admit, even by External Secu-
rity Team standards.''

''And by then, there *was* no team and you had taken
Griff's place in Special Ops.''

''It had long been assumed you were dead. And frankly,
we weren't quite sure what to do with you when you turned
up alive. Especially after you recovered enough to claim not
to know any more about what had happened to you than we
did.''

''So you decided to find out,'' Josh said.

Had that been what all of Steiner's manipulation was
about? Just an attempt to find out what had happened three
years ago?

''Not quite as you're imagining, perhaps. We tapped some
sources, asking them to try to discover any information that
might explain your supposed death and subsequent resurrec-
tion.''

''Sources where?''

There was a long hesitation, during which Steiner's eyes
never left his face. Evaluating? If he had been, he apparently
reached some conclusion. Steiner lowered his hands, letting
them rest, still joined, on the surface of the desk.

''Sources within the current Russian government. They,

too, have a vested interest in anything that happens in Vlad-istan.''

"And *they* provided the information you needed?''

"What we know about your...odyssey was compiled in a rather piecemeal fashion. There are still parts missing, but I have no doubt that what we have learned is correct.''

"I'd like to hear it,'' Josh said.

He realized from his physical response to Steiner's words that he really *didn't* want to hear this. His mind had known that whatever had happened to him or whatever he had done was better unknown. It had resisted his every effort to un-ravel the mystery that was about to be laid out for him by a man he didn't know. A man who didn't like him. A man who had probably just as soon he really was dead in a snow-laden grave somewhere.

"The operative known as Joshua Stone,'' Steiner said, "was captured by a rebel patrol while on a mission in Vlad-istan. The separatists suspected he had participated in the theft of a particularly toxic nerve agent. They were not pleased to discover that he didn't have it with him when he was taken. And even less pleased when he refused to tell them where he had hidden it. Given the situation, the rebels needed that nerve agent to repel the Russian invasion. They were rather desperate for it, actually. And not...patient, shall we say, with the man who had stolen it and refused to tell them where it was.''

"Did he?'' Josh asked, beginning to feel the same sense of disorientation he had felt after hypnosis. As if this should mean something to him. As if it should trigger some mem-ory.

And it didn't. The only memories that had surfaced were ones that had evolved out of his dreams the past few nights. And those had concerned the woman who had been his part-ner.

He had tried to contact Steiner this morning because he

had been told that once the dam of repression began to break apart, the rest of those memories would come. And because he had known that he and Paige would need the agency's protection when it did.

"Stone understood what was at stake," Steiner said. "His mission had been to prevent the rebels from using the nerve agent against the advancing Russian forces, undoubtedly provoking a nuclear retaliation. And if there is one thing one could say about Cabot's operatives, it's that they seldom failed."

Which must mean… "I didn't tell them," Joshua Stone said softly.

Although his voice was controlled, there was again an internal reaction. A deep sense of relief that he hadn't failed. Not Griff and not Paige. And for a man who hadn't known about the existence of those two people until a few days ago, it was surprising to realize how fearful he had been that he might have let either one of them down.

"When the Russians overran the rebel capital, they found a prisoner who had no identification. A man who wouldn't talk. Or couldn't talk. A man who seemed…locked within his own mind. They had no idea who he was or why he was there, but judging by the ferocity of the rebels' attempt to keep him out of their hands, the Russian commander decided Moscow should have a chance to decide why the separatists felt he was so valuable."

"They took me to Russia."

"For more than two years you were incarcerated in one of their…hospitals."

"Hospital?" Josh repeated, reading the nuance of that pause.

"For the criminally insane," Steiner said, his voice low.

The head of Special Operations would know about the conditions in those hospitals. Josh did, although none of what he was visualizing felt personal. Not as if it had happened to him. What *had* happened to him?

"From there, things become…less clear, I'm afraid. When rebellion threatened again in Vladistan, it seems that the story of the man who wouldn't talk resurfaced somehow. The government in Russia is corrupt, I'm afraid. Everyone is open to bribery. And so, someone bought you."

Josh resisted the urge to repeat that phrase, too. There was no need to give Steiner any more satisfaction in his story than he was taking. Nausea churned in Josh's stomach because he knew the worst was coming. He knew that with a certainty that was black and faceless and terrifying.

"Who?" he asked, fighting to keep his voice steady and his face controlled.

"A powerful criminal element has taken over Russian society," Steiner said pedantically. "It has invaded every aspect of commerce and the government."

"The Russian mob," Josh said.

"The potential for profit from that missing nerve agent is enormous. All they needed was to force you to tell them where you had hidden it. As soon as the rebellion threw the region into chaos again, they could easily retrieve it and then sell it to the highest bidder. In today's terrorist-mad world, the bidding would be astronomical."

"And it hasn't been," Josh said flatly. "Not yet."

If the so-called Russian Mafia had gotten that information, this conversation and everything that had happened during the past few days would not have taken place.

"They couldn't force you to tell them. Not to tell them anything, apparently. And they almost killed you trying."

"But they didn't. Because then there would be no hope of ever recovering what they're looking for."

"Or perhaps they decided to get what they want a different way," Steiner said. His chin was resting again on his tented fingers, his lips slightly pursed.

"By giving me back to you?"

"They knew that we also wanted to recover the toxin. All they had to do, or so they thought, was to sit back and watch."

"Watch me or watch you?" Josh asked bitterly, finally realizing what had been going on.

"Both of us, perhaps. As I said, it took us a while to put together what had happened to you. And before we had the final piece of the mystery in place, I'm afraid we had already put *our* plan to help you recover your memory into effect."

"Paige Daniels."

"There were indications in the incident report that she might be the key to helping you regain your memory. And we were pressed for time. Things were becoming heated in Vladistan again. We needed a resolution."

"And you didn't tell her what was going on."

"We weren't sure she'd cooperate if we did. It seemed better if she believed the idea—and the quest—were hers."

This was only what he had suspected from the first. That Steiner had manipulated Daniels into seeking him out. There were a couple of things about Steiner's account, however, that didn't fit. A few loose threads.

"The men filming me? Were they yours?"

"Ours," Steiner corrected, his voice amused. "After all, we are still on the same side, Stone."

"Why tape me? And why pick someone inept enough to get caught doing it?"

There was a second's pause, brief but telling, before Steiner answered. "It's so hard to get good help these days."

Not that hard, Josh thought. Not here. And those two had been spectacularly inept. "You *wanted* me to see those men. That was their instructions, wasn't it. To let me see them."

"And what purpose would that serve?"

"The taping was a sham. A decoy. Those men had only

one job. They were there to make sure I'd listen to whatever Daniels told me. Their job was to put *us* on the same side. To make me believe that what she was telling me, all that business about spies and missions and nerve agents, might conceivably be true."

"If Ms. Daniels could convince you that you *were* Joshua Stone, we hoped you would want to recover your true identity. And to discover what had happened to you."

"And Daniels was the perfect one to help me accomplish that, of course," Josh said bitterly.

"She had been your partner. And she had also been something more. It seemed that if you were going to remember anyone..."

"And if I did?"

"We had planned to be near enough to be aware of when that happened. Unfortunately, you retained more of your former skills than we'd counted on. When the gangsters attempted to take Daniels at the hotel that night, we...lost touch. The two of you simply disappeared."

"And Culbertson? Who killed the doctor?"

"I would assume the people who were following you."

"They didn't follow us to her house."

"Dr. Culbertson *was* the likeliest candidate in the area if you decided to try hypnosis to recover those memories."

"And yet you didn't provide any protection for her? Knowing the kind of people who were after this information?"

"You're the ones who endangered Culbertson, Stone. Please don't blame me for that. Obviously, you underestimated your opponent. And it cost the doctor her life."

There was a surge of regret, but Josh knew there was still something about this he hadn't figured out. Something Steiner didn't want him to figure out.

"Who called the cops?" Josh asked. That call had always bothered him, despite the possibility that one of the neighbors had seen something suspicious and picked up the phone. "Did your people put in the 9-1-1 call the night Culbertson was killed?"

And he knew by the flicker of surprise in those black eyes that he was right. "The Russians didn't follow us to Culbertson. *They* wouldn't have assumed I'd see a hypnotherapist. They just tried to beat the information out of me. Hypnosis was *your* solution, Steiner. The CIA's. And that's why we tried it again.

"Culbertson called the agency to check on Daniels' credentials and somehow you got wind of it. You sent somebody to persuade the doctor to tape the sessions and provide you with a copy. That's what you meant when you said they were watching you. They followed *your* people to Culbertson. And your people were coming back to pick up the tape when they saw someone else enter the house. Instead of intervening and exposing themselves to the Russians, they put in an anonymous call to 9-1-1. But by the time the cops arrived it was too late for the doctor. In the meantime, we'd shown up, just in time to encounter the murderer and get caught by the cops. Your people must have been having a fit when they realized what was about to happen."

"That's speculation," Steiner said calmly.

"Your people led them to Culbertson and then didn't intervene, even when they were killing her. Because they didn't want the Russians to know they were there? Or because they didn't want us to know? I guess that really doesn't matter. Ultimately, you're responsible. You set this into motion, sitting here like some malevolent spider spinning a web of deceit. You tricked Daniels into hunting me down, without giving her any warning about what she was up against. You set her against the same people who had put me into the hospital for months—"

The tirade was abruptly cut off by his realization of what had been bothering him about Steiner's explanation. It took him a few seconds to run the sequence through his head, making sure he was right. And as he did, the cold eyes of Griff Cabot's replacement watched him.

"And after you had done that, you let them know what Daniels was doing. You set her up to come after me, and then you sent those bastards after her. They weren't watching me. They couldn't have been. Not if the agency had done its job in creating a new identity for Joshua Stone.

"And according to Rombart there was nothing to tie Thompson to Stone. Daniels is the only thing that did that, and you gave them the nudge that sent them after her. I never told anybody her name. I never told them anything about her," he said with absolute certainty. "I locked it all so deep inside my head that I couldn't tell them. You're the bastard who gave them Daniels."

"And why would I have wanted to endanger her?" Steiner asked, his voice expressing nothing but a mild interest.

"To get those old juices stirring," Josh said, figuring it out as he talked. "You knew that danger gets my adrenaline pumping. All those psychological profiles they did on us. And in this case you had something else going for you. My protective instincts. You thought that if there was anything that could bring Joshua Stone back to life, it was putting Daniels at risk. I had proved that to you during the last three years."

"I assure you—" Steiner began, only to be cut off when Josh stood up, moving so quickly that the heavy chair he'd been sitting in overturned behind him.

"Shut up, you lying bastard," he said leaning across the desk to grab a fistful of Steiner's shirt. Using that handful of material, he pulled the head of Special Ops out of his chair, so that they were face-to-face. "I wouldn't believe a word you said, not if you swore to it on your mother's grave."

Steiner eyes were unchanged, as cold as they had been from the beginning. Josh could see neither fear nor anger in them, and he had expected both. He had *wanted* both. He wanted Steiner to be very afraid of what was about to happen to him.

"Then I take it you aren't interested in this?" Steiner said, his hand finding a piece of paper on his desk and pushing it toward Josh.

There was something in the tone of the question that made Josh's skin crawl. A cold surety he didn't like. Whatever bait Steiner was dangling in front of him, he was absolutely certain Josh would take it. And Josh didn't like that certainty because he knew there was only one thing that would make him listen to anything Steiner had to say. Only one thing that would make him respond to the pull of the puppet master's strings.

Slowly he released the hold on Steiner's shirt, pushing the assistant deputy director back into his chair. Pushing the bastard away before he lost all control and killed him.

"We received it this morning," Steiner said.

"What is it?" Josh asked, knowing he didn't want to know.

"It's a ransom note. Surely you've been expecting one."

"I want their names," Josh said softly. "I want the names and the current phone numbers of the men I worked with. Hawk. Jordan Cross," he said, remembering the ones Daniels had mentioned. Those names had meant nothing to him then, but as Daniels had once been, those men had been his partners, members of Griff Cabot's team, a bond forged in danger and in absolute trust. "I want a way to contact whoever is left of the EST."

"I can give you something better than that," Steiner said, his voice unshaken, "but you'll have to trust me."

"Trust you, you son of a bitch?" Josh jeered. "Give me one good reason why I should ever trust you again."

"Because I'm your only chance of ever seeing Paige Daniels alive. And because you know it."

Chapter Fifteen

He knew their names because Paige and later Steiner had spoken them. A man called Hawk, whose blue eyes were as cold as the assistant deputy director's, but in a way that said danger rather than deception. A gray-eyed Jordan Cross, who smiled at him, seeming relaxed and at ease. Grey Sellers, tightly coiled power, and obviously as dangerous as Hawk. And Drew Evans, whose quiet hazel eyes managed to express an understanding for what he had been through that Josh hadn't expected among this group.

He didn't recognize any of them, and he realized from the sharp sense of disappointment he felt studying their features that he had really expected to. His eyes shifted again, moving from face to face, examining each, as if a closer look might tear through the frustrating veil that still covered his past.

"I need your help," he said, hoping that at least one of them would agree to join him in trying to rescue Paige Daniels. He couldn't do it alone, not in the time he had been given, and because this was too important to trust to anyone else.

None of them replied, although their eyes continued to meet his. It was clear from what was in them that they weren't afraid of what he was asking of them. They were no longer agents, however, and no longer involved in the unceasing battle they had once fought under Griff Cabot's command. None of these men owed him their help. None of them owed him anything.

The silence built until a door opened somewhere. There were footsteps, and the eyes of the men Steiner had called to this meeting at Langley began to focus on someone behind Josh.

When Josh turned toward the latecomer, he finally found a face he recognized. The face, remembered from his dreams, of the one man who shouldn't be here. A man he'd been told was dead.

"Griff?" he said, his inflection full of disbelief.

"I'm sorry you weren't told, Josh. Steiner has a penchant for secrecy," Griff Cabot said. "And all too often he's mistaken about which secrets he should keep and which he should reveal."

Cabot held out his hand as he approached, and without hesitation Josh put his into it. The grip of Griff's fingers was firm, and just as the weight of the weapon had been the first time he'd touched Paige's gun, it was also familiar.

"Welcome home, Joshua Stone," Griff said. "I can't tell you how glad I am that you made it back."

Just as he had known Steiner was lying, Josh knew that what he heard in that deep voice was the absolute truth. To Cabot he wasn't an inconvenient ghost, but a friend.

"Daniels said that, despite what anyone else said, you never doubted me. Thank you."

"I never had any reason to doubt you. I'm only sorry we didn't get you out. And believe me, we tried. At least, we tried until…" Cabot paused, and Josh knew the hesitation had something to do with Cabot's own agency-engineered death.

"Just a couple of old spooks," Joshua Stone said, smiling at the man who had sent him on that long-ago mission.

A mission that had led to nearly three years of unmitigated

hell, during which he had been passed from torturer to torturer, all of them seeking what this man had told him to guard. And Josh knew that even if he had failed in that duty, the dark, compassionate eyes of Griff Cabot would not have condemned him. They would have welcomed him home exactly as they were now.

"I don't think the word *spook* is supposed to be taken quite so literally as you and I seem to have taken it," Griff said smiling. And then, abandoning a topic that was obviously painful for both of them, he turned to the other four men.

"I take it you've already become reacquainted with the members of Phoenix?"

"Phoenix?" Josh repeated, wondering if this was a term he should know. He couldn't remember Daniels mentioning it.

"The Phoenix Brotherhood. All of us in this room have, in one way or another, risen from our own ashes. The CIA destroyed our identities, and we have…reinvented ourselves, I suppose. I suspect we've done it in a way that most of us prefer."

"*Reinvented* yourselves?"

"We use the skills we learned with the agency for other purposes now. There's still evil in the world, and we recognize its existence. We've simply chosen another way to fight."

"Then… I had hoped you'd be willing help me with this," Josh said, holding out the ransom demand that had been passed to him through the CIA. If Cabot was searching for evil, the people who held Paige Daniels would more than qualify.

Cabot scanned the note, and his eyes lifted to Josh's. "*Could* you give them the location?"

Slowly Joshua Stone shook his head. "Not even to save her life. I can give them my own, but I can't tell those bastards where that toxin is. Not now. Not yet. And by the time my memory returns… *If* it returns…''

He didn't finish because Griff knew what would happen if Josh didn't meet their demand. In exchange for Paige Daniels' life, the Russian mafia was demanding the location of the missing nerve agent. When they had successfully retrieved it from Vladistan, they would let her go.

''I know that what I'm asking means nothing to any of you,'' Josh added, his eyes again meeting those of these hard men, tempered by their encounters with a different kind of evil. ''You have your own lives, outside the agency, and no reason to risk—''

''Daniels was one of us,'' Griff interrupted. ''One of the team. That alone would give us a reason. As does the situation in Vladistan. Just because we no longer operate on the international level doesn't mean we don't know or care about what goes on in that arena. Besides, we've had experience at this kind of rescue, even when the odds seemed as uneven as these. Let's concentrate on getting Daniels away from her captors, and then we'll worry about retrieving the nerve agent.''

THE COMMAND CENTER Cabot had set up in the basement of an old summer house in Virginia would have rivaled the war rooms of a few countries Josh could think of. And the planning had been as meticulous as Josh could have hoped for.

Griff had told him that Steiner had committed some of his people to the search, which had provided the background information they needed to zero in on Paige's captors. In this country, the Russian mob operated primarily out of New York City, which was where, they had discovered, they were holding Paige.

The few hours Josh had been given to respond to their demand had ticked away as Griff and his Phoenix agents had feverishly worked to put something together—a plan which was based on material that was coming into the command center in bits and pieces even as they devised it. And there was no margin for error. Everyone involved understood that.

Josh could only hope they hadn't forgotten anything. Or made any mistakes. And hope that *he* wouldn't, he thought, as he opened the door of the rental car and walked across the parking lot, his footsteps echoing in the midnight darkness.

The waterfront warehouse where the ransom note had told him to come looked deserted in the pale light cast by the street lamps. Every access to the bottom floor had long ago been boarded up, except for one metal door, which had a padlock hanging from the hasp. Josh's eyes skated along the row of industrial-sized windows on what appeared to be the second story.

Thanks to someone in the agency, they had been furnished this morning with the architect's original plans for this building. Josh now knew that those windows didn't open onto a second level, but looked down onto the warehouse floor below. And if everything went according to plan, they would play a major role in what was about to happen.

If everything went according to plan. And his job might prove to be the most difficult. He had to convince the mobsters to bring Daniels here, rather than take Josh somewhere else. Of course, a demand to see the merchandise in an exchange like this should not be unexpected, certainly not by the people they were dealing with, noted for their lack of trust. Whether they would accede to his demand in this case, however, remained to be seen.

Fighting a gut-clenching fear that it was all going to go wrong, Josh walked up to the metal door. The padlock was unfastened, although it would have been difficult to determine that from a distance. He slipped the lock out of the hook and held it in his hand a moment, feeling an overwhelming sense of dread at finally putting this into play.

Opening the door would be like lighting the fuse to an explosive. Once begun…

Except *they* had begun it when they'd taken Paige Daniels and killed two CIA operatives. And killed Dr. Culbertson. All he and Griff's men were doing was trying to finish it.

He pulled the hasp back and hung the padlock over it. When he opened the door, its rusted hinges protested loudly. Warning enough for whoever was waiting inside that he'd arrived.

And as soon as he closed it, a command came out of the darkness. "Arms out," the faceless voice ordered, the accent heavy and, he thought, Eastern European. "And spread your legs."

This was something they had expected. And prepared for. Josh obeyed and was competently patted down. They didn't make him strip, but it wouldn't have surprised him if they had. He was ready for that as well, but apparently the mobsters weren't concerned about anyone listening in on this conversation.

Of course, if Josh had been wearing the traditional wire, they might have discovered it during the search. He wasn't, and it was highly unlikely they would have found the nearly invisible hearing aid-sized microphone he wore in his ear, no matter what.

"I want to see Daniels," Josh said, when the one who had done the searching stepped back, fading into the darkness. "No deal unless I verify she's unharmed."

There was a small silence, and then a light came on halfway across the warehouse. An ordinary brass floor lamp had been positioned beside a straight chair. Paige Daniels was sitting in it, her hands behind her, a strip of duct tape across her mouth.

Josh could see her eyes squint and then blink at the painfully sudden brightness. As he watched, they slowly widened, focusing on him. She looked pale and her hair was disheveled, but he couldn't tell much about her physical condition.

Forcing his eyes away from her, he turned back toward the man who had issued the orders. The face that swam out of the dimness jolted him. He couldn't place it, but he knew this was someone he had seen before. And knew that remembering where might be crucial. Beside him stood the heavyset man who had tried to force Paige into the Mercedes that night, holding an Uzi with a casualness that indicated he was very comfortable with it.

"And now you have seen Daniels," the man whose face he couldn't remember said mockingly. "Shall we deal?"

Not yet, Josh thought. He had been trying desperately to keep track of the passing minutes in his head. Not quite yet. He turned instead to the man holding the machine gun.

"What happened to your friend? The one in the lake."

There was another silence, this one lasting for several seconds. The man's porcine eyes rested on Josh's face without the least trace of interest. It was the other one, the one with the accent, who finally answered him.

"Anyone stupid enough to shoot at you, Mr. Stone, didn't deserve to live. You, and what you know, are too valuable a commodity to be destroyed in a mindless fit of rage."

"I hope you'll remember that," Josh said, his eyes moving to the Uzi. The man laughed, but his massive companion never moved a muscle. Josh wondered if he even spoke English.

And he wondered how many minutes had passed since he had entered the building. He usually had a knack of judging things like that, but time had slowed, especially since he'd seen Paige.

He also tried to estimate how many of them there were, but the only light was from the street lamp outside, filtered by the grime that covered the windows, and that tightly focused cone of light surrounding the chair Daniels was sitting in. He knew there were at least three men, but the shadows on the perimeter of the huge concrete floor might well conceal a dozen, or a hundred, more.

"Of course, we have no such qualms concerning the woman," the man continued. "And although you have a remarkable tolerance for pain, I wonder how great your tolerance is for *her* pain."

"Just about zero," Josh said distinctly, fighting a surge of hatred that made him want to kill the bastard just for uttering the threat. And there was no doubt that's what it had been.

The man smiled, and again the image of his smile—another time, another place—flashed through Josh's mind. And then it was gone. Where he had seen this man before didn't matter now, he reminded himself. All that mattered was making sure he had given Griff and the others time to get into position, once they had been assured through the hidden mike that Paige was here.

"Then we won't need a demonstration," the leader said. "And now the location, if you please, Mr. Stone.

"How do I know she'll remain unharmed after you have it?"

"We will simply wait here together until the nerve agent is retrieved. You may watch over her yourself."

"I don't understand," Josh said.

"Our people can be across the border to where you were captured and back out in a matter of hours. The more exact your instructions, the quicker their retrieval will be. And the quicker the two of you will be free to leave."

The scene of his capture—a demolished village—flickered in Josh's brain like summer lightning. As with the earlier image of this man's face, it was there one second and then it was gone. And he wondered how this man could know where he'd been captured.

"This map should help," Josh said, reaching into the neck of the black turtleneck he wore under his jacket.

As he pulled the tightly folded sheet of blank paper out, the eyes of both men followed his hand. He continued the motion, changing it in midair to a flick of his wrist.

The small square of paper flew where he'd directed it. Into the face of the man holding the Uzi, who spoke a profanity, in very idiomatic English. Before the word was out of his mouth, Josh had wrested the machine gun from him. Continuing the same motion, he swung it so that the stock struck the man with the accent in the face. He heard the cheekbone snap like a dry twig, despite the noises now coming from the other side of the room.

Then Josh began to run, sprinting toward the small circle of light where Paige Daniels sat, the perfect target. The most crucial seconds of the whole operation, the time when she would be most vulnerable. And the timing was absolutely critical.

As soon as Josh said the word "map," four men rappelled off the roof and came crashing in through those tall, industrial size windows. Although he never wasted energy looking that way, Josh knew that at least one of them had made it, the sound of breaking glass an accompaniment to his run. The fifth man, Griff Cabot, whose terrorist-caused injuries would prevent him from entering in that fashion, would be coming in through the front door.

The shooting started before Josh could reach Paige. He ignored it, concentrating on the spotlighted figure before him. Time had slowed again. He seemed to be running through quicksand, each step taking him nowhere. No nearer to his goal. He was aware of broken glass scattering across the floor in front of him, glinting in the light from the lamp over Paige's head.

Her shoulders were hunched, and he knew she must have been struck by the shards. As long as nothing else hits her, he thought, his lungs burning with his exertion. So short a distance. So why the hell was it taking him so long?

And then he was there. He resisted the urge to wrap his arms around her and carry the chair backwards. Given the hard floor, there was too great a potential for cracking her skull that way. He skidded to a halt, and juggling the Uzi, picked up the chair and laid it on its side. As he did, he kicked out, upsetting the lamp, which rolled to a stop. Still burning.

He straddled Paige and the chair, praying that son of a bitch really had given orders not to kill him. He halfturned, aiming at the lamp and sent a spray of bullets in its direction. Despite the noise of the gunfire around him, he could hear them pinging against the flimsy metal of the pole and watched them slash the shade. Incredibly, the bulb continued to burn.

Despite the din, he heard the shot that took it out. Sharp and clear above the clatter of the automatic weapons, it came from above his head and to his right. Raising his eyes, Josh saw a rifle in the hands of one of the figures outlined against the light of the windows. Not his weapon of choice, not for this kind of fight, but the man who wielded it obviously knew how to use it. More effectively than he had the Uzi, Josh acknowledged.

His attention was drawn to the other side of the room by the sound of running footsteps. In the sudden darkness all he could see was a rush of shapes materializing from the shadows. Obviously holding to their orders to avoid hitting him, they were firing at the men coming in through the windows.

Josh aimed the Uzi at the approaching figures and pulled the trigger, sweeping the gun back and forth. The charge broke, as the forms scattered back into the safety of the shadows.

He realized that his and Paige's position in the center of

the floor was probably hampering the men above them. They were equipped with night-vision goggles. They could see into those shadows. If he could pick up the chair and get—

And then, into the lull that had fallen after he had taken his finger off the trigger, the man with the accent shouted, "Kill them all." It took a split second for the meaning to register, and when it did, Josh did the only thing he could think of. He shifted his position, kneeling behind the chair and laying his own body across Paige's, their positions forming a compact cross.

"Tuck your head," he ordered, and felt her obey, forehead burrowing into his ribs. He laid his left elbow over her head, pulling it closer, and put his finger on the trigger again.

All hell broke loose. In the thirty seconds it lasted, Josh emptied the rest of the machine gun's clip. He could hear the periodic crack of the rifle behind him. The rhythm of those shots seemed as regular as a heartbeat, coming as rapidly as the shooter could squeeze them off.

Josh waited to be hit, knowing there was no way he could escape that deadly hail of fire. And when the first bullet struck, his adrenaline was so high he felt the impact of the blow to his left arm, but no pain. The second one hit high on his chest. In response he pressed Paige's head more tightly against his side and ducked his own, putting the now-empty Uzi over it.

For a few seconds bullets continued to bounce off the floor around him, sending chips of concrete flying. Gradually, they, and then the echoes of them, faded away. An eerie silence settled over the cavernous building. Josh held his breath, listening to the stillness. He could feel Paige breathing, her ribs and arm moving under his stomach, and he mouthed a prayer of thanks.

There were sounds behind him, and he turned his head to watch as the four former members of the External Security Team used their ropes to rappel down the wall. Footsteps echoing, they began to walk across the floor, weapons ready to meet any threat.

Paige was struggling to raise her head. He moved his arm, looking at her for the first time. Her eyes were wide and dark, her face paler than he had ever seen it, but she was alive.

When he began to push up, he became aware of the pain. Aware that he was bleeding. A wave of lightheadedness swept over him. He swayed, putting the Uzi on Paige's hip, propping on it to hold himself upright. She turned her head, and he recognized the emotion in her eyes. Fear and concern for him.

"It's nothing," he said reassuringly.

She made a muffled sound, and it finally dawned on him that the tape was still across her mouth. He tried to reach over to pull it off, using the hand that wasn't on the Uzi, but he couldn't get his arm to move. Something seemed to be wrong with it. Shot, he thought. That's what was wrong. He'd been shot.

"Sorry," he whispered, feeling disoriented again.

"All right here?" Jordan Cross asked, leaning down and putting a hand on Josh's shoulder.

Josh turned his head to answer him, moving slowly because of the sudden vertigo. Cross's face wavered before him like a heat mirage. He blinked, trying to clear his vision.

"Josh?" Hawk questioned, stooping down beside him.

Josh didn't know who caught him as he toppled. Someone did, because he didn't hit the floor. They eased him down on it, and by then, Griff was there. Cabot unzipped his jacket and used a knife to cut up the front of his shirt. Josh could feel the cold metal of the blade, sliding along his skin. And he could hear someone running. Neither made much of an impression, however.

The lights came on overhead, and he looked up, staring up into the metal beams that crisscrossed the top of the

building. The pattern they made against the ceiling seemed
to pull him in like a vortex, but he knew there was something else he should be doing. Something besides that.
Something important.

He forced his eyes away from them. Griff was still kneeling beside him, pressing something against his chest. Hawk
stood guard above them both, blue eyes searching the room,
that deadly accurate rifle poised and ready.

"Josh?"

He turned his head and found Daniels kneeling on his
other side. Her fingers shaped his cheek, turning his head
toward her. She put her mouth over his. The kiss was insubstantial, making no demand. Despite how much he
wanted to, he couldn't respond. And when she raised her
head, he realized she was crying.

"You hurt?" he asked, pushing the words past dry lips.

She shook her head, and her eyes sought Griff's. Josh
didn't follow them in time to see whatever was in Cabot's
face. And then his former commander turned his head toward the metal door, which had just creakingly announced
its opening.

"On their way," Grey Sellers said. "Five minutes."

He saw Griff's mouth tighten, and then Cabot's eyes lifted
quickly to Hawk, who shook his head, a tight, negative gesture. When Cabot looked down at Josh, however, he was
smiling.

Josh relaxed, trusting this man, as he had always trusted
him. He turned his head again so he could see Paige's face,
and she was smiling at him, too. He hadn't let them down,
he thought, remembering the relief he had felt when Steiner
had confirmed that. He had never let either of them down.

"You hold on, Josh," Cabot said. "You hear me? Just
keep breathing. In and out. That's an order. You didn't let
them beat you before. Don't give up on us now, damn it."

He wasn't sure exactly what Griff wanted him to do. Not

beyond the breathing part. That much had been pretty clear, and so, holding Daniels' eyes until he couldn't see them anymore, he concentrated on that.

THERE WAS an enormous neon cross on the front of the hospital they carried him to. His eyes had opened when the wheels of the ambulance gurney bumped out onto the pavement, and the first thing he saw was that cross above him, gleaming like blue flame against a midnight sky. The neon gas in the tubing flickered and sputtered against the backdrop of the brick. And the image of another blue cross flickered into his head.

"The crucifix," he whispered.

They were hurrying now, bumping along over the asphalt, leaving the cross behind. Josh didn't want to lose the thought, but he wasn't sure there was anyone near enough to hear him.

He tried to hold onto the image at least, as he had held onto Griff's words, fixing it on a brain that felt sluggish and exhausted. He didn't understand because he hadn't run that far. Just across the room to Paige. Not far enough to be this tired.

"Daniels," he said, not sure his voice was loud enough to reach her, even if she were near. She had held his hand in the ambulance. Whenever he'd opened his eyes she'd been there. And now when he needed her most...

"Right here, Josh," she said. "I'm right here."

He turned his head, finding her face. She was almost running, trying to keep up with the gurney.

"I put it behind the crucifix."

"What?" she said, a small crease forming between her brows.

They were inside now, the automatic doors opening with a whoosh. He knew that soon they would make her go away. They would put him to sleep and he'd lose this. Lose the image of that blue cross, which had seemed like a sign. Just like the crucifix had.

He had needed a place to put the cylinder in case they ran into a rebel patrol. The small church had been the first building he'd entered, looking for a safe place for them to spend the night. Ironically, it had been the most intact building in the village, and given that so much of what had sparked that rebellion had to do with differing cultures and ethnicities and religions, it had struck him almost as an omen.

Before he had gone back out to tell Daniels they couldn't spend the night in the church, he slipped the sealed vial in its protective metal case out of his backpack. He had pushed it behind the small slanting bar at the bottom, the weight of the heavy enameled crucifix holding it tightly against the wall.

If the villagers came back after the invasion, this would not be something they would burn or discard in cleaning up the rubble, inadvertently setting off a neurological disaster. No one would tamper with the cross, and he thought the toxin would be safe. And as far as he knew, it was still there. Still safe.

"In the church," he said, the ceiling lights flying by over his head. "Village. Behind the blue crucifix."

He saw her eyes widen, and she nodded. "In the church," she repeated. "I'll tell Griff."

And then, Joshua Stone allowed himself to give in to the fatigue he had fought. He released the image of that neon cross, shining in the darkness, and slipped willingly into the midnight blackness that lay beyond it.

Epilogue

"There's something I've always wondered about," Paige said, watching Josh ease the metal case from behind the slanted bar of the blue enameled crucifix. "Something about that night we spent in this village."

When the nerve agent was finally in his hand, his fingers closed around it. He held it a long moment, before he slipped it into the pocket of his field jacket, and turned to her.

She could tell by his eyes that he had been thinking about the long years that stretched between the time he had put it there and today. Maybe remembering more details about what had happened to him. The doctors had been right. As soon as the barriers began to crumble, barriers Josh himself had constructed to protect the dangerous secret he guarded, more and more of those memories had returned.

"I've told you everything I remember about my capture. Not my finest hour," he said, his eyes lightened with self-deprecation.

Josh had gone out to investigate a noise and discovered that the curious soldier had returned. Josh had lured him away, realizing belatedly that the rebel hadn't come alone. The three of them had overpowered Josh, and beaten him unconscious. And although he had both guns, he had never gotten off a shot.

Knowing him, Paige wondered if that had been a deliberate choice. Josh knew she would come if she had heard the shot and awakened to find him gone. There had been no shot, and she had safely slept through the entire episode.

In their excitement over finding the man everyone had been searching for, the three comrades had thrown him on the back of their truck and taken him off to headquarters. And Paige had escaped the nightmare Josh had been forced to live through.

And then that same soldier—the same one who had almost discovered them in the cellar—had later become involved with the mob. He had undoubtedly been the one who had told the Russian Mafia about the man who wouldn't talk, the man they had later bought from corrupt officials and tried to beat the secret out of. Physical torture hadn't worked any better for the gangsters than it had for the separatists.

"Not about what happened that night," she said. "At least not then. About what happened before."

There was a small silence, and Josh said, "About our making love?"

She glanced through the opening in the stones where a window had once been. Outside, standing guard, were the men of the Phoenix Brotherhood. They didn't have to be here, just as they hadn't had to help with her rescue that night. But when Josh had said he was coming back to finish the job he had begun—a job he *needed* to finish—they had volunteered to provide an escort.

She pulled her gaze back to Josh, and found that he was still watching her. Waiting for her response to his question.

"When you held out your hand, you looked at me... I've always wondered what it meant. Whatever was in your eyes."

"What did you think it meant?"

"At the time, I wasn't sure. Later, I thought maybe it

meant that you *knew* you were leaving. And that was why…'' She stopped, her eyes considering the men outside again.

"You thought that's why I made love to you that night? Because I knew I was leaving?"

"You'd never given me any indication before that you had ever thought about me like that."

"The circumstances weren't appropriate for that kind of relationship. And besides, you weren't encouraging."

She looked back at him. The peculiar sensation that Joshua Stone's small, enigmatic smile always caused moved in her chest. "I was scared," she admitted.

"Scared of me?"

"At first. And then, while we were working together you were so damned professional. Cold. And yet, because of your reputation, I kept waiting for you to make a move."

"I had a toxin that could wipe out a quarter of the population and a partner who didn't like me. Professional was a necessity. And I wasn't *cold*. Not the term I'd use, considering what you were doing to me."

"What term *would* you have used?"

"Hot and bothered, maybe. If I were in polite company."

"If that's true," she asked, trying to think if it had been, "why didn't you give me any clue?"

"I thought I gave you a pretty good one. The only problem was we got interrupted. By a space of about three years. If you'll remember, however, when we met again, it didn't take us long to pick up where we'd left off."

"And the next morning you had disappeared again. I have to tell you…'' She didn't have to tell him, she realized. She had already admitted that she had doubted his motives once. She didn't have to do it again.

"You thought I'd walked out on you."

"We'd made no promises. Not either time. I'm not trying

to—'' She stopped again because that wasn't the whole truth. And because that's something she had always needed—the truth about how he felt. The truth about where their relationship would have gone if he hadn't disappeared.

''You're not trying to what?''

''Elicit any, I guess,'' she said, looking down at her hands.

''What if *I* were?'' Josh asked.

She glanced up, trying to read his eyes. ''Elicit promises?''

''Or solicit one,'' he said, smiling at her.

''What kind of promise?''

''We make a pretty good team, Daniels.''

She nodded, holding his eyes, not even daring to hope this was going somewhere. Somewhere important.

''Griff has asked me to join the firm,'' he said.

That threw her because it didn't seem to fit what they'd been talking about. ''The Phoenix? Are you going to?''

''I guess that depends on you.'' Josh's gaze focused briefly on the men outside before it came back to her. ''They're probably wondering what the hell we're doing in here that's taking so long,'' he said, grinning.

''This *is* a church,'' she admonished.

''You think *that's* what they're thinking, Daniels?''

''I didn't mean that,'' she said, feeling blood suffuse her throat. ''I meant you should watch your language in a church.''

''Marry me,'' he said.

Again, the non sequitur caught her off guard. ''*Marry* you?''

''Or at least agree to, before those guys get antsy and desert us. I'm not looking to repeat what happened before. Except one part of it. I'm definitely looking for a repeat of that.''

She said nothing, thinking about all the hours she had spent remembering him. Thinking about that night. Wondering if he would ever have asked her this. And now that he had...

"A permanent partnership, Daniels. God knows, I'm no bargain. There are holes in my memory big enough to drive a truck through, and I set off more airport alarms now than I did before. But if Griff's willing to take a chance on me... I guess I thought you might be, too."

"Since Griff and I are responsible for most of the things you just mentioned, we *ought* to be willing to take a chance on you," she said. "I know I am. You've never let me down yet."

"Not out of gratitude," he demanded harshly. "Not because you think something stupid like I saved your life or because you feel responsible for what happened to me. There's only one reason to make the kind of promise I'm asking you for."

"Because I'm in love with you?" she asked softly.

"That's close enough for government work," Josh said, sounding relieved. He leaned forward and cupped his hand around the back of her neck, pulling her toward him. Just before their mouths met, he looked down into her eyes, his blue and very intense.

Exactly the same way he had looked at her that night, she realized. The same look that had been in his eyes as he had knelt on their parkas and held his hand out to her.

"And just so there's never any doubt about my motives, Daniels, I guess I need to say it, too."

Her eyes filled with tears as she looked at his face, so changed by all that he had endured, tempered by a fire she didn't even want to imagine. "You put your body over mine, Josh, taking bullets to protect me. I don't need declarations. If I haven't figured out by now how you feel about me, then I'm in the wrong business. I don't belong in intelligence. Do you think Griff's got room in the Phoenix for another recruit?''

''I don't know, Daniels. Why don't we ask him together?'' Josh whispered, just before his lips closed over hers.

* * * * *

*If you enjoy Gayle Wilson's books,
be sure and look for the upcoming reissue of her
Rita Award nominated Historical Romance,*

THE HEART'S DESIRE—

*the unforgettable story of a strong-willed
widow who helps a cynical nobleman
to overcome his torturous past.*

*Available in December 2000 at your
favorite book outlet.*

The romantic suspense at

HARLEQUIN®

INTRIGUE

just got more intense!

On the precipice between imminent danger and
smoldering desire, they are

When your back is against the wall
and nothing makes sense, only one man
is strong enough to pull you from the brink—
and into his loving arms!
Look for all the books in this riveting new
promotion:

WOMAN MOST WANTED (#599)
by **Harper Allen**
On sale January 2001

PRIVATE VOWS (#603)
by **Sally Steward**
On sale February 2001

NIGHTTIME GUARDIAN (#607)
by **Amanda Stevens**
On sale March 2001

Available at your favorite retail outlet.

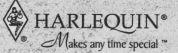

CELEBRATE VALENTINE'S DAY WITH HARLEQUIN®'S LATEST TITLE—

Stolen Memories

Available in trade-size format, this collector's edition contains three full-length novels by *New York Times* bestselling authors Jayne Ann Krentz and Tess Gerritsen, along with national bestselling author Stella Cameron.

TEST OF TIME by **Jayne Ann Krentz**—
He married for the best reason.... She married for the only reason.... Did they stand a chance at making the only reason the real reason to share a lifetime?

THIEF OF HEARTS by **Tess Gerritsen**—
Their distrust of each other was only as strong as their desire. And Jordan began to fear that Diana was more than just a thief of hearts.

MOONTIDE by **Stella Cameron**—
For Andrew, Greer's return is a miracle. It had broken his heart to let her go. Now fate has brought them back together. And he won't lose her again...

Make this Valentine's Day one to remember!

Look for this exciting collector's edition
on sale January 2001 at your favorite retail outlet.

HARLEQUIN®
Makes any time special ™

Visit us at www.eHarlequin.com

PHSM

HARLEQUIN®
makes any time special—online...

eHARLEQUIN.com

your romantic
books

- ♥ Shop online! Visit Shop eHarlequin and discover a wide selection of new releases and classic favorites at great discounted prices.

- ♥ Read our daily and weekly Internet exclusive serials, and participate in our interactive novel in the reading room.

- ♥ Ever dreamed of being a writer? Enter your chapter for a chance to become a featured author in our Writing Round Robin novel.

• • • • • •

your romantic
life

- ♥ Check out our feature articles on dating, flirting and other important romance topics and get your daily love dose with tips on how to keep the romance alive every day.

• • • • • • •

your
community

- ♥ Have a Heart-to-Heart with other members about the latest books and meet your favorite authors.

- ♥ Discuss your romantic dilemma in the Tales from the Heart message board.

your romantic
escapes

- ♥ Learn what the stars have in store for you with our daily Passionscopes and weekly Erotiscopes.

- ♥ Get the latest scoop on your favorite royals in Royal Romance.

THE SECRET IS OUT!

HARLEQUIN®

INTRIGUE®

presents

By day these agents are cowboys;
by night they are specialized
government operatives.
Men bound by love, loyalty and the law—
they've vowed to keep their missions
and identities confidential....

Harlequin Intrigue

Harlequin American Romance
(a special tie-in story)

HARLEQUIN®

Makes any time special ™

Visit us at www.eHarlequin.com   HITC